THE SOUL OF DISCRETION

This Large Print Book carries the
Seal of Approval of N.A.V.H.

A CHIEF SUPERINTENDENT
SIMON SERRAILLER MYSTERY

THE SOUL OF DISCRETION

SUSAN HILL

THORNDIKE PRESS
A part of Gale, Cengage Learning

GALE
CENGAGE Learning·

Farmington Hills, Mich • San Francisco • New York • Waterville, Maine
Meriden, Conn • Mason, Ohio • Chicago

GALE
CENGAGE Learning®

LIBRARY OF CONGRESS CATALOGING-IN-PUBLICATION DATA

Hill, Susan, 1942-
    The soul of discretion : a Chief Superintendent Simon Serrailler mystery /
by Susan Hill. — Large print edition.
        pages ; cm. — (Thorndike Press large print crime scene)
    ISBN 978-1-4104-7678-4 (hardcover) — ISBN 1-4104-7678-2 (hardcover)
    1. Serrailler, Simon (Fictitious character)—Fiction. 2. Large type books.
I. Title.
PR6058.I45S67 2015
823'.914—dc23   2014045896

Published in 2015 by arrangement with The Overlook Press

Printed in Mexico
1 2 3 4 5 6 7 19 18 17 16 15

To my friend Mrs Green
(Candida Lycett Green 1942–2014)

PART ONE

ONE

April 2007
Lafferton, and a night in early spring. After a week of frosts, the wind had swung to the west, bringing milder air. Snowdrops and crocuses were over, daffodils were flowering. Quiet, empty streets. No footsteps.

Jeff Barclay and Robbie Freeman sat on a low wall near the bus stop in the square, finishing off a shared kebab. They only had enough money for one, and a tea. Robbie screwed up the greasy paper and lifted his arm to throw it into a nearby bin. But his arm froze in mid-air.

'What?'

'Bloody hell.'

'*What?*' Jeff shoved him so that he almost fell off the wall. Robbie did not protest or shove back, he just stared at the entrance to the Lanes, the cobbled pedestrian-only street to their left.

'Shit, did you see that?'

9

'Didn't see anything. What was it — a ghost?' Jeff snorted.

'No.' Robbie said quietly, getting off the wall and walking towards the Lanes. 'I saw a kid.'

'What sort of kid?'

'A little kid. It . . . it had no clothes on.'

'You're taking the piss. I never saw any naked kid.'

Jeff levelled with him as they reached the top of the Lanes. There were old-fashioned lamps at either end and a couple of shops had lighted front windows. The whole street was empty.

'Stupid.'

'No. I saw it. There was a little kid, it sort of — just ran and then it vanished.'

'Yeah, right. Come on, let's see if there's anyone outside the Magpie.'

But Robbie was walking slowly away from him, looking closely to right and left. In the end, Jeff followed.

'How could there be a kid?'

'I know what I saw.'

'What are you on, Rob? You start seeing things, you got a problem.'

There was a passageway between the deli and a smart clothes shop, and as Robbie looked into it, he saw a quick movement — something pale. He ran down, but he had

10

to push past two wheelie bins, and by the time he had got through, if there had been anyone, they'd gone.

'Cat.'

'No.'

'You're mad.'

'No.'

'Oh, for fuck's sake! I'm off home.'

It was another five minutes before Robbie followed him. They walked slowly along the kerb, thumbs out every time a vehicle went by. Not many did.

'Wanker.' Jeff gave two fingers to a speeding car. Robbie said nothing. His head was full of what he knew he had seen — not imagined, not hallucinated, seen. A child, maybe three or four years old, naked, slithering out of sight into the shadows, dodging down the alley and passageway. He couldn't get it out of his mind.

A patrol car took the call at twenty to three.

PC Bev Willet sighed. 'Wind-up,' she said.

'Sounds like it. But just in case — hold onto your hat.'

It had been a quiet night. Even a wind-up was better than trying to keep awake with more plastic coffee. The car raced up the bypass.

'How old did he say?'

'Little kid, three or so. Couldn't say if it was a boy or girl.'

'And *naked*?'

'Naked.'

'They piss me off, these hoaxers. I'd have them dunked in the canal on a freezing night.' Bev snorted as she pulled up at the entrance to the Lanes. One taxi was in the rank, the driver asleep with a copy of the *Sun* over his face. He didn't stir at the sound of the patrol car.

'Talk to him in a mo. Come on.'

Ten minutes later they had scoured the area, including every alley and passageway, every wheelie bin and recycling area.

'Diddly squat,' Bev said.

'Pisses me off, this sort of thing.'

'You said.'

'Only why would he invent *a naked child*, for heaven's sake?'

'Guaranteed to make us move fast.'

'Right. Just someone's idea of a good laugh then. Better go and wake up our cabby.'

But their cabby had been out on jobs all evening and then fallen asleep. He was going home now. He'd keep an eye out.

'His face said it all.'

'Wind-up.'

'Wind-up.'

■ ■ ■ ■

Jess Honeywell's baby woke for a feed at four. She picked him up out of his crib and moved the curtain aside briefly to look out at the night. Starry, with a big moon. A front-bedroom light was on a few doors down. Another wakeful baby. She and Katie Green sometimes chanced to look out at the same time and then they'd wave, sharing the small hours of new babies. They had propped one another up through pregnancy and the first weeks and went on doing so now, meeting almost every day, walking their buggies together, swapping notes. It had made all the difference. St Luke's Road was in the grid of small Victorian terraced houses known as the Apostles, friendly, neighbourly, and near to the shops, coffee bars and restaurants of Lafferton's centre. They were lucky, Jess thought as she dropped the curtain, even if the houses were small. She hated the idea of being stuck out in the sticks, even with bigger rooms and a garden, but no life nearby and needing a car to get you anywhere. They couldn't afford a car. Matt walked to work.

The Green bedroom was in darkness, the moon shining on quiet pavements, but as she turned, Jess thought she saw something move. Turned back and lifted the curtain again. No. Trick of the light. Nothing. And then her hand went to her mouth. Noah was grizzling himself back to sleep but she barely noticed.

Matt was hard to wake and when he did, he stumbled out of bed assuming he had to pick up the baby and was almost able to do so in his sleep.

He came awake fully as Jess shook his arm.

'What? You've been dreaming —'

'NO. Matt, go down, go out there . . . I was not dreaming. You've got to go.' Noah cried again as her voice rose. She picked him up and sat on the edge of the bed, putting him to the breast and gesturing to Matt to hurry.

It was not that he refused to believe her, just that he was still not fully awake, and he felt foolish, standing half dressed and in slippers, looking up and down St Luke's Road and seeing nothing, Nothing at all. But she had been wide awake and he knew that she thought she had seen . . .

And then he saw.

The child was squatting down behind the gate of a house opposite.

'It's OK,' Matt said. 'It's all right, it's all right.'

He went through the gate and stopped. Later, he said that he would never forget the child's face until his dying day. Later, he could not sleep because the face was in front of him. Later, he was haunted during his waking hours by sudden flashbacks to the child's face as it looked up at him.

'It's all right. Dear God. Listen, I won't hurt you. I'm going to look after you, OK?' But even as he spoke, gently, quietly, the child tried to shrink into a hedge, as if it might find a safe place among the rough bare twigs and earth.

Very slowly, Matt inched his way, his hand out, talking softly in what he desperately hoped was a voice of reassurance. The child continued to shrink from him and now it turned its face away from him out of fear.

It was a girl. She was perhaps four years old. She was filthy, she had smears of blood on her arms and legs. Her long, fine, fair hair was matted to her scalp. She was completely naked.

There was silence and stillness and fear for long minutes before the child lurched forward, the hedge catching at her again as she moved and drawing fresh pinpoints of blood, and then she was clinging to Matt, climbing up him like a terrified small animal and pressing her little body to him. He put

15

his arm round her carefully and edged backwards down the path. She did not move, only clung fast to him. Matt hurried across the road, back into the house, calling to Jess. But she had already seen him through the window and only seconds later, blue lights turning, the police car stopped outside.

TWO

May 2007

Year 2 at St Luke's Primary School had been talking about Things I Like and Things I Don't Like, as part of the week's topic on food and drink. Sue Norwood had found it informative. Most of the likes were as expected — sweet things, crisps, sometimes the odd grape — and the dislikes she could have predicted — milk, green vegetables, stew, runny egg. The next part of the topic would be more challenging — why we should try the things we don't like again, in case we find we do like them after all. Why we shouldn't eat too many sweets, even if we like them very much. Why our bodies need a variety of foods, including green vegetables . . . they would dutifully chant the 'dislikes' list and promise to try them again, go home and forget all about it. They would still come to school each morning carrying a half-empty pack of sticky sweets and an egg would never pass their lips. Some of them had even picked up on the words 'wheat' and 'dairy' in the same breath as the words 'allergy' and 'intolerance'.

But they were still one of the best classes she had ever taught, alert, funny, loyal to one another and relatively well behaved. One or two had problems, including the boy who still wore nappies and the girl who never spoke, problems which were not easy to solve, and ought to involve the parents.

Sue sighed. She knew that the parents of the boy who still wore nappies would never come through the school gates, let alone come to see her.

The silent child was sitting at the far end of the second table now, head bent to the paper so that her face was barely visible. Glory Dorfner. There were some colourful names in Years 1 and 2 but what parent called their child 'Glory'? And why not? she asked herself smartly. Better than . . . well, better than quite a few.

The classroom was quiet, apart from the odd sniff, cough and shuffle. They were drawing and labelling with some glee six things they disliked to eat or drink. She stood behind Alfie Starman. His ears needed a wash, but his careful picture of a cabbage was very good indeed and she said so. Alfie glanced round, flushed with pride and pleasure. Rikki O'Mara kicked him in the shin. But, as Rikki would have said, if challenged, 'in a good way, Mrs Norwood'. She had a soft spot for Rikki.

Glory bent her head even further and her arm was curved across the paper to hide it. Sue waited a moment. She could feel the child's tension.

'May I see?'

Glory shook her head slightly.

'Shall I guess?'

The child was absolutely still.

'You don't like — chips?' Shouts from all sides, arms waving. Everyone liked chips. 'All right, I know. Chip pictures, all of you.'

Much giggling.

'But maybe Glory doesn't like chips.'

Silence.

'I think you don't like — tea?'

Silence.

'Tomatoes?'

Sue did not continue. She waited a moment, went round three others, looking, admiring, querying. Then got a spare low chair and sat next to Glory. But the child was immovable. She said nothing. Would not lift her arm.

It was early evening before she finally

opened the big folder containing Year 2's work, setting the pile on the table next to a box of gold paper stars. Alice was marking Year 12 English essays, swearing from time to time.

'OFFS, Damian Cross, try reading the text.'

Sue smiled, and turned over the next sheet.

For a second, she thought it had ended up in her folder by mistake, except that she could not possibly imagine how.

Glory could barely write and what she did manage was still in mirror-writing. Well, that would sort itself out, it always did.

'I don't like . . .' was in smudged dark pastel, large letters copied in almost violently.

Sue felt her face flush as she looked at the drawing.

Then she called Alice over.

'Police,' Alice said almost immediately.

'What on earth can they do?'

'Or family welfare officers . . . NSPCC? I don't know, but you've got to show this to someone.'

'Maybe Glory's parents . . .'

Alice gave her a look.

'No, you're right.'

'Take it to Eleanor first thing, cover your

back. Let her decide.'

Alice went back to the essays on *To Kill a Mockingbird,* muttering as usual about wishing they could read a more challenging novel, vowing yet again to start them on *Great Expectations* the moment they were done with the set text.

Glory's picture seemed to come in front of every one of the others that she looked at. She gave up. Turned on the news.

'I wonder if they've found out about that little girl yet?'

Alice just nodded, head down in her essays.

'Look at me,' Sue said, hands on the table in front of her.

Alice looked.

'I'm seriously worried about this child. I mean it, Al.'

'I know, hon, I'm sorry. And so you should be.'

'I'm going to the police station now.'

'Want me to come with you? I can leave these.'

'No, it could take half the night. I'll be fine. Finish those. I'll ring you.

THREE

September 2007

It seemed such a little time ago. They'd often gone out, had a drink at the Ox, met friends for bingo, a walk to the Hill when the evenings were light, even a spin in the car to one of the village pubs. They'd gone to a film occasionally, had a fish-and-chip supper on the way back. Having no children, sorry though they both were, meant a bit more money for them to enjoy treats together. Tom had worked hard all his life, she'd had part-time work so that she could be in, with his tea on the table, when he got home.

Jean Mason stood waiting for the kettle to boil. Such a little time ago. She remembered everything. And Tom remembered nothing. Most days now he didn't even remember her. Most days there seemed no point in even going to see him because it upset them both. He kept asking her who she was and why Jean hadn't been to visit him, she couldn't think of a thing to say to this man she no longer knew. This wasn't Tom, the Tom she'd known since they were both eleven, the person she'd shared her entire adult life with, day in, day out. So who was it?

She poured boiling water into the teapot and took her tray through. They had never been a noisy couple, and the street had always been a quiet street, but now it was uncanny, the empty silence. They had lived in the flat above the shop for the last ten years, since their old street had been demolished. When they came, there had been a dozen shops in the row — launderette, baker, butcher, greengrocer, hardware, and then a Chinese takeaway, a minicab office. Below them had been a wool shop, then a toy shop, then a cafe. One by one, they'd all closed. Now there was a charity shop at one end, a letting agency office at the other, and in between, nothing but windows boarded up. It was lonely and it was bleak and Tom had said they'd try and find somewhere else. But where else was there? So long as he'd been well she hadn't minded. She minded now.

She started to watch a crime drama but it was too violent, turned over to a comedian who was too crude. The last ten minutes of a cookery programme was entertaining enough, but after that she switched off.

She would go to bed with a book she'd bought from the charity shop. *Travels with my Elephant* — she loved animals, she loved reading about places she would never see. Tom would have picked it up, smiled, teased her about it.

Now, he had forgotten how to smile.

A child was screaming.

She went to the window but the street was empty and silent. She opened the window. Nothing.

It had stopped.

Maybe it was a cat. A fox. The foxes still came scavenging round.

As she was getting into bed ten minutes later, she heard the scream again and this time it was in the street. This time, there were people — a car, pulled up outside the boarded-up shop next door, two men, one of them pulling a small child by the hand. They were too far from the street lamp for her to see clearly and in a few seconds the child was pushed into the car, one of the men in the back with it, and the car was moving away, accelerating fast as it reached the corner.

24

Then nothing. The street was silent, empty, dark. Jean wondered if she had been hallucinating, or was half-asleep, and somehow begun to dream while still awake.

Did that happen?

She went back to her bed but when she tried to read, the image of the child being pulled towards the car came between her and the words, and the sound of its cry seemed to echo again and again through her head.

She wondered what she should do.

She knew what she ought to do but her story sounded so fanciful that she could not bring herself to make the call.

It was four nights later that the child screamed again. There was no car in the street; the sound came from somewhere nearby but indoors. And almost as soon as she had heard it, the noise stopped quite suddenly. Then nothing.

Jean lay for a long time, listening, but the only sound she heard was the beat of her own heart.

She had fallen deeply asleep by the time the car drove up the street, lights doused, and stopped outside the empty shop next door. She was asleep when the child, silent now, was carried out and driven away.

■ ■ ■ ■

There were no neighbours left to talk to. She was used to it by now. She had never been unfriendly, it was just that she and Tom had been company enough for one another, but now she remembered the sounds she had heard, of the child screaming in the night, she needed someone to talk to — just no one official, not the police or anyone else in authority. She had not been over to see Kath Latimer for months, partly because she found it hard to deal with questions about Tom, questions to which she didn't really have any answers, partly because it was either a long walk or hanging round waiting for one of the few buses that went anywhere near Spalding Green. But Kath and Dennis Latimer had been the closest to best friends that either she or Tom had ever had, all at school together, all living in and around Lafferton most of their lives. Dennis had died ten years earlier and then Kath had shut herself away, before moving to be near her sister in Bognor. It had been a disaster, they had fallen out and Kath had returned to a smaller house in her old road.

'I feel bad about you,' Jean said later that

morning, sitting in Kath's tiny cluttered front room with a cup of milky coffee. The budgerigar hopped to and fro, to and fro, on the bar inside its cage until Jean had to look away, it irritated her so much. 'Does he never settle down?'

Kath glared. 'He's perfectly happy.'

'I'm sure. Just seems a bit restless.'

Funny, Jean thought, how you forgot things. There had always been a budgie — it was one of the things that had put her off visiting. Tom had never been able to stand them either. The only way they managed to stay friendly was if Dennis and Kath came to them, then halfway through an evening, Kath would say she was worried about Charlie or Pippy or some other silly thing, so they ought to get back.

Kath got up and fiddled with a stick of millet on the side of the cage, pursed her lips and made a tweeting noise. The budgie hopped about madly, tweeting back.

People's lives. Jean finished her coffee. People's narrow lives.

They couldn't find anything to say.

'I suppose there's no real point in you visiting him, is there? As he doesn't know who you are. No point in troubling him.'

'It doesn't trouble him, he likes me to go.'

'Are you sure?'

Jean was not sure but would have cut out her tongue rather than say so.

'I wouldn't dream of not going.'

'Well, I suppose if it's a comfort to you, it's worth it.'

Was it? A comfort? Worth it? Worth what?

She had made a mistake in coming. Kath was the last person she could confide in about the sounds she had heard. In any case, sitting here in the hot room with the hopping budgerigar, she wondered if she *had* heard anything. Sometimes, you hovered about the edge of a dream, sure you were awake and heard a sound that was never there. Kath would have made her feel a fool.

But she stayed for a second coffee, and a chocolate shortcake. It would have been rude not to when it was so long since she'd made the effort. It was only when she was finally waiting for the bus into town that it occurred to her Kath could equally well have come over to see her. She never did.

The sound of the child's scream, real or dreamed, stayed with her. She did some shopping in town, caught another bus, walked the last half-mile, and all the time, it was there, in her head, it kept repeating

itself. It wasn't the sort of sound you forgot.
If it had been a sound.

FOUR

July 2010

Kath never admitted to sleeping in the afternoon, but nevertheless, when the phone rang and rang on that Sunday, she did not hear it and it was almost half past five when she picked up the message.

'Kath? Are you there? Kath?' Jean's voice sounded odd. 'Can you ring me please, Kath? I don't feel well . . .'

There was no reply when she called back, and none fifteen minutes later. Kath panicked and called a taxi.

The hospital said Mrs Mason was in intensive care and could have no visitors, unless Kath was next of kin. She waited for a couple of hours before she was told that Jean's condition was stable and that she could come back tomorrow.

'And,' the woman said, 'do you have contact details for her next of kin?'

It seemed terrible to say that so far as she knew, there were none. No Tom any more. No parents, sisters, brothers, children, aunts, uncles. She had no idea about cousins. 'But I've known her many years and I've never heard her mention one.'

No next of kin. No relatives. No one. How could that be? On her way home Kath felt both exhausted and guilty. She and Dennis had been friends with Jean and Tom for a lifetime, yet there was nothing left to show for it.

She was back at the hospital the next day.

'I want you to do something for me.' It took a long time for her to form the words.

'In my bag . . .'

Kath pulled the handbag out of the bedside cupboard. Jean had no movement in her arms. 'No, I don't like to rummage about it your bag.' But Jean was so agitated, she opened it. Not much. Purse. Pension book. Compact, worn shiny, the words *Love from Tom* hardly visible any longer. Pen. Diary. A small red ruled notebook.

Jean nodded. 'Take it home with you. Keep it.'

'Where do you want me to keep it?'

'Safe. Just safe. Don't throw it out.'

Jean closed her eyes and drifted off. Kath waited ten minutes longer but it was clear she wouldn't wake for a while. She put the handbag back into the cupboard, and the red notebook into her own.

When she got home, she opened the notebook and glanced through. Dates. Times. A line or two in Jean's writing. Then she locked it into the bureau drawer, on top of her birth certificate and her will.

FIVE

The duty sergeant flipped through the red soft-covered notebook. Dates. Times. The entries had been made over the last three years, mostly two or three times a month. He began to read, but after a couple of pages, looked across at the woman sitting on the bench opposite his desk.

'Mrs Latimer?' She got up. 'I think you should have a word about this with someone from CID. I'll take you into an interview room and someone will come down.'

'So I didn't do the wrong thing?'

'You did absolutely the right thing.'

She only had to wait a few minutes.

'Mrs Latimer? I'm DC Bethan Waites. Can I get you a tea? Coffee?'

They both had tea. 'Wise,' the young woman said, sitting down on the small, uncomfortable sofa next to Kath. 'The coffee's disgusting. Actually the best is the hot

33

chocolate.' How many times had she gone through this bit of beverage chit-chat to help settle the interviewee down? But oddly, it usually did.

She's young, was all Kath thought. Not pretty but nicely presented. Emerald-green jacket, dark skirt, plain blouse, hair neat.

'Do you ever wear a uniform?'

DC Waites smiled. 'Not any more.'

'Very nice.'

'It is. Now . . . the duty sergeant filled me in briefly but I'd like you to tell me about this notebook — I didn't get the full story before he had to take a phone call.' Not true. They never got the full story. Starting over was what CID did.

Kath told it. 'That was in late July . . . she never left the hospital. It was awful to watch her . . . couldn't do anything for herself and then another stroke meant she lost her speech. It was a blessing when the next one came and carried her away.'

'I'm sorry. Always hard to lose an old friend — just as hard as losing a relative sometimes.'

I wonder how many of either you've lost though, Kath thought, at your tender age? How do you know what's hardest?

'So Mrs Mason died when, exactly?'

'The third of September . . . early hours

of the morning. I wish she hadn't been alone. I do wish that.'

'Yes, indeed. But maybe she . . .'

'Didn't know anything about it? That's what I tell myself. You see . . .'

Bethan was adept at getting them back on track without apparent rudeness or any sense of hurry. It was a useful skill.

'And it's now the twelfth of October. Why didn't you bring the notebook in to us sooner?'

'I just forgot all about it. Truth be told, I'd forgotten about it more or less as soon as she gave it to me for safe keeping and I put it in that drawer.'

'Did Mrs Mason give you any idea at all why she wanted you to have it and keep it safe for her?'

'No.'

'Did she give you anything else to look after?'

'No.'

'Did you read through the notebook?'

'I glanced inside. None of it meant anything except . . . well, some of the things she wrote down worried me — that's why I brought it to you. These things about hearing children . . . hearing them crying . . . hearing a scream . . . seeing . . . I don't know. It upset me.'

'Yes,' the young woman said. 'Did Mrs Mason ever write things — stories or poems or that sort of thing? A lot of people do. I was wondering if these were notes for some sort of story . . .'

'If she did she never mentioned it and I knew her for over sixty years. She wasn't like that.'

'Like what?'

'Well . . . arty. Fanciful.'

'Right. Did she keep any other sort of diary?'

'Not that I know of. I shouldn't think so. She had a kitchen calendar, same one every year, from the Donkey Protection place . . . she had it hanging up in the kitchen but that was just, you know, hairdresser, dentist sort of thing.'

'And there's nothing else you can think of to explain this notebook? Anything about Mrs Mason that might help us?'

'I just can't think of anything. I'm sorry.'

'Please don't be.'

'It's only . . .'

Kath fiddled with her coat button. 'I feel I've let her down, somehow . . . I don't know . . . she gave it to me to keep safe and I've . . . looked into it, brought it here, shown it to you. I feel as if I've . . .'

The DC put her hand briefly on Kath's.

'No,' she said quietly, 'you haven't let her down, you haven't betrayed her. You have done exactly what she would have done if she had been alive.'

'Are you sure about that?'

'Yes.' The young woman held her gaze. 'I am.'

PART TWO

Six

'Good morning, Superintendent.'

A Tuesday morning in late May and there were four others round the table in the meeting room at Bevham HQ. The only one already known to Serrailler was the Chief Constable, Kieron Bright. The man who had succeeded Paula Devenish was the youngest in the country ever to be appointed Chief, a fast-tracker who had swiftly worked his way up through the ranks and then served in a high-security special unit before being an ACC for under two years. He was impressive, taller than Simon, fit, shrewd, and he had hit the ground running. The force had felt the shock but responded to it well. Simon had expected not to like the man but he did — liked and respected. The only area of disagreement they had was over drugs ops, which the new Chief had pepped up and which Serrailler regarded as

41

a waste of time and resources. They had agreed to differ. 'I respect your arguments, Simon,' the Chief had said. 'I've met them before and in quite high places. But they're wrong. It's my mission to bring you over to my side.'

The mission was not yet accomplished because there was never time for the luxury of exhaustive debates.

The Chief had called him in, without explanation, but Serrailler was fairly sure this was not going to be about drugs ops.

'Thank you for coming over. I'm sorry I wasn't very forthcoming but this was not for any sort of communication other than face-to-face. I'm only in for the first few minutes and then I'll leave you with the officers here to give you a full brief. I don't think you've met any of them before.'

Simon looked round again quickly. Blank and all unfamiliar faces. 'No, sir, I'm sure not.'

'Right. This meeting is to discuss a very sensitive covert operation. It isn't going to be an easy one. But I wanted to say that the operation has my full support, and that I suggested your involvement because you're not only one of the most experienced but also one of the most trusted officers I've ever worked with.' He looked straight at

Serrailler. 'That isn't bullshit,' he said.

'Sir.'

'But in the same way that you've never met the people here before, I know you've never done anything like this op before.'

So the Chief had been through his career file. Serrailler had done most things in his time, except terrorism ops. Right. The Chief left. Coffee was brought in. The room went still.

'I'm DCS Lochie Craig. I work in the Child Exploitation and Online Protection Centre.'

'DCI Linda Warren. Also from CEOP.'

'DCS Harry Borling.' He gave no more information.

Not terrorism then. Child protection was something Serrailler had been involved in from time to time, as almost all police officers were, but as he had risen through the ranks he had left much of it to the specialists. He said so now.

'This is actually a side shoot from CEOP, Chief Superintendent.'

'Simon.'

'Thank you. And it's Lochie.'

The other two nodded. Everyone relaxed slightly.

'First off, I'd like you to look at some images. Three men. No names for the moment.'

He passed his laptop across the table. The older man in the photos was clearly related to one of the younger ones — they were probably father and son, Simon thought. The older was in his late sixties or early seventies, with thick white hair, a strong jaw and a beaky nose. The younger man — late thirties? — had brown hair, worn slightly long, the same nose, softer jaw. Their eyes were exactly the same shape — the family resemblance was strong. The third man looked rather less like the others but he had the same beaked nose as the first. Probably mid-forties. Simon looked hard at each of them for several minutes before passing the laptop back.

'Well,' he said, 'I'm certain I've never seen any of them. My memory for names is OK, but for faces it's extremely good. I don't recognise them at all.'

'Good. Glad we've got that out of the way. Right, let me go into detail.' Lochie Craig was a balding, burly man in his fifties. A measure of strain had become moulded onto his features but he spoke calmly enough.

'Lafferton, 2007.' He had his laptop open.

'Hmm, 2007. That was the year of the serial murders here. I don't remember much else, though there must have been plenty of other stuff going on.'

'There was. In April, a girl approximately four years old was found wandering the streets at night, naked and distressed. She was sighted twice before being brought into safety by a resident. She was initially taken to hospital, later into foster care and finally adopted. She had been physically abused, badly enough to need surgery. Her identity has never been discovered. No one came forward despite widespread appeals — no parents, family, neighbours, no one. She suffered almost total blanking of the events and we could never even find out her name. She now lives in another part of the country and is settled with her adoptive family, but, inevitably, she is scarred in most senses and has educational and emotional problems.'

'I was certainly aware of the case,' Serrailler said. 'Even in the middle of very complex murder inquiries, it couldn't fail to be noted.'

'Right, case two. A child called Glory Dorfner presented some artwork in her primary-school class. It depicted crudely drawn figures engaged in sexual activity. One was of a small girl apparently being buggered by a man. The other was of a small girl performing an oral sex act on a man — the male's sexual organ was made to appear much larger than the rest of the figure. The child's teacher came to Lafferton Police Station. Officers and members of the social services child-protection team visited Glory's house an hour after the teacher reported with the drawings. The child was asleep, but there was sufficient concern and a certain amount of evidence of her being sexually abused to warrant her being subject to an emergency court order and taken into care immediately. Her stepfather and her stepbrother were subsequently found guilty of sexual abuse, and computers and other material were taken from the home. These contained hundreds of images of child abuse. This case is being looked into again at the present time, because of certain new evidence and in spite of the fact that the two men are still serving sentences.' He paused to pour himself a glass of water. Drank it.

The faces of the other two were impassive. They had heard all this before, and far worse. They dealt with child abuse every day of their working lives and it was beyond Serrailler to know how they coped with it.

The DCS looked at him. 'OK?'

Simon nodded.

'Right. Case three. Mrs Jean Mason of

Plimmer Road, Lafferton, died in 2010, and while in hospital during her last illness she left a notebook in the safe keeping of her friend, Mrs Kathleen Latimer. Mrs Latimer looked at it and brought it into Lafferton Police Station. It took a little while to work out what the list of dates and times meant — there were notes, but they were not very full. Do you know Plimmer Road?'

'I do and I didn't realise anyone still lived there. It's been a derelict bit of Lafferton for a long time. Shops closed, didn't reopen, got boarded up, accommodation above them was usually empty. There was a plan for its redevelopment but once the recession bit every developer pulled out. I haven't been along there for a while but I doubt if anything has changed.'

'Mrs Mason had lived above one of the shops for upwards of thirty years. Her friend Mrs Latimer, who died last year, was interviewed several times and said that the Masons had never wanted to leave. When they first went there it was a bustling area of shops, offices and residential, and Mrs Mason had stuck it out while everything shut up round her. But according to the notebook, she started to hear sounds from the disused shop next door — children crying, children screaming — then she recorded seeing cars draw up and men get out with small children, and, twice, men coming out of the shop carrying a child. She knew the property was empty.'

'Did she call us in?'

'No. And she didn't tell Mrs Latimer anything, just asked her to keep the notebook safe.'

'What action was taken at the time?'

'I've a copy of the report here, if you'd like to read it.' He handed over a single sheet of paper.

A routine patrol car had checked out 11 Plimmer Road, at 4 p.m. on 20 October. The shop had formerly been a bookmakers with living accommodation above but was boarded and padlocked. The garden behind was overgrown and needles and other drug paraphernalia were found, none recently used. Steps led from the back door down to a cellar which was also boarded, and bolted. The patrol reported all this and then left, but one of the patrol officers wasn't happy and reported to CID. It was over a week before anyone investigated — low priority at a time when they were overwhelmed with a murder inquiry. Two officers went to the shop equipped with a rammer and broke down the cellar door. An outer room contained some old cardboard boxes and newspapers, but was otherwise empty. A door, slightly concealed by an old wooden chest, was then discovered and that led to an inner cellar. Here, a camera and other recording equipment were found, together with some rugs, a couch, a couple of upright chairs, plus cigarette butts, sandwich wrappers, empty plastic coffee cups and drinks cans. Unfortunately, no one had the presence of mind to make this inner room a crime scene. But all the items were removed, bagged and taken for forensic examination.

Serrailler put the sheet down. 'Findings?'

DCS Lochie Craig looked at his laptop.

'There was a small amount of footage left on one of the camcorders — probably test images, perhaps when the equipment appeared to have a fault. They were blurred and disconnected but there was enough to show us that children were being filmed during the course of sessions of sexual abuse. Nothing else except a feast of fingerprints — they were obviously either planning to return or sure they were safe and undetected. Cups, recording equipment, chairs . . . clear prints were taken from all of these. There was also some DNA — on the rug, on the sofa — taken from semen and saliva and also from blood.'

There was a pause. Their faces were still

impassive, even that of the woman DCI.

Serrailler felt anger and nausea bubble up into his throat. He suppressed them.

'Fingerprints lead anywhere?'

'Only one set. A man called William — always known as Will — Fernley. Mean anything?'

'No, nothing at all. He isn't local, is he?'

'Not local to Lafferton, no — the family live in Devon. William is the third son of Lord Fernley.'

'Sorry, no, I've never heard of him.'

'Fine.' The laptop lid was closed.

'Linda, would you like to take over at this point?' Craig poured another glass of water and drank all of it.

She was probably in her early forties and, until now, she had sat listening with that impassive expression. Now, though, she looked directly at him with a warm, open smile.

'This isn't an area you're very familiar with and I know it can be difficult. We deal with it every day, we get used to it, but we don't get hardened, Simon — the minute that happens, it's time for a transfer to another line of work. Not everyone can cope with it — it takes its toll. On the other hand, it is so important, it's vital — and we owe it to the children to stick at it, so we find ways

50

of coping and continuing. I want to say this now because if you do take on what we're hoping you will, you need to understand that fully.'

Simon nodded.

'Do you have any questions at this stage, before we get down another layer?'

Did he? How the hell did you light on me for whatever it is? Why? It's something I've steered clear of for the whole of my career, I'm not well informed about CEOP, so why me? But whatever the answer and then whatever you're going to ask me to do, it's no. No.

He folded his arms. 'No, no questions,' he said. 'Carry on.'

SEVEN

'Yes, you are interrupting, and I'm very glad about that.' Cat Deerbon led Emma, manager of the Lafferton bookshop, into the kitchen.

'I brought you the Julian Barnes,' Emma said, glancing down at a parcel on the table in Amazon packaging. 'And what did *they* send?'

'Oh God, sorry. I needed a textbook quickly.'

'And cheaply.'

'Emma, I do try to be fair but that textbook would cost seventy-five pounds from you and I got it for less than half. I just can't afford not to. But I've almost finished my thesis and then I won't need any more ridiculously expensive tomes. Coffee? Glass of wine? Slice of my humble pie?'

'Don't be silly. Coffee would be good, thanks, Cat. I'm sorry you didn't get to the book group. Are you feeling better?'

'Fine. I swear I felt more sick than in my entire life, and that includes three pregnancies. Short but ugh.'

'Judith didn't make it either.'

Cat looked at her sharply. 'Did she say why?'

'Only that she wasn't well. It was probably the same bug.'

Cat did not reply, just scooped coffee into the cafetière.

'How are the young ones?'

'Felix has the bug, he's in the den wrapped in a fleece with a bucket to hand. He missed school which he really minded. Hannah is rehearsing for *The Sound of Music.* Sam — well, as Sam rarely speaks, only grunts, I can't be sure but he seems OK — he's going to the under 18 county cricket trials tomorrow.'

'I'm impressed — that and the hockey.'

'No, his cricket isn't as good and he's only fifteen. He won't get in but it'll be good experience for next time. I am sorry about Amazon, Emma — you do understand?'

Emma sighed. 'I wish I didn't.'

'How is business in general?'

'So-so. Children's books are doing well — I could almost live off those sales, but not quite.'

'But you have to stay open. You've worked

so hard at that bookshop, Lafferton couldn't do without you now.'

Emma made a face. 'Try telling that to the people who come in, browse for ages, make a list and go home to order online.' She failed to keep the note of bitterness out of her voice.

After Emma had gone, Cat went to check on Felix, who was asleep under his fleece. She woke him and managed to get him to stumble upstairs and into bed, with only a quick wash. He had a little more colour in his cheeks so the bug was probably on the wane. He'd had a growth spurt but he was chunky, not a beanpole, like Sam. Like Simon. Chris would have loved him, of course, but been surprised by him too. He was a thoughtful, inward-looking boy, and a good musician. But he was also lacking in confidence, young for his age in some ways, and he clung to her as Sam and Hannah had never done. Cat loved his quiet company. She knew she needed to be on her guard against loving it too much and encouraging his clinginess.

She went back to her desk and the expensive textbook and set it beside her laptop. She ought not to feel guilty, but she did. Emma had to make a living and her bookshop was not making much profit. On the other hand . . . Cat's anxiety about her finances came to haunt her every night. She sometimes dreamed of bank statements.

When Chris died, he had left her a modest pension and the proceeds of a life insurance policy, whose value had declined steadily, and now it was worth less than half what it had been immediately after his death. They had never been a rich couple but hadn't had to worry about money either, and as a new widow Cat had found that financially things could continue more or less as before. Now, her income had slumped. The school fees were a drain, since she was no longer a regular GP and the hospice job had folded. Her private pension income from Chris had paid the bills. Now, it was in danger of not paying them.

Molly, her medical student lodger, had qualified and left to work for a year in Vietnam, so her room was empty. She had lived at the farmhouse free in exchange for help with babysitting and some cooking but any replacement could simply pay rent. That would help but only a little. Locum work as a GP was quite well paid, but it was insecure as well as unrewarding, and her job as medical officer at Imogen House had more or less ended when the hospice had changed from being one with bedded wards to day care only. She had a small retainer — the operative word being 'small'. She had spent the past year working on her PhD, attached to the Cicely Saunders Institute at King's in London, and she had found it absorbing, but that cost money, it did not generate any.

She needed to talk to someone about her situation, but, other than the bank manager, who was there? Not her father, not Judith. Simon? But a member of the family might assume she was asking for a loan or a gift and Cat was emphatic that she would never do that, she just needed a listening ear and some suggestions. Yes, Si then. The problem was that he was either taken up with work, as ever, or with Rachel — even more so now that she had moved in with him. Cat was anxious not to make any more demands on his time.

She sat fiddling with a pencil, jotting down odd, rather unconnected sums on paper, getting nowhere.

Chris. The loss of him overwhelmed her again in a way she had half forgotten. It was not linked to an anniversary or any physical reminder, just a pure sense of loss, a desperate longing and missing which seem to search every corner of her heart and mind, only to find them empty of him. After all

this time, she thought, and it is still yesterday. So I know it will never be any different,
I will never stop being knocked over by the
force of this feeling.

And I'll never forget him, I know that too.
Immediately after her husband's death, she
had been panic-stricken that in time the
memory of him might actually fade away
completely. It was a small comfort to be
sure now that it would not.

EIGHT

They broke for ten minutes. More coffee came in. Serrailler returned a couple of calls. Then back.

Linda Warren was working from written notes, not a laptop, but she did no more than glance at them occasionally.

'The Honourable Will Fernley was charged with and convicted of possessing pornographic material relating to children, and to being party to actual child abuse. It was clear that the inner cellar room had been used to film children being abused by adult males and Fernley's fingerprints proved that he had been present. But he had a clever defence and there was no evidence to prove absolutely that he had been involved in the abuse itself. But the case was kept open because there had to be others involved, and because of the other two cases we had on file — that of the small girl found wandering and of Glory Dorfner,

58

the child who did the drawings. There were no immediate links — but three cases of that kind in one area and within a few months of one another would always arouse the concern that they could be linked.'

'But still no proof?'

Lochie Craig shook his head. 'Not really. But Glory Dorfner was six, whereas the naked child had been younger, around four. The difference in age is crucial. Glory remembered things and over time, and with very patient counselling, she volunteered some snippets of information. She remembered being taken from home one night in a car, and being led down some steps to a dark room — maybe this cellar room in Plimmer Road. She remembered a camera. She remembered three or perhaps four men, apart from her stepfather. She remembered . . .' He cleared his throat. It was the first very slight sign he had given that even he was disturbed by some of the things he had to deal with in the course of his work. 'She remembered being sodomised, she remembered penetrative sex, she remembered having to have oral sexual contact with two men, as she had been forced to do with her stepfather. It took weeks to get all this from her. It's a sensitive business, as you know, we have to be extremely careful

59

not to make matters worse for the child, or to cause her any more distress, and perhaps most importantly, not to lead her to tell us about things that did not actually happen. In the last resort, we can never be a hundred per cent sure but the officers who got to know Glory and talked to her over a long period were certain that she was telling the truth and describing actual events. When they suggested one or two invented scenarios which were different from those she had described she always rejected them — she said, "No, I didn't have to do that. No, he didn't." She was as trustworthy as a child of six can be. It was an appalling case. Though there was no evidence, it did seem possible to link our one conviction — of Will Fernley — to another offence. Then the case of the child found wandering naked — well, there will always be a question mark over it and we won't get anything more directly from the girl. There was never much chance of that. But she was examined and semen was found on her externally and internally.'

'DNA?'

Craig shook his head. 'Yes, we got it, but it was no match either for Fernley or for anyone else on the databases.'

'Presumably it's stored so a match might

still come up.'

'That's what we always hope.'

'How long did he go down for?'

'Eight years, of which he has served five.'

He leaned back and folded his arms. Met Serrailler's look and held it. Linda sat very still. The third officer had taken notes on his laptop during the whole session, and hardly spoken a word.

'Simon, I'd like you to take a moment to think again, because it is absolutely crucial. Are you certain that you have never met Will Fernley or any member of his family?'

'Well, I meet a lot of people in the course of the working year, I've taken the Chief's place occasionally at public functions and so on. But that has always been within the county and I am as certain as humanly possible that I have never met any of the Fernley family.'

'Good. So we can proceed.'

NINE

She had been a couple of times to the house before but never felt relaxed there. It had something to do with the air of formality Gerald Hanbury always gave out and with his wife's slight imperiousness, and perhaps more to do with their elegant, beautifully proportioned home. Cat much preferred to meet Hanbury, the chairman of Imogen House, in her office there, not because she felt more in charge but because it was her own and fairly neutral territory. Today, though, he had asked her to lunch — it was just the two of them, his wife, Judge Nancy Cutler, being away on circuit. They had eaten in the pale green silk-lined dining room, where the tablecloth shone as white as in a washing powder advertisement and the napkins were card-stiff. The ceilings of this Queen Anne house were high and their two voices sounded brittle. But the asparagus, lamb cutlets, lemon mousse were good, if somehow predictable, they had had a single glass of Sancerre each, and were now back in Gerald Hanbury's study. It was a relief to find it slightly untidy, the armchair cushions less than perfectly placed.

'I have the impression,' Hanbury said, pouring her coffee, 'that things at the hospice have — how shall I put it? — not quite bedded down. Am I right?'

She had been prepared for this as the reason for lunch. Routine business would have merited an email.

'I'm afraid you are.'

'I thought we were going to save money by becoming a day-care hospice only.'

'We have a lot of money, though of course we're never flush with it. But this isn't about money. The transition was never going to be smooth but with hindsight we could have taken more time over it and perhaps planned it better. Staff don't feel settled — they know we haven't got things right yet. As you know, we had to shed a few of them when the wards closed but those who stayed aren't finding it easy. They miss the bedded wards, they keep referring back to them, as if they find day care only very much second best.'

'And do you?'

'Gerald, you know that in some ways yes,

I do, but I don't regret it.'

'I know that you have less responsibility —'

'I have less work.'

'Yes, and that must be frustrating when you were so heavily involved and put so much time and energy into the hospice during the old regime.'

'I recognise perfectly well that we had to change. Financially, we simply couldn't have continued as we were.'

'Indeed. And we can't go back. But I'm not happy and I realise that you're not either.'

'Are you suggesting I resign?'

'Good heavens, no! I'm hoping to give you a bigger role — though when I say "I" of course the job wouldn't be in my sole gift, even if it existed yet.'

'I'm still the medical director.'

'And you would continue as such. But we need to sit down and work out exactly what a day-care hospice does and does not do, how we can bring everything together and play to our strengths. We must stop looking back and we also need to be clear about the way forward. Hospice at home, for example? Listen, Cat, what I have in mind is this. The role of medical director, because it is less demanding, should be expanded, at least for the short term. You would take on a strategy role, to look at how we do things now and how we might do them in future, what we should and what we shouldn't be doing, and plan out a whole new strategy for Imogen House. It would involve your travelling round to look at other hospices, see how they organise their units.'

'That isn't a medical role, it's a managerial one.'

'To a certain extent, yes, but you know far more about what patients actually need than someone brought in as a pure administrator and who has no medical expertise. It would not be managing budgets and doing HR, it would be researching, assessing, planning for what would be the very best for future patients.'

'It needs a lot of thought.'

'Of course. But you are the ideal person for this — you have known the hospice from its inception, you know Lafferton and its communities, you're passionate about providing the best palliative care — who better to do this?'

'But as you've said, you can't just offer me the job.'

'No, it would have to be advertised. That shouldn't present us with any problem.'

'Has this been discussed by the full board?'

'Informally. I would put it to them as a firm proposal at the next meeting.'

'Whether or not I decide to apply?'

'Whether or not. We need to turn this round. Income is down, we have fewer legacies. People sense that things are not right and they have plenty of other worthy causes.'

Cat sat back in the deeply comfortable chair.

'I know, I know,' Gerald said. 'Here we go again. Poor Cat, you've been through this too many times. But I truly think that if we get things right now we'll be on a very firm base going into the future. And we absolutely do not want to lose you. Your experience and commitment are far too valuable.'

Instead of going straight home she drove out to Hallam House.

She found her stepmother lying on the sofa under a duvet, looking pale and reading *Love in a Cold Climate*.

'Oh, darling, it's lovely to see you but don't come near me, I'm toxic.'

'If it's the sickness bug, we've had it. Let me make us a cup of tea.'

'Not for me but could you bear to get me

66

some cold water and ice? I can keep that down if I sip it. I'm so sorry.'

That was something else, Cat noted, going into the kitchen. If she had ever felt an apology necessary for any reason Judith would never hesitate, but lately she had become someone who apologised too much, for things that could not possibly be her fault — like being ill. Whether or not her father had ever been physically violent, he could certainly be a bully and she did not like to see the self-confident stepmother she loved and admired become cowed.

Now, though, Judith seemed only to be cowed by the virus, and when she had sipped her iced water, she sat up and rearranged her cushions.

'Tell me what's going on in the great world, I'm starved of gossip.'

'This isn't goss, sorry, but I do need your take on something.'

'Good, that's exactly what I feel like, reclining here and giving out advice, so tell.'

Cat told and noted that, as ever, in setting out the proposal and how it seemed to her, she clarified her thoughts, saw the pros and cons and could begin to assess them.

'You need to mull it over for a while,' Judith said, 'but you have that advantage because it doesn't seem as if this is going to be a rushed appointment anyway — can they even afford to make it?'

'I suppose if they gave the job to me they would simply add to my salary — no idea how much — whereas if they opened it up they might have to advertise at a higher level.'

'That hardly seems fair. Don't sell yourself short, you're worth a lot to them.'

She couldn't afford to be too demanding either, but Cat could not possibly say that to Judith. Her financial worries were hers alone.

'You'd miss dealing directly with patients.'

'But I do so little of that now anyway. And I would still be medical director. I'd see some patients when I was in the day clinic.'

'Have you decided yet about sending Hannah to the performing arts college?'

'Still wondering.'

'She's got some talent and so much ambition, you can't refuse her now.'

'She's also only thirteen. Long way to go.'

'But she'd continue with her all-round education, and if she doesn't take up the place, she'll be so angry and frustrated she might down tools and refuse to do schoolwork at all.'

'Tell me about it.'

Hannah was more than capable of doing

exactly that. Her two elder children were nothing if not strong-willed and single-minded.

'Is it that you can't bear her to go away to board?'

'No. Not that at all.'

'So it's the money.'

Cat was silent.

'If I could afford to pay for her, you know that I would.'

'I wouldn't dream of letting you. No, either I pay or she can't go.'

'Then there will be university for Sam in three years or so.'

Cat got up. 'So if the new job is offered, I may have no choice.'

Ten

'Will Fernley spent the first years of his sentence in a category A prison,' the DCI said.

Serrailler had been with the officers from CEOP for well over an hour. He did not yet have any idea why.

'He had a tough time, as you may imagine — all sex offenders do and paedophiles come off worst of all. He was transferred because it was thought the risk to him was unacceptably high and things have been somewhat better for him.' She looked at Simon over the top of her bright-blue-framed spectacles. 'I think the word to stress is "somewhat". Whether it was partly or wholly out of fear that he might be attacked again, late last year he applied to be sent to Stitchford TC prison. His application was approved but he has had to wait until recently to be allocated a place. He's been there for three weeks and gone through the admissions programme. That finished last Friday.'

'How much do you know about TCs?' Craig asked.

More coffee had been brought in, this time with biscuits, and Simon selected one as he looked across the table.

'Only a little. TC stands for therapeutic community. Prisoners ask to be admitted — as you say Fernley did — and they undergo a rigorous year of therapy — or perhaps longer, I'm not sure — which is designed to make them address their crimes, to understand why they committed them, to try and face up to all that — and so maybe to change. I know the success rate at a TC like Grendon, for prisoners who complete the therapy and are later released after serving their time, is impressively high.'

'In other words, it works. It does — sometimes. But TCs used to be much more about equipping and preparing prisoners for their new lives outside and a fresh start. Nowadays, it's often lifers in for a year — and it can be up to eighteen months, by the way — for an intensive therapeutic programme. But they then go back into the mainstream prison system to finish serving their time. There's much debate about the point of a TC for lifers. I have no opinion either way.'

'Sex offenders would seem to be the best candidates for TC,' Linda continued, 'though the jury's out on that too. A lot of psychiatrists — and prison and police officers come to that — feel they are incurable, untreatable, and that it's just a case of damage limitation. I'm inclined to agree but only partly. I have known of successes.'

'And what's wrong with damage limitation?' Simon said.

Neither of them replied.

Serrailler leaned back in his chair, arms folded. Waited.

'So, Fernley is in Stitchford at the beginning of the programme,' Linda said eventually. 'We know that he committed offences against children going back some ten years, quite probably a lot more. We also know that he had — maybe still has — paedophile contacts across the country and abroad. We know that he was part of a paedophile ring based in and around Lafferton and we know he was involved with them in what we have called the Plimmer Group. They bought the building in Plimmer Road —'

'Bought it?'

'Yes — we're sure they have some members with plenty of spare money — Fernley himself to name but one. They bought the house, via an agency, they left it untouched except for the cellar and its inner room and they used this for their filming over approximately three years.'

'But Fernley's home is in Devon.'

'Yes. And some of the others will have come to Lafferton from all over England. They communicated remotely, via computer, but they met up in two or threes when they were making their films. Then they split again.'

'So — who are "they"?'

Craig finished his coffee, pushed the cup and his open laptop away from him, and leaned on the table, looking directly across at Simon.

'That,' he said, 'is the one thing we do not know and are determined to find out. That is what Will Fernley could tell us but never has — he's stayed silent throughout, from his arrest until now. But we know he knows and if we could get information on at least the leaders of this ring, we will be a long way towards closing it down and laying hands on shoulders. He's the key, no doubt of it.'

'I'm not trying to teach my grandmother, but have you discovered nothing from a trawl through computer hard drives and so forth?'

'Fernley had a laptop in his house but there was absolutely nothing of any interest to us on it. We ripped the house apart — his family home and his London house — found nothing. Whatever he had, he got rid of and we've accepted that we'll never find it. We do sometimes come across links with other computers we've seized but that's always a long shot and so far no joy at all. And we pick up an awful lot of laptops, as you may imagine.'

'Fernley said nothing to his lawyer?'

'Well, confidentiality and all that but we think not, nothing beyond what he had to tell him in connection with his own involvement in the cellar ring. And he stayed absolutely silent, or said "no comment" to every question, in every damned interview. He smiled nicely — he's a decent-looking bloke and he's got a very charming smile — but he didn't say a dicky bird. We've got nothing. We've spent hundreds of man hours on these cases and he's all we've got. Meanwhile, they're out there, whoever they are and however many of them. They are continuing to abuse children and recruit members to their ring and spread porn. And we've got to take them down.'

He banged his fist hard on the table. His face was creased with anger.

'I'm with you, of course I am, but where do I fit in? Presumably the cellar room is no longer used.'

'No. They're somewhere else.'

'On my patch?'

Craig shrugged. 'No idea. We have to get Fernley to talk. Short of an accidental find — and of course they happen — he's our only hope.'

'So you need someone to get close, try and open him up. Who?'

'You,' Linda said.

'Sounds good. I can take a couple of days, get a walk along the coastal path too. I know it well over there, though I've never been to Stitchford.'

Linda Warren and Lochie Craig glanced at one another.

'Do you know much about it?'

'Nothing beyond the name and that it's fairly new.'

'Stitchford was opened five years ago. It's relatively small and it's purely a therapeutic facility — no main prison. And it's privately run. It was talked about for years, decades even, but there was never the money and a lot of people didn't agree that it should exist at all, at least as an independent unit. In the end, though, a Home Secretary arrived who was very keen on privately run prisons and on the TC model in particular. There was an old wartime RAF base in the hinterland of north Norfolk which was disused and ripe for development. It was sold to a large private conglomerate who also run hospitals as well as two other special prisons and they built a shiny new set of buildings. They got an architect who had worked on the design of therapeutic communities in Holland and in Canada and he came up with an intergalactic complex. Sorry — I'm a bit of a cynic. Anyhow, there it is. It's a class-A facility so the security is very tight and it's a bit like Dartmoor — miles from anywhere and then just a few scattered villages. No dual carriageways or motorways for miles, no trains, one bus a millennium.'

'Fine. I'm happy to drive over there.' Serrailler was still baffled that it had taken a special visit to Lafferton by three officers to arrange it.

But Craig shook his head. 'There would be no point in your arriving as yet another cop to give him a grilling. He's never played ball before and he wouldn't do it now. He's never talked to anyone. Which is why you are being asked to do a covert op. You would become a prisoner, a sex offender who had served some time in a main prison and applied to do the intensive course at Stitchford. Two months max, then you'd be hastily transferred — i.e. spirited away in the middle of the night.'

'Essentially,' Linda said, 'you would be a sex offender, you'd attend all the group therapy sessions and community meetings — be a prisoner among sixty others, living as a prisoner, working as one, the whole package.'

'And trying to befriend Will Fernley — only him?

'Yes, though you'd socialise and spend time with others — it would look odd if you didn't. But Fernley is the one with a head full of names and all the info we need on the other members of his ring, where and how they're operating — because we know they still are. They're extremely clever, however — expert at hiding themselves and warning one another if there's the slightest wind that anyone is on to them. They operate on such a closed system that even with all our technological resources we haven't got into it.'

'And this is the ring who filmed their child abuse at the cellar room in Plimmer Road?'
'Yes.'
'I wonder how many times you hear offi-

cers say it's unbelievable — evil and sickening.'

'Every day,' Linda said. 'But "evil", "sickening", "pornographic", "abusive", "horrifying", are words you will learn not to use if you take this on. As of course are words like "scum", "castrate", "flog" . . .'

Serrailler leaned back again and closed his eyes. Behind them were images, swirling and expanding and receding.

They waited, not interrupting him, not pushing for an answer. But at last Craig said, 'If you decide to say no, that's it. We move on. This won't be an easy one. You need to be 110 per cent certain and committed. It will scour you. It will challenge you emotionally and psychologically and it won't be without risk, though obviously you would be as safe as it's possible to make you.'

'How many officers have you approached to date?'

'None. You're our first choice, Simon. You've done covert ops, you've been through the training process, you've been screened. You know the ropes. You've also been SIO on child abduction and murder cases. Above all, you're the right match. You're the man we think can get close to Fernley and extract the info we desperately need — if anyone can.'

Linda leaned forward and looked at Serrailler for a long moment. He read everything that she was about to say in her expression.

'Yes,' he said, 'understood.'

Understood, that the ring was as active as ever. Understood, that if they got even a snippet of genuine information they'd act on it and get results. Understood, that this sort of challenge was the real excitement of police work to him and when it came along, he was hungry for it. He felt as he did when a call for SIFT (Special Incident Flying Taskforce) came and he had to drop everything and go. The adrenalin had already started pumping through him.

'We can give you twenty-four hours,' Lochie Craig said.

'I don't need them,' Simon said. 'I'm in.'

Eleven

I was happy. I was happy when we met again, I was happy when I came to live with him here. I was happy when we married, and after we married. I was happy for — what, two years? At least.

I was happy.

I knew perfectly well that he was not the easiest man in the world. I knew he could be moody, irritable and demanding, I knew his irrational dislikes and that he needed to have things just so. I knew. But I was happy because he seemed to become softer, easier, less selfish. Because he was such good company. We laughed a lot. We enjoyed some of the same things and were happy to give one another space. We spent weeks in a camper van touring round America and we could not have been happier. We got along. We rubbed along. We . . . I . . .

Judith sat with the doors open onto the garden, a rug on her knees, book open on her lap. It was almost half past six and the last of the westerly sun was on the wide border beneath the wall. Meriel's border. She had planned, planted and tended it, as she had the rest of the garden. Meriel's garden then. And that was fine. She felt happy and blessed to have inherited it, though she herself didn't do a great deal. A young man called Olly came every week and looked after the beds and borders, the shrubs and the lawn, as if they were his own. Meriel would have liked Olly. They would have spent contented hours working together, discussing what might suit here and ought to come out of there, what needed cutting back, what was doing particularly well.

Judith liked to think of it. She had no disturbing feelings about the past in this place, about Meriel, about the family. There had been no doubts, in spite of Simon. He had resented her at first, but in the end, he had warmed to her and accepted her. She was his father's wife. She was not Meriel but she was his stepmother and she loved him and, eventually, he realised it. Now, they were as close as they could ever be.

Now.

Now that she was unhappy, and had been

so for the past year and a half. Now that Richard had become hostile, distant, cold. And occasionally — only occasionally, she told herself, only once or twice — had been violent towards her. It was not his fault. He found retirement difficult, he found her different ways hard to adjust to, he flared up for no reason but, but, but, of course, his temper flickered and went out just as quickly. He was not at heart a violent man. He was troubled and much of it had been her fault. She needed to understand him better, be more sensitive to him, give way, be less self-absorbed.

A swallow sat gracefully on the telegraph wire at the far end of the garden, forked tail dipping up and down to balance itself, and Judith had a moment of agonising awareness that it was free to stay there or to go, free to do anything until, in September, that strange communal instinct drove it to leave with the others for Africa and the sunshine. And mingled in with her flash of awareness was longing. I could do that. I could do that. She caught herself in mid-thought and was frightened.

'You not getting ready?' Richard stood in the doorway.

'Darling, I told you, I can't come. I'm still feeling nauseous and when I stand up I go giddy. This really is a knockout bug.'

'Funny I haven't caught it. Eat a couple of cream crackers, then go and get changed. You'll feel all the the better for it.'

'I doubt it and it would be such a nuisance for you if I was ill when we got there and you had to bring me home. You'll enjoy yourself much better on your own.'

'You just don't care for the Freemasonry.'

'I've no problem with the Freemasons, darling — don't forget Donald was one.'

'How does that make a difference?'

'It made me used to it. I've simply continued. I really don't feel well enough for a formal dinner.'

'Ladies' night is twice a year. People will wonder if I have a wife at all.'

'They certainly won't if you just tell them I'm ill.'

He clicked his teeth irritably and went out. She looked at his back. Straight, as if he had been a guardsman, hair grey but still thick. Shirt collar neatly settled into his sweater.

I was happy. I was very happy and I loved him. Not in the way I loved Donald. Who was it said 'the arrow only strikes once'? That was true, but it had not prevented her from marrying for a different sort of love, and for friendship and company. Why not?

She had met an old friend whose husband had had both hips and then a knee replaced. 'He's not the man I married!' Yvonne had said, laughing.

He's not the man I married. No. Or was he? Had it taken all this time for the real man to reveal himself or had he changed radically for some reason impossible to fathom?

She closed her eyes, feeling nauseous and giddy again. Poor Felix was still suffering from it; Cat was better but pale with dark shadows under her eyes.

'I haven't caught it.' He made her feel that catching a virus was her own fault. He was more careful. She had done it on purpose to get out of ladies' night.

She felt tears prick. That was because the illness had made her feel weak and vulnerable, of course, but she had cried more in the last year than in the last thirty and she had not always been able to blame a virus.

'You look very handsome, darling. A dinner jacket well becomes a man.'

Richard grunted. 'Have you seen my black wallet?'

'Yes, on the dressing table.'

'It certainly is not.'

'It was there this morning. Do you want

me to — ?'

But he had gone, running up the stairs — he could still do it.

'Yes?'

He did not answer, merely patted his pockets.

'Have you booked a taxi?'

'Naturally.'

'I am sorry, darling, but have a very good evening.'

'Eat something bland and get to bed early.'

'I will.'

The sound of the cab turning into the drive.

He left.

What have I done? Judith asked herself. What is it? When did it begin, this aloofness, this curt way of talking to me? What did I say, do, or not say, not do? We were happy. I was happy.

Something had flipped over to show a dark side. Never flipped back.

What did I do?

TWELVE

'Yes?' Shelley Pendleton twirled round. Tim was brushing the sleeves of his dinner jacket and barely glanced up.

'Fine.'

'Oh thanks.'

'No, sorry — you look good.' He hesitated.

'What?'

'Is it a bit low at the front?'

'Too revealing?'

'Some might think so.'

'Do you?'

'Not the point, I'm your husband.'

'You mean stuffy Masons — great master and all that.'

'Grand master.'

'So I should wear something high up to the neck with long sleeves, preferably in beige.'

'I didn't say that. You look good, OK? Come on.'

'It's boring when you don't have a drink.'

'It's boring when you have too many so watch out, Shell.'

'I'm ignoring that. You could have a couple of glasses.'

'If I'm driving it's much easier to have none at all. I don't mind.'

'I know you don't and I never understand it. You need it to get through the evening.'

'You mean you do.'

'I don't drink too much.'

'Not in general you don't. It's when you go out. Something comes over you.'

'Boredom usually.'

She dreaded going, dreaded it all the way to the hotel where they held all their silly meetings and the functions in the big dining room. But once they hit the place and she was repowdering, combing and adding a bit more mascara, in the ladies' cloakroom, she started to feel better. She always did. There was a buzz. There was the smell of *Giorgio* and *Poison* and *Paloma* and the sideways looks at every other woman's dress. So many in Eastex and Betty Barclay, Shelley noted, women over fifty playing it safe by becoming their mothers. She had spent silly money on a Stella McCartney, but she could get away with it all right. *Was* the front too low? She hitched at it. But it wasn't designed to be hitched, it was designed for a cleavage. She let it go again.

There was more buzz outside and on the stairs going up, the men, always good in DJs. This was when it started to get even better. A couple of glasses and it would be great. She gestured to Tim to give her his arm.

'Good evening, Richard.'

Richard Serrailler was a step or two above them.

'Tim. Shelley, beautiful as ever.'

Tim dug his elbow into her ribs. All right, so she did think Richard was handsome. Sexy even — not as sexy as his policeman son but he would do. She'd felt quite a pang when he had married again. Nobody had seen that one coming.

'Where's Judith?'

'Caught some bug from the grandchildren. So I can have Shelley all to myself.'

'I don't think so.' But Tim had seen someone across the room — networking, obviously. That's what the Masons were all about, networking, mutual backscratching. Oh, and charity, of course. There would be the usual, amazing raffle, in which Shelley had once won a Balenciaga handbag. All for charity — Masonic charity, naturally.

'Good, your husband has deserted you in a timely manner — let's go and find a drink.' Richard took her elbow and steered her through the crowd.

Nice, Shelley thought, the most distinguished-looking man in the room apart from the old Lord Lieutenant, though he had gone over rather suddenly into old age.

Richard waylaid a passing tray of champagne and handed her a glass.

'I hope we're sitting together.'

'I haven't looked. I always get next to some —'

'Old bore? Or a thigh pincher?'

'Usually both, I find.'

He had taken her arm now and led her to the seating plan. 'Now this is a bitter blow. I'm on B, you're D.'

'Never mind, we can wave to one another. And there's always the interval before they draw the raffle. I'm so sorry Judith is ill by the way — please give her our best.'

'It's nothing. She likes to cosset herself.'

Then Tim was back and someone was taking Richard Serrailler away for a quiet word.

They edged between bodies towards table D.

Judith woke from a short, deep sleep into the sensation of being in a storm at sea, the sofa pitching and tossing, the floor a green swell. She made it to the downstairs cloak-room and remained there for almost half an hour, sick and faint, the walls coming in on her and expanding again like balloons being pumped up.

Cat was writing up some dissertation notes, with Wookie the Yorkshire terrier squeezed on her lap against the edge of the desk, when the phone rang. He jumped off, eyeing her resentfully.

'Darling, I'm so sorry to bother you but is there anything I can do for this damn bug? Can I take something? I thought I was getting better but I'm worse and Richard's at a Masonic dinner.'

'Have you got any sachets of rehydrating powder?'

'I . . . I don't think so, no.'

'OK, get a glass of water, put in a teaspoon of salt and one of sugar and sip that. Do you have a temperature?'

'I'm shivery, so probably yes.'

'Could you hold down some paracetamol?'

'I can try.'

'I'd come over but I'm on my own with the children. Go to bed. I'll call in after I've done the school run tomorrow. And ring me again if you feel worse. Better still, get Dad home.'

'No, no, I'll be fine, and besides, he would be furious.'

So what? Cat thought, shifting the cat Mephisto off her chair. Not long ago you wouldn't have hesitated and he would have come back, grumbling perhaps, but come all the same.

She tried to settle down to work but after reading the same paragraph three times without taking in the meaning, she rang Silke, the au pair she used to share, and who still sat occasionally. Silke was up, watching 'TV schlock'. She was at the farmhouse in ten minutes.

'Did you lose consciousness?'

'I was very giddy. I remember coming upstairs. No, I don't think I passed out completely.'

'Headache?' Cat sat beside her, holding her wrist. The pulse was slow and Judith's eyes looked slightly sunken. 'You're dehydrated and you shouldn't be on your own. I'm going to call Dad —'

But Judith gripped her wrist tightly. 'No. Please. Do as I ask — *please.*'

THIRTEEN

Rachel stood by the tall windows of the sitting room in what Simon still thought of as 'his' flat. He came in, then stopped abruptly.

The two white sofas, placed adjacent to one another, had been moved so that now they were facing, and instead of being pure white, they had brilliant scarlet, purple and emerald-green throws of fabric over the backs. The colours were in themselves arresting and vibrant. But not in his room.

'No?'

To give himself time, he walked back into the kitchen, got some ice and dropped it into a glass, then filled it with two measures of gin and a little tonic.

'Drink?'

'Not just now thanks. I wondered if we could eat out — or is it too late for you?'

'Not too late but don't we have anything in the fridge?'

'Yes, fine.'

He sat on the nearest sofa and looked across at the other. No, he thought, absolutely not.

He got up again.

'I'm sorry. I just loved the colours — I wanted to . . . to make my mark I suppose.'

'Not the colours so much,' he said, 'but I just can't have them arranged like this. I like them as they were. This way round doesn't work at all.'

'OK,' Rachel said brightly, and started to haul one end of the first sofa round. Simon took over, and they were back to their original positions in seconds.

'I dare say you were right the first time. Sorry, darling.'

'No problem. And yes, let's eat out by all means.'

'There's the new dim sum place in the Lanes.'

'No. I need proper sustenance.' He drank. The colours of the throws jazzed in his eyeline.

Rachel moved to sit beside him. He put his arm round her.

'I wonder if you should get something to do.'

'To do? You mean, work?'

Rachel's husband had left her a valuable house, which she had rented out, a chunk of capital, an even bigger chunk of shares, and a good annual income. She was not a lazy woman but she had no need to work and she wanted to take her time about finding the right thing, whether paid or voluntary. She had trained as a solicitor but only practised for a few years and hated it.

What concerned Simon most was that, with time on her hands and no money worries, she might make more radical changes to the flat than simply moving the sofas about and buying a couple of throws.

He was unprepared for what she did say, when they were having their first glass of wine in the bistro.

'Si, your flat is lovely but it's nowhere near big enough for us both, is it? I thought we might look for a house. No hurry, we want to make sure it's absolutely the right one.'

He was so appalled he took too large a gulp of wine and had a coughing fit. By the time he had recovered with water, he was calmer — a little.

'Absolutely not. Not even up for discussion.' He looked into her violet-coloured eyes and saw distress and knew that it was unavoidable. 'Rachel, the flat is my haven — it's my security, my safe place, my oasis . . . whatever you like, it is. It's where I can be my real self and I could no more leave it than climb Everest. Actually, I would probably climb Everest sooner than leave the close. I'm sorry if it feels small but you've made it smaller with your stuff. It should be fine for two people.'

'You want me to take my things away?'

The waitress came with his steak, her salmon. He ordered another bottle of the house Merlot. More water, giving himself time.

'No, I didn't say that.'

'I can, easily, of course I can. You should have said. Most of my other things are in storage, the rest can go there too. No problem. But — I wonder why you can't imagine your bolt-hole somewhere else. If we found the right house —'

'I can't.'

Rachel hesitated. He could see that she was uncertain what to say next, how to react, that she was upset and puzzled, he recognised it and couldn't help her. But he hated himself because it was like this all over again. It was always like this.

'Rachel . . .'

'I'm sorry. I feel stupid. I've done this all wrong.'

'No, of course you haven't. I'm sorry I'm difficult about it. I really do try not to be difficult about a lot of things but this is just non-negotiable.'

'I didn't understand. Not properly. I shouldn't have brought my stuff and put throws all over the sofas and changed your pictures.'

'Changed my pictures?' He saw her eyes fill with tears. 'Rachel . . .'

'Leave it. Eat your food, it'll get cold. I'm really sorry.'

He poured her wine. 'Drink,' he said, 'now. Just don't choke.'

She did not smile.

'Drink.'

She drank.

'What kind of a shit am I?' Simon said.

'No kind. I wanted to ask about something else.'

'Ask anything.' He put his hand over hers. 'Go on.'

'I'm afraid of how you'll react.'

'Jesus, please, Rachel — don't be afraid of me. Really, don't.'

'It's nothing major.' She looked up at him anxiously. 'Can we talk about holidays?'

'Of course we can talk about holidays, for Christ's sake.'

'I just wondered if you had any leave blocked out — so we might book to go away somewhere? I haven't had a proper holiday since Kenneth's illness. I haven't had one for years. It was always the odd weekend when I could get care for him — well, you know all that.'

'A holiday,' Simon said slowly. 'A holiday would be beyond good.'

Her face lit up with relief and delight.

'Only problem is something that came up today which means I won't be able to commit myself to definite dates.'

'But you have to — you get leave.'

'I do but not always when I want it and this has made things very fluid for the foreseeable months, maybe till the autumn. I just don't know.'

'So what is this "something" that's come up?'

'I'm afraid I can't tell you.'

'Oh. Yes, well, I understand. But you must have some idea when it will be and roughly how long for?'

'No,' Simon said. 'I have absolutely no idea at all.'

He looked at Rachel, and saw her struggle not to show disappointment. She was right, they ought to have a holiday, two or three weeks far away. But his holidays were not her holidays. He walked and spent hours drawing and next leave he had been planning the Norwegian fjords and the Northern Lights. Rachel loved sun, white sand, reading for hours with a long cool drink beside her. Romantic evenings. Those were things she had not had for many years with Kenneth, things she deserved. Things he realised that he too could not, or would not, give her.

She was looking out of the window into the empty Lanes in the lamplight. Phoney old-fashioned-style lamplight, but pleasing nevertheless. She was as beautiful in profile as full face, and she was sad.

I don't deserve you, Simon thought but did not say. Too much of his life had contained the unsaid. That would not change.

'There just are some things I can't tell you. You do understand that?' he said, his arm round her shoulders as they walked back.

'Yes. If it's the job that goes without saying.'

'What else would it be? This assignment is open-ended — they often are.'

'Will it take you away?'

'Yes.'

'Far?'

'I can't say.'

They walked through Cathedral Close, where the huge old magnolias had finished flowering and the trees were in first fresh leaf. He could never leave here. Not for anything. Or anyone.

'I was thinking that you won't want to be on your own in the flat for weeks on end,' Simon said.

Rachel did not answer. Was she afraid to look at him, for fear of reading something in his face that she was desperate not to know?

FOURTEEN

All right, women could be bores but never such bores as men, Shelley thought. The neighbours seated to her left and right were the usual, old, well-meaning bores, pillars of the Lafferton Masonic Lodge, intent on telling her everything about their working lives. Not even the grandchildren, she thought, accepting a second refill of Côtes du Rhône from the waiter, not even holidays. Why do they think I'm interested in taxes? Why do they think I want to know about traffic regulation? Why do they never ask a single question about me?

The food was edible but undistinguished, the wines better than at most of these deadly events. She looked for Tim and saw him listening with interest to the woman on his left, a large woman in electric-blue lace with eyeshadow to match. Tim knew how to behave at dinners, taking equal notice of the one on his right, then on his left, and never, ever ignoring women.

She could not catch his eye but then she saw Richard Serrailler looking in her direction. Shelley smiled slightly. Richard winked.

She drank half her glass of red wine quickly. The noise level had risen, the main course plates were being cleared away with too much clatter. It was only nine thirty. Another couple of hours had to drag by before they could think of leaving.

Between the dessert and the coffee, Shelley got up, smiling to her neighbours vaguely, and headed for the cloakrooms, through the wide doors of the banqueting room and down a flight of stairs. The buzz from the big room was shut out and it was blessedly quiet. Corridors to hotel rooms went off left and right, all empty. Even the turn-down teams had finished and left. Who, in heaven's name, designed cloakrooms like this? A small lobby led into a huge plush-carpeted, plush-wallpapered outer room, with lines of mirrors, pink downlit basins, scent and handcream in expensive brand bottles that were probably only refilled with the cheapest, sets of tortoiseshell-backed brushes that no one used. Gilt chairs. Two plush-covered sofas.

She had not needed to come down here,

she would just have gone mad if she hadn't got away for a few minutes.

She took her comb and hairspray out and as she did so, the door opened an inch or two. Shelley glanced in the mirror. Probably some other woman bored out of her skull. 'Ladies' night' — how many 'ladies' actually wanted or enjoyed it?

The door opened another inch.

'Richard? This is the Ladies!'

He came in swiftly, and immediately took one of the gold chairs and jammed it against the door handle. Shelley stared at him.

'What the hell are you doing?'

'Now now . . . you know perfectly well. Naughty girl.'

She was still in a state of confusion when he had grabbed her round the waist and pushed her onto a sofa.

'For God's sake, Richard, you're drunk — get out of here, what are you thinking?'

'You know full well what I'm thinking — exactly the same as you, and no, I am not drunk. Careful not to be or it would have spoiled everything.'

The next few minutes were like none Shelley had ever known. She felt Richard's strength and determination, panicked, bit him, lashed out, only to have him press his hand on her mouth, swearing.

'Listen, it's extremely ill-mannered of you to flirt with me, send out clear signals, to the extent of leading me out of the dining room with an obvious look . . .'

She tried to speak, furious and struggling, but his hand pressed harder and then she was afraid that he might actually smother her. She went limp.

'That's better . . .'

His knee was in her groin, his hand pushing up her skirt. Fear, disbelief, shock, nausea, fury . . . but she knew better than to try and fight such focused strength and instead prayed for someone to come in, rattle the knob, push the door hard enough to overturn the chair. But no one came. The room was oddly silent, muffled by the plush furnishings. She heard a sound coming from her own throat, and then the grunts from his, tried to struggle again and felt his elbow jab her so hard in the stomach that for a few seconds she could not breathe.

And all the time, round and round in her head, round and round, was the thought that he had spoken the truth, that she had flirted with him, not just tonight but often in the past, exchanged looks, let his hand linger on her shoulder or her back, smiled with her eyes looking into his. What did she expect then? What else did she expect?

FIFTEEN

'How long has he been in your sights?'

They were in room 9, a bland office in a bland office block in south London — Jed Nichols, the DCI attached, and Serrailler. Nichols was Afro-Caribbean, taller than him, lithe and very focused — Simon had never met a man more intense about his job, more dedicated, more . . . the word 'enthusiastic' seemed wrong in context, but it was right. He wore jeans and an open-neck denim shirt. Purple Converse trainers. A thin gold wire bangle on his left wrist, thin gold earring in his right ear. Simon had liked him on sight, as he had bounded down the stairs to meet him in the lobby.

'We ought to be several steps ahead of them,' Jed had said, 'and we're not, we're always, always behind — a combination of this being a rapidly expanding area of crime, an explosion of people with Internet access and technological expertise, plus the usual . . .'

'. . . lack of resources.'

Jed had nodded.

Two laptops open on the desk. No pens, no paper. No waste bin. No traces. They took their empty paper cups away and dropped them in a container outside.

Will Fernley.

His face was on Simon's screen, several times over. The images ranged from his official police and prison ID photos, to more personal ones. Will as a teenager, leaning on a gate. Will as a young man at Oxford. Will with an older man, both walking across a field carrying shotguns. Will in a touched-up professional portrait, aged thirty. Will in morning suit as someone's best man. Will, presumably, with a jacket over his head and handcuffed, being led by two shirt-sleeved police officers.

He was rather gentle-looking, with an engaging smile, clean-shaven, light brown hair, worn slightly long — a young man at ease with himself, confident, relaxed, open, his expression without any angst. An untroubled face.

They spent a few minutes looking at it in silence. Then Jed leaned back, hands behind his head.

'Thoughts?'

Simon looked one last time, then turned away. 'First thought is an odd one maybe. I am still absolutely certain that I've never seen him in my life before — as I said to Lochie and Linda. Quite certain. But looking at these — I know him.'

Jed nodded.

'He's a type,' Serrailler said. 'A classic upper-middle-class, public-school- and Oxbridge-educated son of a country land-owner. He's pretty conventional though he probably sports jeans rather than pink cords — his dad wears those — and he wouldn't be seen dead in tweeds except when shooting. Or brogues. He's easy to talk to, gets on well with most people, affable, good host. He's an open book. I know him.' He paused and looked out of the window onto a section of corrugated roof. A pigeon. A rectangle of blue sky. Like being in prison, he thought. Better get used to it. 'But obviously I don't. I don't know the half.'

'You do know the half and you're spot on about it. You probably even know three-quarters. It's the hidden part you don't know. No one does. Has anyone ever known? Fernley himself doesn't know because he won't let himself. Most of the time he can't admit that this part even exists.' Jed jumped to his feet and paced a few times round the room. 'Or so the psychs would tell us.'

'You don't agree?'

He shook his head. 'Not my concern. It'll be yours though. You'll be the one who hears all about that hidden person. You'll have a deeply hidden persona of your own before long. Listen —' he leaned over Simon, hands on the table — 'I know there's a why, I know there's a whole string of whys — but what I'm here for — what we're all here for — isn't to dig out the why, it's to dig out the truth — the facts. Who. Where. When. How. Not Why. That's someone else's job. We're here to catch them. To stop them doing any more damage. We're not even here to prosecute and punish — we pass that on. I want to ferret out every one of these child abusers and every scrap of information they've got about the others. Who. Where. Everything we do in here, every day, is about that. You know what abusers are? Thieves and robbers. They rob children, they rob them of their innocence and their trust and their sense of self-worth. They rob them of their childhood and a childhood is something you can never get back.'

His voice had grown not more strident but quieter and quieter as his words became more passionate. Now, he went silent and did not catch Serrailler's eye.

You, Simon thought. That's why. Somehow, sometime, it happened to you.

'This is only a sample of what Fernley had on his computer. You ever seen any of this stuff before?' He held up his hands. 'Not a leading question, sorry — but you haven't worked in this area much and your average CID officer doesn't come on it very often, not in this category. We're dealing with level 5 child pornography.'

'I know.'

'You wouldn't be on this job if you couldn't cope with looking at it, goes without saying — all the same, it doesn't make for easy viewing, Simon. One tip — it's a weird thing, but it takes on a life of its own. It'll try to burrow its way into your head, into your memory, into every corner of your waking and sleeping. Don't let it. There's a trick you'll learn, with experience — not sure how it's done, to be honest, you just find yourself doing it and you get better at it. You watch and you let it slide over the surface of your mind but you don't give it permanent space inside your head. Make sense?'

'Perfect sense.'

'Only with that knack comes the risk —

that you'll stop being disturbed by it and start to get used to it, which is one thing, but getting used to it must never mean "accepting". You *never* accept it, you never tolerate it, you never stop being 110 per cent focused on eliminating it from God's earth. Right — leave you to it. Back in an hour.'

It was one of the most draining hours of Serrailler's life. He began by reminding himself of Jed's advice and had to remind himself of it several times as he viewed the material from Fernley's laptop. When he had finished going through it, sometimes flipping over images so fast he barely noted what they contained, he closed the computer and instinctively drank an entire glass of water. He did not let his mind recall what he had seen. Instead, to steer himself in another direction entirely, he tried to remember a poem — any poem — and hit upon one he had learned at school.

Day after day, day after day,
We stuck, nor breath nor motion;
As idle as a painted ship
Upon a painted ocean . . .

After a while, he recalled the whole of Coleridge's *Ancient Mariner* and repeated it twice, so that the images in his head were of the bearded old man, the huge bird, the still ship and the sea under a burning sky.

'OK?' Jed looked into Serrailler's face the moment he came through the door.

'Yes.'

'So?' He set down two cups of black coffee.

'If I was up for this at the start . . .' He realised that he was clenching his fist round the paper cup.

'Good man. You won't have to look at this stuff again. No point.'

'What's next?'

'Read through the account of Fernley's trial. Not that he gives anything away. Read his file — everything we know about him down to the brand of boxers he wears, everything we've got about his life, from birth. It's all been put on disk. You don't have to stay here to go through it. You sign it out and keep it on your person at all times when it isn't in the laptop. You sign it back in when you're done.'

Jed signed him, his laptop and 'all material' out of the building, the reception clerk took his pass, the door locked behind him and he was on a scuzzy London backstreet, with the sound of metal on metal from a bodywork repair shop and the smell of rain on dirty pavements.

Dearest Simon

I hope you reached wherever you were going safely and I do understand that you can't make contact. Of course I do. It's your work and I have never, ever minded it taking you away for long hours or days and even weeks — as maybe this will? — because you are so totally committed to your job. How could anyone mind that?

But this isn't really about work, as maybe you already realise, this is about something that's gone wrong and someone who longs for that not to be the case and to know how to put it right. I love you — that is the simple truth. It's not something fleeting or shallow. I don't doubt that you love me and that you have committed yourself to our relationship in a way you have perhaps never done previously with anyone. Yet I feel what was a hair's distance between us is widening to a gap and I don't want it to become a chasm.

I need you to talk to me and tell me what you want me to do, how you want me to be with you. I need you to tell me because I just cannot guess — or not all of the time and then it is only about unimportant things. What have I said or done that makes you uncomfortable or unhappy? What has happened to distance you?

I love you so so much and it is lonely and bleak without you, but all this makes it much worse. It isn't that you are absent in person, it's that I feel your absence from me in some deeper way. Even when you're there. We were so happy together — even through the hardest time, we seemed so able to cope and support one another, because we loved. What's changed?

If you can find a way to communicate — preferably to talk, but if not, email is fine — just tell me what has happened, what I have done, what you want me to do. I can't bear any sort of coldness to develop. We're too close for that and I love you too much.

I am working at the bookshop all next week, to give Emma a break. Wish me luck.

You thought I wouldn't like to be in the flat by myself and I did wonder, because of the empty offices below and no one about at night. But I love it. I love the flat whenever I'm there, but best of all with you — that goes without saying.

Look after your so-beloved self.

Rachel

He had checked into the office block that was a standard chain hotel, showered, changed, glanced into the bar thinking he might get a drink before heading out to eat, saw what it was like, and just headed out. He had walked a mile or so before finding a decent Thai restaurant, eaten well, drunk a couple of cold beers, and walked back. He felt perfectly at ease — just glad he was a copper and six foot two.

He stopped at a late-night supermarket and bought a bottle of overpriced Famous Grouse. Put up the Do Not Disturb notice on his door, then locked it. Half drew the curtains, though there was only the playground of a junior school opposite, with black metal poles at intervals between twelve-foot-high wire panels. He gave the room a quick check, sat down at the flimsy table and opened up his laptop.

Dearest Simon . . .

He read the email through, then read it again more slowly and as he read he felt the

113

long-familiar knotting in the pit of his stomach, the needles of panic and anxiety probing their way into his mind.

Dearest Simon . . .

He closed his eyes. Images. Images. He opened them again. Got up. Poured a whisky and ran the tap until the water was as cold as he could make it. Sluiced it round his throat. Topped up his glass.

Images.

Let them slide over the surface. Don't let them burrow.

He read the email again.

Listen, you jerk — this is the woman you fell in love with. The woman with the heart-shaped face and violet eyes. The woman who had an affair with you while looking after her sick husband, and who never once made you feel bad about that. The woman who would marry you tomorrow, love and look after you for the rest of your life, maybe even have children for you. The one woman who actually got through to you so far as to come and live with you in your sacred space.

Rachel.

So now what?

What do you want?

He could answer that immediately. He had no idea what he wanted but he knew what he did not. He had always known that. He did not want a wife, a family, an invasion of his space, a dependent being, someone who tried to second-guess him or look into his mind, let alone his soul. He did not want to be disturbed or disarranged or invaded. He loved Rachel. Yes, he could answer that easily enough, but in his own way, on his own terms. He knew himself too well and far better than anyone else knew him. Cat thought she knew him but she didn't, his mother had once thought so, but had also come to understand that she didn't. Rachel? Maybe she knew him better than he thought, but if she did, he couldn't cope with it.

Dearest Simon . . .

What had she done? What had happened between them? How could she start to put things right? What, why, how, supposing, if . . .

Please. Please. Simon?

The image he had now was of her face and her eyes and the expression in them, the last time he had seen her — puzzled, thoughtful, anxious.

He had to let that image glide over the surface of his mind, too, and leave it there.

He looked at the email again, without reading it. She wanted a reply. Deserved a reply.

He had none.

He took the disk out of his inner pocket and inserted it into the drive. The machine whirred softly for a few seconds, then the screen flickered.

He began to read about Will Fernley, the man he must get to know as well as he knew himself.

SIXTEEN

'I've read up on Fernley's trial,' Simon said. 'He wasn't giving an inch.'.

'He's a bloody mute. Except when he's talking about anything else under the sun and then he's quite chatty — full of charm, looks you in the eye. Mind you, that was then. Five years banged up has probably changed all that.'

Simon set down his fork and leaned forward slightly. They were surrounded by men and women in the same line of work, no one would be eavesdropping, but his instinct always told him to play safe.

'Listen, Jed — I'm doing this because you have drawn a blank on everyone connected with Fernley in this Internet ring. You've chased every lead, then every shadow until you've started chasing yourselves. And as this building we are in houses all the people in the country capable of breaking into just about any of these set-ups, you will have thrown every bit of expertise you've got at it. I'm your last resort.'

'Pretty much says it all.'

They left the canteen and headed out for a walk along the Embankment.

'Fernley stayed shtum — no names, no places, no admissions — helped get himself a long term as a result.'

'How has he been inside?'

'OK. Keeps his head down, polite, affable but he watches out. Nonces have to. Plays a top game of table tennis. Reads a lot — he orders up psychology and philosophy books via the library. We've got as much inf as we can but you'll find out more, hopefully. Whether you'll get close enough to have him open up further I have my doubts, to be honest. But as you said, last resort.' Jed stopped. They leaned on the wall and looked out over the river. The tide was low, water dark, litter and driftwood spoiling the sand and shingle edges like a rash.

'We're working on your legend this afternoon. Harry's coming in on that. The one you used last time you did a covert ops won't do because that was very different circs.'

'Firearms.'

'Right.' Jed looked down. 'Dirty old river,' he hummed. 'I'd have given my back teeth to have written that song.'

'You do that? Music?'

'Gigs. Clubs. Out of town mostly. I sing my own stuff.'

'Play anything?'

'Sax. I try to go to New Orleans every year — play in the bars, join up with whatever jazz is out on the street. One day I might not be back.' He held open the door for Simon. 'One day — when we've cleared the rats out of all these sewers.'

It was after seven before the three of them had thrashed out his full identity and legend — the man he would become for his time at Stitchford Therapeutic Community Prison.

'You know how it goes. From the moment you're picked up — you are no longer Simon Serrailler, no longer a detective chief superintendent, no longer a copper. You are Johnno Miles. Anything catch you out the last time?'

'Yes — when someone calls out your real name, and you automatically respond. Harder than forgetting to reply to your new one.'

'No use saying there probably won't be any other Simons because there could be four. You'll be aware. It's a decent legend I think — we've got a good blend of true and

119

false, and as much of the true as we dare keep. OK, last thing. This.'

A small padded mailing envelope. From it Jed took a cheap black plastic watch.

'Snoopy!'

'Yeah, sure you've used one before. But this is state of the art as of about three months ago.'

'Three years at least since I had one.'

'Long time in surveillance terms. Right . . . this works on GPS, like they all do now. These pretend-fancy knobs? Three are recorded messages. The first is "A-OK". This knob starts the recorder and you can speak up to eight words, it holds and relays them to my receiver which will be backed up by my deputy, Al Morris. When I'm off he's on and vice versa. Four of these pressed in quick succession . . .'

'Red emergency.'

'Same as before, yup. Then all hell gets let loose. It also tracks you constantly and it's pretty tough but it's not completely inde-structible. Other signals from similar devices could conceivably interfere with it but there aren't likely to be any of those in your nick. It's showerproof but it won't cope with submersion.' He handed it over. 'It looks cheap, like you got it with a tank of petrol, so not worth nicking, and they don't have much of a thieving problem in Stitchford, interestingly.'

Harry stood up.

'And that's it, Johnno Miles. Best of luck. Next time we meet you'll be yourself again.'

At six o'clock the following morning, 'Johnno Miles' was sitting on the hotel bed, holdall beside him. At five past, the call came telling him a taxi was waiting and by half past, he was in a safe house in another London backstreet, handing over his bag to a monosyllabic young plain-clothes officer and getting another in exchange. He changed into a pair of dark blue jeans, denim shirt, black fleece, navy-and-white trainers. In the bedroom he checked the contents of the bag. Clean set of underwear, two T-shirts, grey jogging pants, four pairs of socks, two navy cotton handkerchiefs, one pair of sports shorts. Shaving kit. Toothbrush and comb. Lee Child paperback. A pack of ibuprofen tablets for backache. Watch on his wrist.

The second cab picked him up and he was away down the street on a pearly morning with a mist floating over the surface of the river. There was already a build-up of traffic and the runners and joggers were out two-deep. Simon watched them as the traffic lights turned to red and had an urge to leap out, throw his new kit over the wall and set off with them, running away, following the tide. The next few weeks would be hard. Freedom was precious and he was no longer free, the system had picked him up and was conveying him along. He had to go with it.

He wondered what Rachel was doing — in bed, hair tucked into her neck, arm outstretched, breathing quietly, or standing at the window of the flat with her first mug of coffee, looking at the sunlight touching the flying angels on the cathedral tower. Or somewhere else. He had no idea and could not find out. A sense of complete isolation hit him, as he realised that very few people in the world knew where he was and where he would be for the next weeks and even months. The Chief would be too busy with other things to spare him a thought, the prison governor would be fretting, wondering if he should have authorised this under-cover operation at all. But Jed would be concerned, thinking about him, silently wishing him luck. Jed was his contact, listening ear, safety net, minder, overseer. His only contact with Jed, though, was a minute electronic device which communicated the minimum of urgent or significant information.

They had left the Embankment and were heading into the tightly knotted streets of the City. He was in the hands of the driver and the plan now. He knew where he would be by the end of the day. That was all. How he would get there, let alone what it would be like, he had no idea.

SEVENTEEN

There were seven of them in the prison van. Simon had been taken to another safe house in the black cab, then conveyed by a small white van to the back entrance of a huge outer London prison. There he had been frisked, his bag labelled and taken away, before he was put into a holding room. Two other men were already there, four arrived later. The room was the usual — stuffy, windowless, green paint, like every interview and holding room in every police station Simon had ever known. They were given tea in paper cups, and a plate of biscuits between them. They waited for four and a half hours. Lavatory breaks had come twice, and each of them was escorted by a prison officer. There was nothing to read, nothing to look at, nothing to do. He glanced at the others occasionally. They sat with their heads down, hands on their knees, staring at the floor. No eye contact between them.

They ranged in age from early twenties through to a couple in their sixties, if not older. They looked wary, defeated, and used to endless waiting. He remembered it now, the waiting, sitting about in pubs, in greasy spoons, in cars, during a covert op, sitting outside police cells, waiting for a balloon to go up.

Waiting.

They shuffled their feet, cleared their throats, sat back, leaned forward again, and closed their eyes. More tea. No biscuits. The duty prison officer left and another took his place. There was no clock. No one told them they could not talk but they didn't anyway. They were rule-bound.

He had met paedophiles often enough but not six together, convicted, serving time for the offence, waiting to find out if this or any other therapeutic regime under the sun could cure them, take the rotten core out of the apple and make it wholesome again.

He caught the eye of the oldest-looking man. Looked away. So, he's thinking the same. Paed. Nonce. Another like me.

The brown linoleum was worn away where feet had rubbed into it.

'Seven for Stitchford? Follow me.'

They filed out, Simon expecting a closed prison van but they were greeted by a people carrier. Climbed in.

'The journey takes three hours. We have a single pit stop, we'll be met at the service station by two prison officers from Stitchford, who'll supervise the break. Then on for the last hour. If you need a pee now put your hand up.'

Two hands.

The doors were opened, and they were escorted out. Three minutes and back.

'Seat belts on please.'

The gates opened for them and they slipped into the stream of afternoon traffic out of London.

Ten minutes or so into the journey the man in the next seat at the back of the carrier offered Simon a mint.

'Thanks.'

'Nobby.'

'Johnno.'

The man in front half turned. 'It's Brian, if we're getting pally.'

That was it. The others went on silently looking out of the windows.

'Where you come from, Johnno?'

'Dartmoor.'

'Shit.'

'You?'

Nobby jerked his thumb back to London.

'Wandsworth?'

'Pentonville. You been?'

'Started out in Exeter, got moved to Dart-moor, that's it, me.'

'Not bad.'

'Yeah, right.'

'How long?'

'Done four and a half.'

'Out of?'

'Nine.'

'Shit.'

'You?'

But Nobby didn't answer.

They hit the M1 and a belt of rain that streamed down the windows, blocking any view. Simon put his head back and closed his eyes. 'Johnno,' he said inside his head. 'Johnno Miles. Johnno Miles. Johnno Miles. Giles John Archer-Miles. Johnno. Johnno. Johnno Miles.'

The driver slammed on the brakes, shaking them all up.

'Christ.' Man in the row in front of them. 'Fuckin' mentalist.'

'Me?' the prison driver asked warningly. 'Or him?'

There was a murmur round the van.

'Good job.' He edged forward again.

'We could play I spy,' Nobby said. 'If we could see out the bleedin' windows.'

Seems normal, Simon thought. People

carrier of blokes going from work site A to D, Tuesday afternoon. Usual mixture. Normal. Motorway full of the same. Instead, six of us are convicted child abusers, two are prison officers, one is an undercover DCS. Six men serving time for offences so unimaginably vile most people would cross the street to avoid coming face to face with any of them, the rest would spit, a couple or more would get out a knife. He caught the man in front glancing round. Brian. He bent his head. You had to get used to that, not making eye contact, keeping your head down. Until now. Until the therapeutic community that was Stitchford, where there would be no hiding place, not for any of them. Not even for Johnno Miles. The only one who was hiding so deep he might never crawl out of the hole was Simon Serrailler.

EIGHTEEN

Prison. He'd been in plenty of prisons but Stitchford was relatively new, purpose-built as a therapeutic community. It housed enough highly dangerous lifers to make it a category A, so that whatever the facade, the reality was maximum security. It looked it.

They were not very far from the coast so that by the time they were nearing the prison a sea fret had rolled over them, shrouding the buildings. First came a mile or so of flat land, concrete runways to either side, a few disused hangars — even now, remnants of World War II still lingered.

'Gawd,' one of the men said.

It was on two levels, concrete and glass, porridge and grey, perfectly camouflaged in the fog. The usual high perimeter fencing, barbed wire bent inwards, cement posts. The usual gate. The usual security. The van stopped and the driver leaned out. A couple of words and they were waved through. A hundred yards to the main gate which opened automatically. Closed behind them. A wide entrance yard. Glass doors. They drew up. A second or two of silence as the engine died and every one of them looked out again, at the prison into which they had struggled and begged and queued to be admitted. Last chance. If it didn't work here, Jed had said, a paedophile was at the end of the road, locked in with himself for good. Or for bad.

They jumped out one by one and started to bend, stretch, jump, easing limbs and circulation.

'Like a long-haul flight,' Brian said.

Simon nodded.

'Wouldn't know,' another said.

Another holding area. Better. Larger. Windows. Tea and a slab of cake. Sports magazines. Plastic flowers and a living pot plant.

The driver and his mate had disappeared.

One of the men got up and went to try the door. It opened.

'Fuck me.'

'How far do you reckon you'd get?'

He hesitated. Sat down again. None of the others had moved, apart from reaching for cake.

How much of prison life was spent hanging about, waiting, waiting, doing nothing? How long now? An hour? Two?

The first two men's names were called before they'd finished drinking.

Then the next.

'Johnno.'

It was not the fact that it wasn't his own name that almost caught him out, but the use of a first name. In prison, you were either a number or a surname.

He stood up.

'Hello, Johnno, I'm Neil. Welcome to Stitchford.'

Hand outstretched. The prisoner he was would not have had anyone proffer their hand to him perhaps for years. Paedophiles expected it least of all. People would sooner shake the hand of a serial killer.

'Thanks.'

This man does not know who you really are. This man thinks you have sexually abused and filmed others sexually abusing children as young as four years old. This man knows you have been sent down for nine years. This man . . .

'I'm a forensic psychologist and head of therapy here. We'll meet each other again tomorrow morning in your introductory assessment. I hope you settle in quickly —

you'll find everyone wants to help you do that, staff and your fellow inmates. Ask about anything practical and someone will tell you — and there's a list of everyday info in your room, plus fire drill and so on. Your daily timetable is in there too. You're on B wing, upper floor, room 6.'

Neil leaned back in his chair. He had a desk in the corner of the room but he was not sitting behind it. Simon had the chair next to him.

'You asked to come here. You know that, but do you also know that about sixty people a week apply for a place in this community and only a couple are selected?'

'I got lucky.'

Neil raised an eyebrow. 'In one sense, you're dead right. How long ago did you apply?'

'Fifteen months.'

'About average. So you understand how much competition there is for a place. Do you know the dropout rate?'

Simon shook his head, though he did.

'High. High because this therapeutic journey is no walk in the park, Johnno. It's tough. It drains you. It turns you inside out. It scours you. You expose in public, out loud, the details not only of what you have done — all of it — but how you felt and feel about that. Therapy isn't a nice lie on a couch with one psychiatrist listening to you talk about your dreams. Forget that. This hurts, there's nowhere to hide and it's relentless. It's why you're here and it's what you do, day in, day out, six days a week. Quite a few men think it'll be a breeze and it finishes them. They'd rather just go back into main prison, with all its misery and risks — and you know what those risks are for paedophiles. They'd face that rather than face up to what they did and what's inside them and bring it out into the open in front of a dozen or more other people. You've been told what happens, you were assessed, you got a place. That's the start and that's good. But start is the word. Beginning. Stage one. Are you up for the rest, now you're here?'

Simon was silent for a minute, looking down. 'I've got no choice. I can't live with myself like this. I've got to stick it out, haven't I?'

'How old are you?'

'Thirty-nine.'

'Get through this, serve the rest of your time and you're young enough to start over.'

He stood up. 'Your kit's over there. Michael's outside, he'll take you up to your room. You've got half an hour.'

■ ■ ■ ■

He had been told only to read a general outline about Stitchford, nothing in detail. That way he would be inquisitive, anxious, alert — like every other prisoner who'd just arrived. He could be surprised, pleasantly or otherwise. He could be whatever he was at a given moment.

He was surprised by the light. Most prisons were dark or in a glare of artificial strip lighting. This one had windows in the roof and high up in the walls, and light-coloured stairwells, walls with bright pictures — presumably done in art therapy. He had been told to make his own decision about art therapy but that to qualify he must show minimum talent and work only in colour. This was not about fine painting, it was about trying to unlock some inner part of himself which had been hidden for a long time. Revelatory, not pretty.

The corridor did not clang, like the metal corridors in other prisons, though footsteps sounded clearly and there was a squeak of rubber soles.

Michael led the way, Serrailler carried his own bag. A man looked out of a doorway, nodded. Someone else came down the corridor wearing a towel and carrying another, trainers in hand, hair wet and flattened onto his head. 'Y'all right?'

'Thanks.'

'Most are helpful, most will be pally. There's plenty of give and take in here.'

Michael had a shaven head and a small spider tattooed on the back of his neck. The first person Simon had yet seen who looked like a prison officer.

Last few doors, at the window end of the upper corridor.

'Here you go.'

The small room that would be his home and refuge for however long it took.

'Looks a bit bare, only you can buy stuff from catalogues — rugs, pot plants, cushions — you earn from whatever work you're assigned and spend it that way. If you want. If you get invited into anyone else's room, take a good look round. Sparky in room 11 — his is like Buckingham Palace. OK, four toilets at the end, showers next door to them — you go when you like and if you're free. No lock-up at night, which might surprise you. Washbasin — you drop down that lid. Light in the ceiling above your bed. You change your bed every week, sheets get left outside your door. Bell goes for your evening meal in about forty-five minutes. Just follow the crowd. Anything you want to know for now?'

'Can I hang my clothes up anywhere?'

'Had a nice wardrobe in your other prison, did you? No, you fold them and put them on the shelf. Jacket hangs behind the door. Do your washing in the basement. There's the bumpf.'

Michael went out, shutting but not locking the door. Someone was shouting loudly on the floor below. Someone else was whistling as they went down the corridor past his room. There was a faint smell of frying fish.

Home.

Simon picked up the duplicated information sheets and lay down on his bed to read them.

NINETEEN

Shelley tried to stop shaking. Tim must not see that anything was wrong. She clenched her hands. She felt sick and when she turned her head, she felt dizzy. She felt a boiling up of anger, hurt, confusion and guilt, went over and over in her mind all the way home, what she had said or done, what gesture she might have made to give him the idea. She could think of none. Tim always accused her of flirting, being too friendly, saying too much, asking too many personal questions. Had she?

Tim talked all the way home and she supposed that she answered. He chatted about the food, the drink, the talk, the woman on his right, the woman on his left, the man opposite, and she dreaded him mentioning Richard's name let alone starting up a conversation about him. He did mention it, and she jumped, but he swerved onto someone else.

As she got out of the car, he said, 'You ripped the back of your frock. How on earth did you do that? I thought it was a new one?'

'It is . . .' She almost ran up the path.

'I'm having a nightcap. You?'

'No. Yes . . . yes, do we have any brandy?'

'Brandy? You never drink brandy. Anyway, no, we don't. Whisky?'

'Yes. Fine. Yes.'

'Are you all right?'

'Just need to rush . . . loo . . .'

'Oh God, I hope the chicken wasn't off. Seemed OK but you never know with mass catering.'

She went into the spare bathroom and locked the door. Still shaking. Still sick. She tore the frock again in her panic to get it off, desperate for it not to be touching her body any longer. Ripped her pants off and threw them into the sink. Got them out again. Dropped them on the floor, shuddering to touch them again and knowing that she couldn't leave them there. She pushed everything into the laundry bag, shut the bag in the cupboard, locked the cupboard.

'Shell? Are you all right?'

'Bit sick, sorry . . . be out in a minute.'

'I've got your drink here.'

Drink? She didn't know what he meant. Drink.

She got under the shower and turned it up as hot as she could bear it. Their own shower was better, the pressure on this was weak but she couldn't go into the bathroom she used every day until she was clean, clean, clean.

She showered for minute after minute, washed every nook and cranny of herself over and over again, washed her hair and rinsed, rinsed, rinsed, hot water, cool water, hot again.

'Are you sure you're OK?'

She came quickly out and into the bedroom. 'Think so. Sorry.'

'Funny — I'm all right and I ate the chicken. I wonder if anyone else is ill — I'll ring round in the morning. Sure you're not just pissed?'

She was shivering again.

'Look, you get into bed, I'll bring you a hot-water bottle. Maybe whisky isn't the best idea.'

Tim folded the duvet back and helped her in. Kind Tim. Thoughtful Tim. Good, loving husband Tim.

Tim can't know. I could never . . .

'Someone raped me,' she heard herself say.

Tim was on his way out of the room. Stopped dead.

'It — I wasn't sick. It's nothing I ate.'

He turned slowly. 'You can't have been raped. You haven't been anywhere to —'

'When I went down to the cloakroom.'

She was shivering so much now that her teeth were chattering. Why had she said it? She wasn't going to tell Tim. Tim mustn't know.

He sat down on the edge of the bed and put his hand over hers. 'Shelley, do you think you've got a temperature?'

She stared at him.

'Just that — listen, you could be really ill — high temperatures can make people hallucinate.'

'I'm not hallucinating.'

'You'd better tell me what you think happened.'

'No. What happened. It happened.' She turned on her side rather than look at him. 'It doesn't matter. Forget it. I just want to go to sleep. It's over with.'

'Of course it isn't. Shelley? Please tell me what happened — now you've started you have to tell me everything.'

'I went to the cloakroom . . . it's got a — you know that place, everything's huge, all the rooms — it's got a sort of outer powder room . . . sofas and mirrors . . . I don't suppose you know what I mean. Never mind.'

'Go on.'

140

'Please, no. I wish I hadn't told you.'

'Go on.'

'Just . . . there was no one in there at all but I suppose he — he must have followed me. Down the stairs. I was in this outer room and . . . he came in.'

'Who came in?'

She hesitated for a split second only. 'Richard,' she said.

'Richard *Serrailler*? You have to be joking, Shelley. Of course it can't have been Richard.'

'It was Richard. Do you think I don't know? Do you think I was so blind drunk I couldn't identify him? Of course I could.'

'For God's sake . . . if this is true . . . I'll have him strung up. What exactly happened? You must go over it, Shelley. You can't make a mistake about this.'

'No, I can't and I'm not. He just . . . pushed me down . . . there was this chaise longue — sofa thing.'

'He must have been extremely drunk.'

Why, she thought, but did not say, why must he have been drunk? To want to rape me? To bother with me?'

'Not drunk.'

'What else? What happened then?'

'There's nothing else to tell you, is there? You know what rape means.' She pulled the bedclothes up higher, wanting to bury herself away.

'Why didn't you say anything until just now, Shelley?'

Why? A thousand reasons and none. She had been too shocked to say anything, too afraid of seeing him again, too disgusted with herself. With him. With it.

'I couldn't. I didn't want to tell you and I don't want to think about it.'

'All right. I'll bring you some tea — be better for you than anything else. I'll think about what you ought to do.'

'There isn't anything to do. It happened. It's over.'

She was half asleep and in the shadows of a dream when Tim came back. She kept her eyes closed, her back turned from him. When she woke it would be morning — no, later morning, it was past two now — and it would be even more over than it had been over immediately after Richard Serrailler had walked out of the cloakroom. It happened. Get over it.

'One thing,' Tim said when he returned, and as if there had been no pause in their conversation, 'I don't know if it has crossed your mind to go to the police, but if it has, forget it. No way.'

Police. It had not, in fact, crossed her mind, but now Tim had said it, she clutched at the word, because it was the right one. Police. What Richard had done was wrong and a crime and of course she had to go to the police.

'Even if you could prove it, which of course you can't . . .'

No.

'. . . They wouldn't do anything and they can be quite nasty to women over this sort of thing.'

Was there any 'sort of thing'? She was raped, that was all. All.

'They would take into account the fact that you'd been drinking —'

'I had not "been drinking" — I had a drink at dinner.'

'Well, more than one, and before . . . and besides, you know him.'

'What difference does that make?'

'It means they'd assume you'd, you know . . .'

'No, I don't — that I'd what?'

'Led him on. It's different with real rape . . . if you'd been attacked in a dark place by someone . . . some man who was a complete stranger.'

'This was "real rape" — whatever you mean by that.'

'Listen, sweetheart, I don't mean to upset you but I did say this — not to have too much drink because when you do, well, you flirt. Don't you?'

Shelley sat up, her shivering over, body quite still, head clear.

'You mean I led him on? You mean I was asking for it? Is that what you're saying, Tim?'

'No, no, of course not . . . but you do and you always flirt with Richard — you've always said he was attractive.'

'I've said no such thing. Or if I have . . .'

'There you are —'

'If I ever have it was only a general remark — you might say someone's wife was attractive, mightn't you? Mightn't you?'

'Well, yes . . .'

'Yes. And does that mean you want to rape her and might even try it? Even do it? And would that be a good reason?'

'Shelley, calm down. Lie down and take a deep breath. I think you're getting this whole thing out of proportion.'

How was it possible to get being raped out of proportion?

But he came to bed, lay beside her, put his arms round her and held her to him.

'Poor darling. Whatever actually happened, it should not have done and I'll sort it. He won't bother you ever again.'

He doesn't get it. He just has no idea. It felt wrong to be close to him, even though she had had a shower. Wrong. But she couldn't push him away.

She stayed in bed until after he had gone to work. He got carefully out of bed, out of the room, out of the house, considerate, thoughtful and without any idea of how she felt. She could not even be sure that he did believe her.

She waited for ten minutes after the car had gone before getting up and having a shower in their own bathroom this time, the power turned on full and almost unbearably hot. She tried to think of nothing but the water sluicing over her, but in fact she thought of Richard Serrailler, going over and over not so much what he had done as how it had ever happened, whether she had 'led him on', even inadvertently, whether a certain amount of harmless flirting ever could be 'harmless'. She had flirted, yes. She had held his eye, smiled, responded to the subtext of his remarks. As she went over it, she understood that. But she had behaved like it before, as Tim had said, often enough — she liked to flirt, though only in what she had always thought of as a safe context. She and Tim had had a rock-solid marriage for seventeen years. Without children, which neither of them had wanted, they had been everything to one another and yet gathered plenty of friends round them. Neither had ever had an affair. It wouldn't have interested them. Yes, Shelley thought now, yes, she had sometimes flirted, because — she stopped soaping herself for a moment — because it was fun. Nothing more. Tim had been known to flirt too. It meant nothing.

She turned the water off and stood there, shuddered, put on her towelling robe, and went back to the bedroom. It was a bright, clear-skied morning, warm, inviting. But her stomach lurched at the thought of going out, of people looking at her, at walking among them, in the streets, for surely they would guess. She looked at herself in the mirror, and looked away, and dressed without looking again. Did her hair and her face and barely looked at either.

But through her head like a regular beat was the insistent thought that she had to do something and no matter what Tim had said, that something was report it to the police. Even if they did nothing, disbelieved her, made her feel a slut, as she had read that the police could — even then, she had to go because unless she did the anger inside her would destroy her. It was corrosive, bitter and hateful. She could not forget the look on his face — gloating, sneering, amused. Whatever they said to her, whatever they did or did not do, even if it led nowhere, to get rid of the turmoil of feelings of anger and shame and hatred inside her, she had no choice but to go to the police.

She started the car. Stalled it. Started it again. Switched off the engine. The clothes were still in the bathroom cupboard and she wanted rid of them, wanted them burned or torn to shreds. She went back into the house, but when she opened the cupboard door and saw the laundry bag she was sick without warning and without the chance to reach the basin. When she had cleaned up, and before she could throw up again, she picked up the bag on the end of a coat hanger, and stuffed it into a black binbag and then into the car boot. Everything felt contaminated. She threw the hanger in the bin.

She drove aimlessly around the streets, into a one-way system, almost colliding with a delivery van, out onto the bypass and back into town, not thinking, not knowing where she would end up, still nauseous. In the end, the thought of the bag was so sickening that she turned back, hit the bypass again, then a road that led towards Starly. She stopped by a gate. A field. No animals. Nothing. No other car came by and she forced herself to drag the bag out of the boot and throw it sideways over the gate into a ditch on the far side.

She was shaking again, and had to sit, head between her knees, to stop herself fainting. But gradually, taking deep breaths and remembering what she had just done, she calmed. When she got back into the car she felt better. It had gone and somehow, a line was drawn. It had happened but whereas an hour before it had somehow gone on happening, over and over again, now it was done and in the past. Over.

She drove back towards Lafferton and home and work, conscious that she had not even opened up the computer to check the morning's emails.

She was shocked when she found herself pulling up in the police station forecourt fifteen minutes later.

TWENTY

Judith, looking better, with colour in her face and her appetite back, sat in the old wicker garden chair podding broad beans. The late-afternoon sun always caught this corner, and as Cat watched her expertly sliding a row of beans from their fleecy bed into the bowl, she thought that two days here at the farmhouse, recuperating, had made a difference to more than just her physical health. She seemed relaxed, less anxious, less touchy. She had spent an hour helping Sam sort out the muddle that was his history homework, read to Felix, who was perfectly able to read himself but still enjoyed the attention, taken Wookie for walks and combed the knots out of Mephisto's undercoat, to his silent fury.

'All done. Shall I bring them in?'

'No, I'm bringing you a drink out.'

Judith rested her head back, smiling.

'Spoiled,' she said, when Cat set down the tray.

'No, you're convalescing. And you're staying for the rest of the week — until you've fully recovered.'

She opened the Sauvignon and poured two glasses. In better times, they would have had a better wine but this was adequate and well chilled. It had to do.

Wookie was sitting at the far end of the garden by a syringa bush, waiting patiently for Mephisto to emerge and submit to being chased, amid wild yelps, back to the house. It was a game the old cat seemed to accept with reasonable grace.

'I'd love to have a dog again.'

'Then do.'

'Your father doesn't like them.'

'My father likes them perfectly well. They used to have a cairn terrier — it was when I was at med school. Dad liked it all right, though it's true they didn't replace him when he died.'

'Funny he's never mentioned it.'

'Pick your moment, tell him you've decided you both need to be fit and having a dog to walk every day is the answer.'

'Perhaps.'

Cat did not look at her stepmother. 'You used to stand up for yourself when you and

Dad were first married. It was one of the things I loved you for.'

Judith just shrugged. 'Have you heard from Simon?'

'No. A text — he's off on a special op, didn't say where . . . some SIFT assignment I expect.'

'I was reading a new book about our spies during the war — he'd have fitted that bill all right.'

Cat laughed. 'There's something I'd like your thoughts on. This idea that I should plan the strategy for the hospice and go and learn more about how the day-care-only ones operate . . .' She sipped her wine. Judith had her eyes closed and her face turned to the sun. She was the ideal listener, never chivvying, never jumping in until she had listened carefully and digested the subject fully. 'Whenever I think about it — and let's face it, I ought to say yes — I feel a grey pall settle on me. It isn't what I want to do.'

'Then you mustn't. There have to be other options.'

'Yes. One came up today — I think. You probably don't remember Ross Dickens?'

'Just . . . GP with the Starly practice?'

'Yes, then left to work in South Africa, came back and joined a practice in London. He was on our old out-of-hours roster —

good doctor. He rang me out of the blue today. He's now married and his wife's a GP. They want to set up a wholly private GP practice here. They've done a lot of market testing and reckon there is more than enough demand. They would do out of hours and link to a practice in Bevham for that too — nobody would be on call more than one night in ten at most. They want to talk to me, with a view to joining them.'

Judith whistled softly.

'Meaning?'

'Meaning there would be a lot to think about before you went ahead but I suppose the first advantage is that you haven't been a full-time GP for a while, so you wouldn't look as if you were abandoning an NHS practice.'

'Chris would never have countenanced it, not in a million years. He was against every sort of private medicine — it became something we could never talk about.'

'All right, tell me the reasons for.'

Cat sighed. 'Money. I'd be pretty well paid. I'd be back doing hands-on medicine — but of course I could do that by joining an NHS practice. Great working conditions. They have a lot of backing — Ross's wife is well off, apparently.'

'So far it sounds good. And against?'

'Conscience. I didn't agree with Chris altogether, but let's face it, private general practice is medicine for the well off.'

'You have put in your fair share of time and expertise and care to the NHS, you know. And why shouldn't people with money have decent doctors just as well as the rest?'

'Hmm.'

'Listen — the main reasons seem to me, one, you'd be doing what you like doing best and are good at, and two, you'd be very well paid. Assuming you could manage the on-call hours, which aren't many — and you know we'd always help there — and that you get on with the other two doctors . . . I can't see any serious reason for you not to jump at it.'

'I know.'

Judith looked at her for a long moment before saying quietly, 'You can't go on living your life by Chris's principles, darling. I know he had strong ones and I admired him for it. You have your own too. You need money at the moment but you're not a money-grubber, no matter what. Big difference.'

Cat put her hand out and took Judith's. 'Thank you. I used to say this a lot after

Chris died but perhaps I haven't been saying it enough recently. I don't know what I would do without you.'

She jumped up quickly, at a sudden idea.

'What if I ring Rachel and ask her to supper?'

'How lovely! Yes, do.'

Meanwhile my father, Cat thought, as she went in to call, is the elephant in the room.

TWENTY-ONE

A tap on the door. 'Johnno?'

A split-split second. 'Hi. Come in.'

'Thought I'd give you the nod — we eat in ten minutes. Canteen is down two flights and along the corridor, but you don't need to know that, just follow the stampede.'

'Great, thanks.'

'I'm Chris, by the way.'

Simon went over and shook hands with the warder. Stocky, hair gelled. Big nose. Dark blue uniform trousers, light blue shirt. No tie. No shoulder tabs.

'Takes a bit of getting used to, this. Can't remember the last time anyone wanted to shake my hand before today.'

'It's all about respect. It's about a totally different feel — technically, this is a prison, right, but first and foremost it's a community, a therapeutic community.'

'Nice.'

'And it's not just about being friendly, but

it helps if things get difficult, anything blows up — good basis.'

'So do things blow up?'

'Not often, and if they do, generally they're well contained. Surprising really . . . there's a lot of hurt feelings, a lot of pent-up anger and frustration . . . It's not an easy ride in here, Johnno.'

'I know.'

'I doubt if you do. Anyway, if things get a bit heated, the background — that this is a community, people respect each other, look out for one another — that all counts. Meanwhile, enjoy the caviar and champagne.'

Which was watery chicken casserole, mashed potatoes, carrots and bread pudding.

So far as food was concerned at least, Stitchford was a prison.

A warder stood up and gave out a couple of notices, then consulted a list. 'Darren Watson, Brian Field, Johnno Miles — you're on pod duty next week, breakfasts.'

A man sidled up to Simon. 'Bad luck.'

Will Fernley. The pleasant face. The relaxed self-confidence. The voice. He hadn't bothered to try an Estuary accent.

'Too right.'

'You new on B?'

Simon nodded but curtly, then looked down at his plate. He caught a glance between a couple of the others.

'There's a knock-up game later. You any good?'

Man on his left. Weasly. Acne. Looked about fifteen, was probably twenty-five. He was familiar with the type. No. He stopped his train of thought dead. He wasn't familiar. He wasn't a copper. He had to guard against pigeonholing this one and that one. It wasn't his business.

'Ping-pong,' someone else said. 'What did you think?'

'Could have been pool.'

'You any good at pool?'

'No. Ping-pong's OK.'

'Footie?'

'So-so. Played basketball a lot.'

He left out cricket.

There was a sudden racket as people all scraped back chairs, dropped cutlery into metal bins.

'Johnno Miles?'

'Yup.'

'You're wanted.'

Simon followed the warder up a floor into the central area. Doors right, doors left, all painted different colours. Bright blue. Grass green. Orange. Yellow. Pale brown. Purple. No red. No black.

'Wait in here please.'

He waited twenty minutes.

The warder came back and led him down the corridor. Footsteps on the landing above. A roar of laughter. Another door.

'Johnno Miles, Governor.'

The blind was drawn. A low-voltage desk lamp, facing downwards.

He was a very large man, almost bald. Navy suit, with the jacket on his chair back. White shirt. Navy and dark red tie.

He came round the desk, hand outstretched. 'Ray Norman.'

Simon hesitated. 'Johnno Miles aka Simon Serrailler.'

'Take a seat. If asked, some of your signatures weren't on the right line or within the box or perfectly legible. Probably no one will ask . . . not this time anyway.'

He sat heavily in his chair and put one knee over the other, fingertips of his hands together. Looked calmly and steadily at Simon.

'I'm going to say this first if you don't mind. I was absolutely and totally against your coming in here but I was overruled. I don't like infiltrators, I don't like secrets, I don't like being party to covert actions. Having given way I've set one or two of my own rules. You're here for a good reason, I grant you, but that is the only reason, and you do nothing unrelated to that reason. You are not here to gather any information about any other inmate, to pass on anything you hear, no matter what it is, other than what's within your remit and concerning Will Fernley. Understood?'

'Perfectly. I've no reason or wish to do otherwise. What I find out from or about anyone else goes no further. I understand your concerns, Governor.'

'Ray.'

'Thanks.'

'Do you want to be Simon in this room?'

'Better not.'

'Wise.'

'If there were any other way at all of finding out who Fernley's co-offenders were, believe me, it would be taken. It's all been tried. Dead end after dead end. Nothing. These guys are out there and they're still offending and you don't need me to tell you the nature of the offences.'

The governor was still looking at him, but it was not a challenging look.

'Have you met him yet?'

'Just now, at supper. We exchanged a

couple of words.'

'So, no time to get any sense of the man?'

'Not really.'

'Want my take on things?'

'I want whatever I can get.'

'Right. We get a fairly broad cross section of sex offenders coming into Stitchford and remember, they're here by choice. They ask to come. Every single man is here because he wants to be and he's waited a long time to get a place, during which time he has been fully assessed. We don't want places taken up by those who think it might be a soft option — it's not of course, but word gets out that you have a nice room of your own with adjacent lav serving only half a dozen others, and you can even buy your own cushions and curtains from a catalogue. We have young men, though we never admit juvenile offenders, we have middle-aged men and older men, though no one over seventy. We have lifers and those on a five-year term — no one comes here who is serving less than that. We have men who have a good IQ and quite a few with decent educational qualifications — we had a couple who had degrees. Men need to be of average intelligence and above to go through all the assessment questionnaires and be able to gain insight into themselves and have empathy with others, and above all to learn. It's about a different form of learning. Self-learning. We have the strictest "no drugs, no alcohol" policy. One hit and you're out, that day, no excuses are heard and there are no second chances. The men in here have seen it happen — and it works. By and large this place has always been clean.

'There's zero tolerance of offensive behaviour towards one another, so any arguments are defused and any violence. Same applies as to drugs and drink — no second chance. We teach respect and mutual cooperation — and that works. So the men — we don't call them inmates, by the way, and we try not to use the word "prisoner" — the men help one another. There are good relationships with staff and my staff pride themselves on openness and fairness, and they believe in respect too, which cuts both ways, but they don't give an inch if there's rule breaking and offensive behaviour. They're still prison officers, all of them except the psychs and the therapists.'

He leaned back in his chair and swivelled it slightly from side to side.

'You are going to join in the therapy, you'll be everywhere Fernley is. You've got your own story. Are you confident about it?'

'Yes.'

'You're Johnno Miles. Your crimes are horrendous. In any general prison you'd be beaten up on a regular basis. You're scum. You're a nonce. What you've done doesn't bear thinking about. But you'll have to describe it, and how you feel about it, many times over. Act it out. Paint it out — we have drama and art therapy and they're important parts of the treatment. You don't have children, I take it?'

'No. I'm not married. Nor gay.'

'Right. I'm not keeping you any longer or it will look odd, but you can ask to see me — the warders make appointments. I don't have an open-door policy, I can't, but I'm about the place a lot and I always see anyone who asks, by said appointment, and I try not to keep them waiting. Your contact has my emergency number as well as the general one. I'll ensure any messages from him reach you but unless there's something urgent there will be radio silence.'

So he hadn't been told about the Snoopy. Jed would have a good reason for that.

'One question. I know you can't talk about cure rates but how successful is this therapeutic community regime?'

'How long have you got? It can work, unquestionably. I have experience of that. In terms of rates of reoffending, in terms of rehabilitation safely into the community . . . in terms of the individual's own mental state . . . it can work, and it works with those men who are desperate for it to work and who can't any longer live inside themselves as they are and who dread their own future if they're unable to change. But for most paedophile offenders in prison, and a lot of them in here, there is no cure. It can't work. There's only damage limitation. Can you find your way back?'

'Probably but if I don't it will just add authenticity. Thanks for your cooperation, Ray.'

He meant it. The buck stopped with the governor, and if things went badly wrong, it was his judgement that would come under scrutiny and his job that would be on the line.

He found his way back. From a games room he heard the pock-pock of table tennis, the click of a pool ball. He hesitated. His instinct was to ignore both and head upstairs to his room to read and think, digest the onslaught of new impressions. But what would Johnno Miles do? Get together with the others for some company? Forget himself in a game?

He edged up to the door and looked in. A

dozen or more men, two games of table tennis ongoing, others watching, cheering or groaning, waiting their turn to play. A couple of them looked up but he recognised no one.

'You in?' one of them called out.

He joined them. A few names. Outstretched hands. Offers of a chair. He had to quell his inevitable instinct to ask questions, speculate on what these men had done, set a distance between them and himself.

'Johnno Miles . . . Johnno Miles . . . Johnno . . .'

'Cheers, Johnno.'

'How you doing?'

'You any good at this?'

He waited for twenty minutes until a space came at the table. He had played a lot and he knew he could thrash an average player but too often threw his game away. Sam usually beat him.

Sam.

A flash of memory — Sam racing into the sea carrying Felix, who was squealing with pleasure, on a family weekend in Devon last summer. He and Cat sitting on a rock drinking bottles of lemonade through straws. Hannah making an elaborate seaweed-and-shell collage in the flat sand.

And in this room, cheerfully playing ping-pong, men who could never be trusted near one of them, never be trusted on that beach full of laughing children.

He smashed a serve across the table.

Three fast games later, the man called Malc shook his hand. 'Sorry, mate.'

Simon's serve had taken him ahead for a couple of games, after which he had played wildly, and Malc had knocked him all over the table.

'I'll get you at basketball.'

'I don't play basketball — not against guys who are ten foot tall.'

Two other players were taking over the table. Simon watched their game for a moment, then left. The place was quiet. Music came from a few rooms along his corridor. As he passed one, Will Fernley came out, carrying a towel. Nodded. Smiled.

'Finding your feet?'

'Pretty much. Shan't know until it starts in earnest, I suppose.'

Fernley smiled again. 'It's not a walk in the park but you'll be fine.'

'How do you know?'

'Hunch.'

'Hope it's right. I'm Johnno, by the way.'

'Will Fernley. Off for a shower. You need a shower as often as you can get one in here.'

165

'Seems clean enough to me.'
'I wasn't referring to the housekeeping.'

TWENTY-TWO

Twelve men in a small meeting room. Blue chairs. Simon looked round at the feet. Trainers. Blue and white. Green and white. Maroon. Navy. One flash pair, brilliant, chalky white. Crocs, bright orange. Just the one. More trainers.

Jeans.

Jeans.

Jeans.

Maroon sweatpants. Standard prison is-sue.

Navy sweatpants.

Jeans.

Jeans.

Jeans

His jeans. His navy-and-white trainers.

Nine o'clock.

They were arranged in a semicircle, two rows. Will Fernley was four away from him. Smart clean trainers, green and white. Good jeans. Arms folded.

Brian. Lemon-yellow trainers scuffed and with odd laces, one grey, one white.

'Morning. Welcome to the newcomers. We have six. I'm George Prentiss, I'm a senior psychotherapist. On my left is Helen Granger, also a psychotherapist, and Andy Mutton, staff member.

'Couple of notices — Kev Cameron is ill, recovering from an emergency appendicitis, as some of you may already know, so drama therapy this week has been cancelled but we're getting a visiting therapist for next. Sorry for those of you who are finding this a real positive in the programme but good drama therapists aren't thick on the ground. One other thing — complaints about the state of the showers. This will be dealt with by maintenance of course, but when you use the showers please try and leave them in a decent state. It's not anyone's favourite on the duty roster but it has to be done — least everyone else can do is make sure they clean up properly after themselves. Sorry to talk to you like teenagers but there it is.'

They sat obediently, taking the stuff in, nodding, crossing and recrossing their legs. School-assembly notices about communal living were dealt with swiftly and efficiently.

How much of a shock must it be for men who had served five or ten years in a normal prison to hear this?

'OK.' George Prentiss put the paper with the notices on the floor beside him, leaned back, crossed his arms. 'Newcomers, as you can see, we mix you up with longer-term residents . . . other places would keep you all separate, like school students at the start of a course. But this sort of therapy doesn't have the same beginning, middle and end, and by having some here who are a couple of months in, you get to understand the whole process. And one of the points of these groups is that you don't get taught things by people like me, you learn primarily from yourself and the others. We're just here to facilitate that, provide a bit of guidance, occasionally some interpretation — we're not teachers or lecturers or medics telling you to take the tablets three times a day.

'For the old hands, this is the first time you've been grouped with your equal number in newcomers. New experience. You don't have all the answers any more than I do but you can help them . . . as you help each other outside of this room. All I ask you to be aware of is that you were starting off in therapy not so long ago.

'Right. This is a two-hour session and this is round one — call it the intro. Any probs?'

A man with long greasy hair and maroon prison-issue tracksuit had a prob.

'Are we going to be forced to repeat everything just for the newcomers? I don't want to go over and over the same stuff every time.'

'No. When it comes to your turn carry on where you left off last time, but if you want to recap for their benefit, you can. Or not. Up to you, Kane. You have any prob with that?'

Kane slumped in his chair, barely shaking his head.

'Right. From the left. Len?'

'What?'

'You start.'

'What with?'

It was immediately clear that anyone spoke as they wanted to, no one waited to be invited. The therapist was not the teacher.

'For fuck's sake, Len, why don't you ever bloody listen? You heard him.'

'No need to bloody swear, I'm trying to clear me head.'

He was probably sixty to sixty-five, grey hair, overweight, scruffy beard and moustache. He leaned forward, hands dangling between his wide-apart legs. Looking at the floor. His fingers twitched.

'I'm Len. You know what this is all about. I've done this before.' He sighed.

'Yeah, well, you gotta do it again. Get over it — we've all got to.'

'Stop bloody harassing me, will you? Did I say I wouldn't?'

'Give him a minute.'

'Right, start again. I'm Len. I've been in here four months. I waited to come here four years. No other option. I'm fifty-four. I've served seven years of a twelve-year sentence but I'm looking at three off for good behaviour. So I'm looking at two years and I need to sort myself out. Two years ain't long.'

His hands were still dangling between his legs and he went on staring at the floor. A few shuffled their feet but no one interrupted again.

'My index is sexual offences against underage girls.'

He leaned back. He was sweating.

'Thanks, Len. Spike?'

Spike might have been twelve years old. Small. Skinny. Bad skin. Smart trainers. Frayed jeans. He sat up straight.

'Spike — my real name's Pete McKinnon. I'm twenty-four. Been here nine months and it's bloody fantastic. I was self-harming, I was stashing pills away, I was working out how you hanged yourself, I was a fucking mess. I got beaten up, I got me head down the toilet and crap pushed into me mouth, I got me skull bust open, I got boiling water poured on me hands. I've served three of a five-year and before that I'd been in juvenile. And I was thinking there wasn't any point and then I got told about this place and I got on the list and it's fuckin' fantastic. It does your head in, you're like a bag turned inside 'out. You wait. Only I've stopped having the dreams, I've stopped — well, nearly — having the — thoughts.'

'What do you mean, thoughts?' Brian. 'Like fantasies — daydreaming?'

'Yeah. We all have them. You talk to anyone. You do. I do. What you done, you daydream about it, then you have like plays in your head where you're doing it again. I did it all the time. I had a job and I got sacked because it's what I did, I couldn't do anything else. And it's stopping. I'm like clean inside my head. Well, almost. Nearly clean. Bit of a way to go but my aim is stick this out, work it out, and I'm aiming on getting parole and getting out and being all right, done with it all. Makes me sick to think.'

He looked around. He wants applause, Simon thought. He's cheeky. He's pleased with himself. He's cocky.

'You haven't said anything about your index.'

'Kids. It started when my sister had her baby, she was fourteen, she had a baby, girl, and I was sixteen, and when it was . . . Index offence, child molesting.'

Spike glanced around again, pert, gloating. He caught Simon's eye, and then quite suddenly put his hands in front of his face and burst into loud, howling tears. Simon felt the tension rise around him. Spike could not stop crying until the therapist brought him up with 'OK, thanks, well done, Spike. Take some deep breaths. Moving on now. Duncan?'

Child molesting.

Rape.

Sex with underage girls. Boys.

Sex with small girls. Boys.

Rape and murder.

They sat, some uncomfortable in their seats, shifting their feet, twisting their hands, others stock-still, staring ahead, no emotion, no facial expression.

'Will?'

Simon sat, arms folded. Don't react. He's no more to you than the rest. He glanced at Fernley. Glanced away.

'Will Fernley. I'm forty. Served five years

of an eight-year sentence. I've been here at Stitchford for just over a year of an eighteen-month term. It's made a massive difference to me — to the way I think about myself and my mindset, to the way I feel about my offences. Everything. This is a remarkable place. I wouldn't have believed how big an impact it's had on me. I feel I'm becoming fully prepared to be rehabilitated into the community and quite safely, which I most certainly was not before I came here.'

He tried to soften his accent but the fluency with which he spoke singled him out as a public-school-educated, public-school-confident man. Once or twice he ran his hand over his hair but otherwise sat easily, one leg crossed over the other like several of the others. Plausible. Easy charm. An apparent openness. Serrailler took him in again, knowing that what they were being presented with was all gloss and surface, carefully honed.

'So just to the newcomers — stick with it because it works. I never thought I'd say that. Oh, sorry — yes. Index offence, child molestation . . . and related issues.'

There was a general murmur of protest.

'Sorry, sorry . . . I don't know how much detail is required at this point. Offences relating to obtaining and downloading child pornography and to organising and running a pornographic Internet, erm, group.'

'Ring,' someone muttered. 'Say it how it is.'

'Yes. Sorry. Ring. But it does amount to the same thing, doesn't it?' He glanced round with a smile at the interrupter.

'This is where it starts,' the therapist said, 'and it starts pretty easily. Basic info, index offence. Then you're going to fill in with some detail, about your offences but mainly where you stand right now in relation to them — your feelings about them and about yourself, then about the victims . . . and we'll come to the past. In time, people in this room will know as much about your life as you do, maybe more . . . about childhood and schooling and adolescence and family and the gradual emergence of the inclinations which led to the offences you committed. But there's a long way to go before you get to those . . . This isn't any sort of a quick fix as I'm sure you now realise. Just a reminder — say what you think and feel, about yourself and about each other, no holds barred, but this whole therapeutic community runs on the basis of mutual respect, so no offensive remarks, no aggression, no verbal abuse. And one other simple but very important rule — you stay seated. Anyone want to say anything before we listen to the new guys?'

'Just, like — good luck. And we're here to support you.'

'Thanks, Malc. Important to hear that. Sorry, one more thing — whole community meeting tomorrow at eleven fifteen. This is a weekly thing — occasionally we have an emergency special, but only if some issue really blows up, and that's rare.'

'Not so rare as all that. What you trying to say, George?'

Laughter from the old hands.

'And the WCM isn't optional. Nobody misses it unless they're at death's door.'

'Or stoned.'

'Not funny.' The skinny boy Spike. Serrailler wondered how much of a problem drugs really were, in spite of what the governor had said. Some would still be daft or desperate enough to risk getting them in somehow, in spite of the one-strike rule.

He looked around again, trying to reconcile what he saw — ordinary men of different ages, in different states from scruffy and without any obvious sense of personal pride, to clean and smart and would-be cool. An average mixture — thin, fat, dark, fair, shaven or not — there were several moustaches and goatees. Cross section.

Then think of what each of them had done. Think of the room full of sadistic, abusive, violent crimes.

'OK, let's start — from the right again. Tell us who you are.'

Brian did not realise for several seconds that he was the one, and in the silence, he half glanced round, looked back. The therapist nodded to him.

Brian's face flushed and then, as quickly, went very pale. He coughed, sat very still, head down.

'It's OK, take a deep breath and just talk.'

Brian looked round again. 'I'm . . .' His voice came out as a croak; he cleared his throat twice. 'Brian Field. I'm Brian Field. Sorry. I come from Manchester. I'm thirty-seven.'

Simon was surprised. The man could have been fifty.

'I was — I had five brothers and four of them died in a house fire when I was nine . . . my dad died in a work accident. My mam worked as a barmaid and left us on our own a lot — I suppose she had to — but there was always a bloke somewhere and she married one of them . . . then he left, then I was coming up teenage and I ran off — no money, nowhere to go . . . stole some cash from my mam and then a couple of purses and that was it. Petty crime just to get by . . . but I'd always had — had these funny thoughts . . . that one day I'd kill somebody. Not a voice or anything . . . I just knew I would. It was like a weird sort of thing I carried round — like a superstition or . . . I dunno. I liked girls. I'd always liked girls . . . I mean, not liked . . . I was interested in girls, know what I mean? How they were — shaped, what they wore under their skirts, what they looked like without clothes. I'd never had a sister, maybe that was it, I dunno. This feeling . . . it was always there. I couldn't get rid of it. I didn't go out with girls, didn't even chat them up because I felt I'd be tempted . . . I'd be some sort of danger to them. I got a warehouse job, which was all blokes. Even then, I kept away from other people. I just stayed on my own and had the odd mate to have a pint with, that was all. Carried on like that for a long time — then I was on the beach at Southport . . . and this girl was there. It was late on, not the summer season, and the sea was miles out, which is what it does at Southport, and there was just her . . . I saw her and I knew what I would do . . . it was like the time had come. It all, like, boiled up . . . I followed her. She didn't look round. She went to the sand dunes and

I followed her all the way. That was it.'

He stopped speaking. Everyone was silent, waiting.

More silence. No one wanted to stop him by asking any questions. The old hands were giving him every chance.

Silence.

'Listen, Brian . . .' Will Fernley leaned forward and gave the man a warm, encouraging smile. 'You shouldn't stop there — maybe just give us the basics — what happened — say what your index offence is, you don't have to go into more detail now. You're doing so well.'

Brian shrugged about inside his clothes, as if he had a violent skin itch. He did not look at Will, and he seemed to have come to a stop and gone into a frozen state.

'Brian?' The therapist.

Brian took a deep breath, then said, 'My index crime is murder — and rape. I raped her and then I strangled her and then I buried her in the dunes.'

No one made any comment. There were no sharp intakes of breath. No one stared at Brian. Serrailler's heart was thumping. He had spent a working lifetime in the presence of men, and women, who had murdered, assaulted with appalling violence, who had raped, abused, used knives, shotguns, ropes and their bare hands. He had always been required to remain calm and focused, not to express disgust or anger, let alone any desire for vengeance. He had fulfilled all those requirements but it had been made easier because he had been in authority over the criminals, had followed them and arrested and charged them and sometimes given evidence in court which had helped to send them down for life. He was trained not to react, to stay on the level emotionally, to be a professional and in control of himself at all times. Brian's statement was nothing new. What was new was the requirement to sit still, listen, take in and empathise, because he was a fellow murderer and abuser, a partner in the therapeutic process.

From now on, he must treat Brian, and every other man in this room, 'with respect', and without aggression of any form, possibly even of thought.

He saw the leg of his neighbour on the left, jeans torn at the knee, black trainers with stark white laces. He gave off a faint smell of deodorant and aftershave. His equal in murder or violent sexual assault of some kind.

He took the deep breaths the therapist had advised for Spike.

'Thank you, Brian. It's tough — everyone knows how tough it is — and it will get worse. Therapy tears you apart and it's a while before you begin to put yourself back together again. Yes — you. I don't do it for you, no one else in this room does it for you. The programme doesn't even do it. You do it, with assistance from the programme and support from the rest.'

The therapist glanced quickly at his watch.

'Anyone want a break? There's water and cups on the table. Five-minute toilet break.'

Two men went to the drinks jug. Brian followed after a moment. No one left the room. People got up and stretched, swung their arms about a bit. Sat down. Brian returned to his seat, sweating heavily. The room settled again.

The therapist looked at Simon.

'Johnno Miles,' he said. 'Your turn.'

TWENTY-THREE

'If you go to the police you'll be treated like dirt.'

'They won't believe you.'

'I tell you now, Shell, the minute you say it's someone you already know, they'll just assume you had a few too many and led him on.'

'Talk sense, Shelley, who are the police going to believe, you or Dr Richard Serrailler?'

'The police will make you feel like a slapper. They're not very nice to women over this sort of thing.'

Of course Tim had said other things. He had believed her, even if he also believed she had had more to drink than she'd owned up to, and he had been upset on her behalf, had comforted her and told her it made no difference at all to how he thought of her or loved her. But he had also told her over and over again not to go to the police.

But it wasn't like that. It hadn't been like that from the moment she had walked up to the front desk in the police station. Thank God it had been quiet, no one waiting, no eyes staring and no ears trying to make out what she said.

From that first minute, when she had been shaking so much and her throat had gone dry and closed, and he had said, 'Take your time, there's no rush,' from the second she had first heard the sergeant's quiet tone of voice, even though she could not stop shaking, she had realised that it was not going to be as Tim had said. It was going to be all right.

It was all right.

The desk sergeant. The small side room and the cup of coffee. The woman officer. 'My name is Lois Dancer.' Everything.

'Let me run you through your first options, Shelley. This is really important. You can remain here, and we'll get a police doctor — and it will be a woman doctor — to come in and see you and do an examination, or you can go over to Bevham, to the centre. Do you know about St Catherine's?'

She had never heard of St Catherine's.

'Right. It's in the old town hall building, not far from the bus station. It's a centre for rape victims and one or two other related crimes. It's not police-operated but police — Bevham, us, and a couple of other forces — refer rape victims there. It's staffed by doctors and specially trained counsellors. Basically, you tell your story on tape, so that they, and we, have a full detailed record of exactly what happened to you. Then you have a full physical examination. The centre is entirely staffed by women. You talk to one of their counsellors and you can make appointments to see her again and she would support you if you decide you want to press charges and be with you through the whole process, especially if the case does go to court. We work closely with St Catherine's and so do the legal teams and you wouldn't be alone making decisions or giving statements or whatever. I really recommend that you go there, Shelley. As I said, you can choose to stay here and we'll call the doctor, but honestly, we don't have the surroundings and facilities they do, and also you might have to wait several hours. The doctor will make it a priority but she does have her other work. At St Catherine's, you won't have to wait long. Can I get you another coffee while you think it through?'

'I have, thanks. I'd like to go there.'

It was an easy enough decision.

'I think that's the right thing to do,

Shelley, you'll be in the best hands and well looked after. But I will have to take a basic statement from you now. When you've told it all in greater detail over there, that statement will be recorded and we will have access to the recording. I just do need to take some information from you now, if that's all right. Take your time. I can give you a break whenever you like.'

'It's all right. I want to get on with this now.'

Name. Address. Date. Place. Easy. Brief description. Easier than she had expected because now she was angry again.

'OK — you say that the person who raped you was someone known to you. How well known — a relative?'

'No, no. A — more an acquaintance. My husband knows him better than I do. I've only met him at social occasions . . .'

Lois was writing. She looked up. 'Thank you. And full name?'

Shelley took a deep breath. Realising. Suddenly, realising.

'Serrailler,' she said. 'Dr Richard Serrailler.'

The sergeant looked quickly down at her notepad, then back. The shock on her face was quickly concealed.

She paused a moment, then said, 'I'm sure

you know the implications of this, Shelley, and some of them aren't necessarily relevant. I would just caution you, though. Are you absolutely sure? Any doubts at all, any possibility of confusion of identity, and you should tell me now. I will support you and so will the rest of the team who look after you but you've named someone of prominence in the community and with a high reputation in the medical world. If you do press this charge I'll warn you informally that it will be — difficult. It will raise the level of publicity and frankly, I'd expect big legal guns to be wheeled out as defence counsel.'

'Are you telling me I should drop this charge just because he's a prominent person? A high-up Freemason, a top doctor? And the father of your Superintendent?'

'No — categorically no. I just want you to be aware that the identity of your alleged attacker will raise the profile of the case and you would need to be fully prepared for that.'

'It doesn't make any difference. It makes me more angry. It makes me furious actually.' Her hands were shaking again but she had raised her voice.

'That's fine, but it would be wrong if I didn't put the position to you and they will probably do so again at St Catherine's. No way will anyone try to stop you and in all other respects it's irrelevant what position your attacker holds or doesn't hold or how he's regarded. Right, that's everything from me. One or two practical questions — have you had a bath or a shower since the attack?'

'Yes. I shouldn't have but I couldn't bear . . .'

'That's all right, it's quite understandable. Hopefully it will still be possible to get forensic evidence from an examination. Have you got the clothes you were wearing — all of them, including underwear and shoes?'

'No. Yes. I've got my shoes.'

'What happened to everything else?'

What had happened? For a moment, she had no idea at all, except that she had not been able to keep them in the house, had had to get rid of them, had . . .

'I threw them away in a binbag but I know where . . . I . . .'

'Could you retrieve them?'

'Yes, unless . . . I ought to but . . . maybe someone has moved them.'

'Right, then the first thing we do is go to where you dumped them. I'll drive you there, and then take you on to St Catherine's. Would you be able to come and pick your car up later? Or maybe your husband could do that for you?'

'No. I'll be fine to do it.'

'No hurry. If you don't feel in a fit state to drive you should just get a taxi home and pick your own car up tomorrow. Give me a couple of minutes to drop this statement off and get a car.' She turned as she reached the door. 'You've done absolutely the right thing, Shelley.'

Had she?

They retrieved the plastic bin liner full of clothes, still where she had left it.

Had she done the right thing?

They went to the house and collected her shoes.

Had she?

They hit the bypass and were halfway to Bevham before the full implication of what she had done and was doing reared up at her and she said, 'I'm not sure about it now. I'm really worried.'

'I can't stop here but as soon as we turn off this road I will. I understand exactly what's happening, Shelley, and I don't blame you. It's just hit home and we need to talk about it again. The way you're reacting now — it's perfectly normal. This is a big deal. You're talking about accusing a highly respected and prominent local man of raping you, and if you press this charge you'll have to go to court and give evidence. It's not trivial. Frankly, I'd be worried if you weren't having second thoughts and you'll have third and fourth. You need to sit calmly and go through this again and ask yourself, do you want him to get away with this? Do you want him to carry on as normal, big guy, everyone respects and all that — this rapist? Is that what you want? I'm not sure you do. Ask yourself, why did you come to the station in the first place?' There was a new edge to her voice, almost a desperation.

'You sound as if you really want me to do this. So what if I just wanted to get at him for some other reason, what if I was making it all up?'

'Are you?'

'No, I'm bloody well not.'

'Didn't think so.'

'Still . . .'

'Still?'

'You seem — you really want me to go for him, don't you? Just wondered why. Do you know Richard Serrailler?'

'No. So far as I'm aware I've never met him.'

They turned off the bypass and pulled up beside a row of new estate houses.

Lois switched off the engine, glanced at Shelley and then away.

'It happened to me,' she said. 'Some years ago, before I joined the police. It was someone I knew and I didn't report it because I was scared and young and I just wanted to forget it. But I never have. I try very hard not to let it influence me, that would be totally unprofessional. I haven't any opinion about this, Shelley. I don't know if you were raped in the meaning of the term or if you led him on a bit and it was more or less consensual. I don't know. All I know is that if you're telling the truth, you have to pursue this, if only to make up for all those people like me who were too cowardly and didn't and as a result sent out the message that it's OK, carry on, rape women, they won't say anything, it won't go any further, there'll be no consequences. You see?'

'Yes. Thank you for telling me that.'

Lois started up the engine.

TWENTY-FOUR

'Sorry, I didn't mean to startle you, but why look at me as if I were an armed intruder?'

Judith stood in the sitting-room doorway, the back of her hand up to her mouth, heart beating too hard.

'I didn't hear you.'

'Because you had the television on too loud.'

'Yes, I suppose that was it — but you crept in so quietly.'

'My dear, I did not "creep" at all. I walked round the house and the back door was unlocked, as it seems to be far too often. Talking of armed marauders, Catherine really should be more careful, living out here by herself. Are you going to sit down?'

Judith backed a little until her legs found the sofa.

'Do you know where she keeps the whisky?' he asked.

'Yes, in the cupboard below the dresser.'

'For you?'

She was about to refuse, but said, 'A small one, that would be nice.'

'Water?'

'Please.'

It was a little after nine. Cat was at choir practice, Felix and Hannah were asleep, Sam in his room watching a rerun of the Ashes on his iPad.

The strange thought, that Richard would not attack her while the children were in the house, zigzagged through her head. But what made her think that he might attack her? He had hit her during arguments, but never simply gone for her out of the blue.

'I'm sorry I haven't been to collect you earlier. I was in London and then Catherine's message said you needed a bit of recuperation and I'm not surprised — these bugs seem trivial but in small children and old people they are often serious if dehydration sets in, as it clearly did with you.'

Judith looked at him as he sat leaning back in the armchair, whisky in his hand, relaxed, pleasant. Handsome. Yes. Of course people do not marry for looks at our age but I had always noticed Richard's — I had even been flattered that he had picked me out, when he could have had anyone. Though she knew that she had not looked her age, as perhaps she did now, had always dressed well because it gave her pleasure, never become slack about hair, make-up, weight. She had paid attention to those things for herself, and out of pride, not to attract a man. But perhaps it had helped.

He was seventy-three, looked at least ten years younger. He had Simon's fine features, and tall, narrow frame, though they did not share colouring.

She looked at him again as she drank. What had gone wrong? They had started wonderfully well, she had been happy. He had seemed happy. No — he had been happy. She was sure. Nothing in particular had happened but almost overnight a different man had emerged from the shadows of the one she knew.

And now?

'I have not behaved very well,' he said. 'Correction — I have behaved very badly. To you.'

'Yes.'

'I am of uncertain temper. That isn't an excuse, Judith.'

'But a lot of people have tempers — not all of them manage to control them but I think most do. I don't understand you, Richard. And that's a hard thing to accept.'

He sighed. 'I'm not sure I understand

myself. I seem to have reached my seventies without attaining much wisdom — about myself, anyway.'

'What are you saying to me? Are you trying to explain — apologise — excuse yourself? Because — you frighten me and I'm not sure how I can get over that.'

They sat in silence. Judith felt a surge of confidence, in her own ability to carve out a new understanding on which their future might be based, in her absolute wish to have everything open and clear between them, and in her belief that if it was not, she could and would walk away from him and from what had started by being a good marriage but which now had a rottenness at the core.

'What do you want to do?' he asked now, speaking very quietly without meeting her eye.

'Stay here for another couple of days. I need to work things out. You?'

'I'd like us to go away — take two or three weeks in the sun.'

'It's sunny here.'

'Indeed. But if we just took the car and drove down through France, stopped where we felt like it, might we not be able to mend things?'

'You are the one who needs to do the mending, Richard.'

'When we went to America we were happy, weren't we, doing just what we wanted, going about, staying a day or a week wherever we wanted?'

'I was happy then, yes. I think you were too.'

'I don't want you to think my irritability always has to get the better of me.'

'More than irritability.'

'It begins there.'

'And should end there.'

He stood up. 'There isn't much to pack up. Catherine will look after the house.'

'Cat has more than enough to do already and it isn't the house that's the problem.'

He was looking at her like a child waiting to be back in favour, nervous, hopeful, half smiling. Did she still love him, love him enough to give in?

'When were you thinking of going?'

'Tomorrow.'

'Goodness, as soon as that? I'm not sure I can be ready by then and why the rush?'

He put out his hand to her and, after a moment, she took it.

'Because this is too important to wait,' he said. 'Nothing matters more.'

When Cat came in an hour later, the kitchen had been tidied and the table laid for the next morning's breakfast, children's school things were ready and Judith's bag was in the hall.

'I've left a quarter-bottle of wine in the fridge. How was Mozart?'

'Good except that too many people were missing — the norovirus has a lot to answer for. Hello, Dad.'

'Catherine. You look to me as if a small whisky would suit you better than the dregs of a cheap bottle of wine.'

'This will do fine.'

Judith looked away from her as she said, 'I've imposed on you enough, darling, and it's time I went home. Your father's suggested we take a break in the sun which I do need and which will get rid of the last bugs, so I have to get back and sort everything out.'

She went out to find her coat. Cat stood with her back to the draining board, watching. There was nothing she could or would do. Judith was an adult, she had to make her own decisions. That things were not yet right between her and her father was obvious. She hoped they might mend but doubted they would.

'I imagine you have no more news of Simon than we have?' Richard said. He sounded more anxious than usual. 'Odd

how these things work. He could be anywhere, doing anything, for any length of
time and nobody is allowed to know. He
might as well be working for MI5.'

'The only thing that worries me is having
no way of getting in touch. What if something happened?'

'I imagine the people at his police station
have ways. He implied that he could be
absent for months rather than weeks.'

'Did he? I didn't think he knew.'

She heard Judith go upstairs, probably to
retrieve something she had forgotten, and
in the few moments she had, she knew she
ought to get his opinion, before he also disappeared for weeks.

'Dad — I need your take on something.'

She told him, as succinctly as she could,
about the private practice offer. He listened
carefully, as he always did about anything to
do with her career. His advice was always
valuable to her, though she didn't ask for it
often.

He was silent for a minute, frowning. 'You
can't worry about what Chris would have
thought. We both know he had a point, but
there are counter-arguments. Two things oc-
cur to me. You probably wouldn't get the
wide variety of medicine that you have in
an NHS general practice, though that's not

to say the well off don't present with interesting illnesses from time to time, but you would have to do rather a lot of pandering to very minor ailments. My only other query is whether it could possibly work here. Private practice used to be very successful — probably still is in parts of London — but it bears no relation to private hospitals, which are largely financed by insurance. No insurance will pay for a private GP. So I just wonder if they've done their sums.' He got up. 'After all, most people would ask why pay for something you can get free.'

Judith stood in the doorway.

'Good,' he said, smiling at his wife. 'You should think hard about this one, Catherine, but you may come to a different conclusion.'

She watched them drive off. It was a balmy night. An owl hooted from the chestnut tree. There were stars. Behind her in the house, three slept.

Whatever happened between her father and stepmother would happen and was no real business of hers. Wherever her brother was and whatever he was doing — much the same. She felt entirely alone but was conscious that for the first time in years she was content to be so. She had let something go.

Wookie had come out of the house to sit

quietly beside her on the step, a small, silky, warm presence, anxious to have company. She picked him up, rubbed his ears and stroked his head.

'Funny little object. You're not a proper dog at all.' Chris would have said that. Then, growling suddenly, Wookie struggled to be put down and raced off into the darkness, barking ferociously.

Cat waited for him to see off whatever ghostly presence he had detected deep in the bushes, and when he returned, still making small grumbling sounds, hustled him inside and shut the door.

TWENTY-FIVE

'Do you have a History section?'

He was in his fifties with wavy grey hair, handsome in a fleshy, full-lipped way. He looked slightly familiar.

'Far wall, in the middle, but Local History is by the door.'

He smiled. 'Not my cup of tea.'

Fifteen minutes and he was still browsing. He had also brought a pile of books to the counter.

'I wanted Antony Beevor's *D-Day* too.'

'That's out of stock again but it will be in tomorrow. I can keep one for you.'

'Would you? That's very kind. Yes please.'

The shop had been busy the day before, mainly with children coming to spend tokens they'd won as school prizes, but Rachel had sold a respectable number of other books, including a couple of expensive illustrated ones. She was pleased. Emma would be pleased. She had discovered that she was very much enjoying being a book-seller. But so far this morning the shop had been dead — two greetings cards and a map, at least until the man in the History section. He brought two more hardbacks to the counter and moved to biographies. Four there. Three children's picture books, which he seemed to pick up at random.

'Would these be suitable for a three-year-old?'

'Well — not really, at three, though I confess I'm not the children's book expert.'

'I'll take your word. This lot then please.'

He wandered around, brushing his hand against other books, spinning the greetings cards round, but it was obvious his shopping was done.

'I'm afraid that's three hundred and ten pounds. I'll spread them across three carrier bags — they're pretty strong. Can you manage?'

'You don't deliver?'

'I'm afraid not. The boss is away and I don't have anyone else.'

'Right. Three carrier bags then.'

The name on the card was the Hon. Rupert P. Barr and the payment went straight through.

'If you leave a phone number I'll let you know when the *D-Day* book has come in.'

201

'Don't bother. If I don't drop by someone will.' He smiled again. It was an engaging smile.

After he had sauntered out, and two people had come in to collect orders, she tidied the shelves, replaced one or two books that had been put back in the wrong sections and tried to remember why the Hon. Rupert Barr seemed familiar.

It was halfway through an afternoon devoted to Lafferton's most irritating customers — one who wanted a book they had seen somewhere and had 'Summer' in the title, another looking for one with a horse on the cover — when she remembered. The former Lord Lieutenant, at whose banquet she had first met Simon, was Sir Hugh Barr. Rupert P. could be a brother.

The banquet was a lifetime ago. It was also yesterday. She remembered every tiny detail about the evening. She had driven home happy. Was she still happy? No, she thought. Not happy, desperate. She had no idea where he was. She also had no idea what he felt and thought, how he saw her and her place in his life, if he had any idea about their future. Did he want her to be in his flat when he got back? Did he want her in his life at all? She had no idea. If he did not, she was certain that she could not bear to stay in Lafferton. There was little else to keep her. But where should she go? She had no ties elsewhere, friends were scattered, family small and distant. She had come here because of Kenneth, stayed because of him and then Simon.

The only thing she might want was to take an interest in this bookshop. It needed some financial input from outside. Why not hers? She loved working in it and she could do that whatever Simon wanted. Was it enough?

The rest of the afternoon was quiet and she spent it working out whether they could fit in a coffee machine, another counter, and a few tables, maybe one outside. Emma was against coffee in bookshops, Rachel knew that it brought people in who might eventually buy a book, and that it also made a good profit in itself, which helped through the quiet times. Emma said that the other coffee-shop owners would resent it, Rachel felt that you could never have too many and that their coffee would be superior, their cakes always home-made and fresh daily. Emma did not bother to respond, but then Emma seemed so despondent these days, so far as the bookshop was concerned.

When Emma came back from holiday, perhaps they could ratchet up the conversation a notch.

TWENTY-SIX

Eating lunch, then mopping corridor floors, exercising round the outdoor track, eating supper, playing pool. Normal. Terrifying. How do you look those men in the eye, hearing what you heard from them, knowing what you now know and can never unknow? How do you face the way they look at you, what they think, how they judge you? And do it again and again. How do you look them in the eye knowing that what you told them is a lie?

He mopped with his head down, ran alone, ate sitting at the end of a table. But playing pool with Martin, five foot four and with a pigtail down to his waist, he had to take the sideways looks, and once, a pat on the shoulder that might have been encouragement, might have been sympathy. Comradely. He shrugged it off and let Martin beat him easily so that he could get out of the games room.

He felt dirty. A criminal, not because he believed the story he had told earlier in the group, but because he was lying and they were believing him. Deceitful. Double-crosser. The words hammered a way into his head.

He did some stretching exercises and then turned on the television, flicked about, turned it off. Picked up a John le Carré, skimmed half a dozen pages without taking them in. Put it down.

'It won't get easier,' Jed had said, 'and you'll never be off your guard, but you will get used to it. Work your way in.'

He had never felt so ambivalent about anything he had done in his entire police career, except once, many years ago, when he had taken part in an entrapment. And what was this but entrapment in another form?

He had to lie and go over the crimes he had heard about in detail earlier, to remind himself why he was here, who he was trying to protect. It worked.

He was about to go and make a cup of tea when there was a tap on his door and Will Fernley put his head round.

'Hey. Just going to make some tea. Want one?'

'Read my mind.'

'I'll get them.'

'White, no sugar.'

The next stage, then.

'Not bad, these honeycombs,' Will said, sitting on the floor with his back to the door. 'You were where — Dartmoor?'

Simon nodded as he drank. Dartmoor because he knew it, had been inside to do interviews a few times, been shown round once, got his bearings.

'You?'

'Wandsworth. Strangeways. You an Oxford man? Know the prison there? Five-star hotel now.'

'I heard. Where were you?'

'The House.'

'Balliol.'

'Leftie then.'

'It's not compulsory.'

Fernley smiled. 'Seriously, Johnno — how are you finding it so far?'

'Weird. Oh, the place is OK — good facilities, food no better.'

'Right. I meant — still, you've only had one session.'

'I thought I was going to be sick. I almost gagged, waiting, then once I'd opened my mouth . . .'

'Right. You didn't say much.'

'He didn't ask for much.'

'That changes.'

'Right. Confession.'

'You Catholic?'

'No, just — what it feels like.'

'Gets harder. They come at you — what do you mean by that? How did you really feel? You're not telling us, you're blaming someone else not yourself, you're pretending, you're joking about it, you've not really admitted it to yourself, not if you can joke — all that and a load more. They don't let you off, they don't miss a trick. You'll sweat.'

'What I'm here for.'

Will looked at him over the rim of his mug.

'Have you been in one-to-one?'

'Therapy? No.'

'It's easier.'

'So why come here?'

'I'm going back a few years. Probably all changed now.'

'What do you mean?'

Will shrugged. 'Or maybe it was who I got. Can't all be top of their game.'

'You're saying there was something wrong with the psych or that it didn't work on you?'

'Well, obviously.'

'Right.'

'Pathetic.'

'What do you want out of it?'

Will didn't reply.

'The thing is, Johnno,' he said eventually, 'I want out. I can't believe you don't want out as well.'

'Doesn't everybody?'

Will shook his head. 'You must have heard of the guys who come out and nick a pair of trainers or something just to get back in because "in" is safe, "in" is home to them, they can't cope anywhere else. Which is extremely sad, but it doesn't include me — or you, I'll bet.'

'Sure.'

'I want out. I want life. This is the only way I'll ever have to get it. In here it's a system like any other system and systems can be beaten. I met a man in Wandsworth, a lifer, armed robbery twice, and he was the safe cracker — and he said there is no safe in the world that can't be cracked. Given time. That was his problem. Time. You don't get it when you've got ten minutes before an alarm goes off or a hostage finds the panic button and manages to work it, but given time and a cool head, he reckoned there was no safe he couldn't crack. "It's a system," he used to say, "and systems are there to be beaten." Interesting chap actually. He was taking a degree in maths. Like safes, I suppose . . . systems to be cracked.'

'This is a bit different.'

'Well, it's a comparison, that's all.' He drained his tea mug and stood up. 'Another?'

'My turn.'

'Or ping-pong.'

'God, the excitement.'

'Five quid I beat you.'

'I haven't got five quid.'

'You soon will have, way you were mopping that bloody floor. Eat your dinner off it. If you do a bad job too many times, they dock your pocket money.'

'Go on about this system,' Simon asked as they went down the stairs.

'Another time. Walls. Ears.'

A couple of men were leaning over the upper-floor banister rail looking down. 'La-di-da.'

'Ignore them.' Will didn't turn his head. 'No worse than school.'

'School!'

They both smiled.

TWENTY-SEVEN

'Brian?'

'Sorry. Sorry.'

'No need. But carry on a bit longer if you can?'

Brian shook his head.

'Recap.'

'Get on with it, you'll get nowhere copping out every time, Bri. We've all been there.'

Brian blew his nose, then wiped it on his T-shirt sleeve. He was a wreck. He had recounted how he had stalked the girl and how he had been excited when she had finally realised that he was following and looked terrified. He had said, 'I just jumped on her. I jumped on her and brought her down. I didn't want her looking at me.'

But then he had stopped, and after a few moments, begun to cry.

'How did it feel? When you brought her down?'

'Powerful.'

'What sort of powerful?'

'You had power over her, you mean?'

'Powerful because she was a lot smaller than you?'

The questions came from all sides.

'No. She wasn't that small. Slim but . . . no, it was just feeling myself jump on her and down she went. I felt — it was the most exciting feeling I'd ever had.'

'Go on.'

'Was that just because you'd jumped her or because you were excited about raping her and excited about killing her afterwards?'

'No. I didn't — I wasn't going to. Not when I followed her . . . not when . . .'

'So why'd you do it? You must have had that urge — to rape her.'

'No. Yes, I suppose I did. I don't know. I don't remember.'

A couple of jeers.

'Leave him, let him have a minute. Give him time.'

'You're almost there, aren't you, Brian?' the therapist said. 'You've followed her, you've felt powerful, and you jumped on her and brought her down and felt more powerful still. Was that a good feeling?'

'It was a great feeling. The best.'

'Better than what came after?'

'No . . . the start of it. I was — you know, I was like the Hulk, I was growing as huge as him, I was a giant, I was mighty — it did that to me, feeling powerful like that.' His eyes were gleaming now, but gleaming with a distant look. He's there, Simon thought. He's given in to it and he's back there now.

No one spoke. They occasionally shuffled a foot or crossed a leg. Waited.

'I knew I was huge and powerful enough to do anything. I had my foot on her to stop her getting away and she was trying to get up, but my foot was a giant's foot, it was vast. She hadn't a chance. Then the rest was easy. I mean, I couldn't have stopped then. I could see her face, I could see her pleading with me and that made the feeling better. I could . . . I knew she knew what was going to happen, and . . . when I had her she just went still, she didn't fight, and in a way that was worse for her. I think if she'd fought me, I'd have gone on feeling powerful and it would have been enough. I'd got enough. I was high on it. It wasn't the sex . . . not really. Only she just lay like a jelly, like a dead flat thing and that made me very, very angry.'

He looked into the middle distance, unaware of the rest of them, his surroundings, the day or the time, only aware of being back there and bloated with power and rage. His hands were clenching and unclenching, and he tapped his right foot fast on the floor.

'Did you know you were going to kill her?'

'No. Oh no. I never planned that. I never would have killed her. I can't kill a spider, me, I have to pick them up and put them gently out of the window. I couldn't kill anything.'

'Only you did.'

'No.'

'You strangled her.'

He sat up with a start, and stared at the man on his left. 'I strangled her,' he said in a small, dead voice. 'I strangled her.'

'How did that make you feel?'

Brian shook his head over and over again. 'I didn't mean to kill her.'

'What did you mean to do then?'

But all he did was shake his head, and then bend forward and put his hands, and then his arms, over his face to shield it from them, and the sight of them from himself.

'What did you do after you'd strangled her? You haven't said that yet.'

'Did you feel powerful when you chucked some stuff over her and ran?'

Brian's shoulders heaved.

'Do you feel powerful now?'

'Brian — not sure I believe you about the sex not mattering. It always matters.'

'Right, let's give him a few minutes. Will, haven't heard from you for a day or two. What sort of place are you in?'

'OK. I'm OK. It's all helping.'

'You were talking about feeling — detached, was it?'

'Dissociated. Yup.'

'Big words, Will, big words.'

'Sorry.'

'Not all got Oxford degrees and that.'

'What's to be ashamed of having one of those? Wish I did.'

'Will?'

He leaned back in his chair, one leg up over the other.

'I suppose it's . . . separating yourself from what — what you did.'

'How?'

'Just happens, doesn't it? I mean, I know, I know about what it meant. I know. Just feel it was someone else.'

'But it wasn't.'

'Right. Listen, I know that, of course I do, and I'm very sorry. I couldn't be more sorry.'

'Sorry's just words.'

'Well, it's a start, isn't it?'

'Yeah, but how long have you been spouting words in here and nothing else? Doesn't seem to get you any further.'

'Oh, it does. I feel a lot further.'

'How?'

'I — I realise it *was* actually me. I'm responsible. I don't like admitting that but it was me. So . . . I'm a lot further.'

'It seems to be more in your head, Will,' the therapist said.

Will recrossed his leg. 'Not altogether.'

'You've never actually gone into any detail, have you? And you never show your feelings about it.'

'What're you afraid of?'

Will sighed, glanced round and acknowledged the comments coming from different people in the room.

'I suppose — I'm afraid of what I did. I mean — of ever being at risk of doing anything like it again.'

'You think you're not at risk of that now?'

'I'm not sure. But I've learned a lot about myself and being in prison hasn't been any fun.'

'Never is for nonces.'

A murmur.

'OK, sorry. Take that back.'

'Thanks, Len.'

'Listen.' A man whose name Simon had

215

not caught leaned forward and looked along the row at Will Fernley. 'You told us your index offence, you told us you were attracted to kids . . . that you'd gone wrong, I think you put it, in that direction. You said you'd been downloading stuff and got sussed. Only — there's a hell of a lot more you're not admitting to us and that's because you daren't admit it to yourself. But if you can't get to grips with it in here you're never going to. This is your one chance, come on, take it. Nobody's sitting in judgement in here — Christ, that'd be a laugh. Only you just sit there and smirk, to be honest.'

'I don't think I was smirking.'

'Whatever. That expression.'

'Will?' The therapist had been focused on him closely all the time he had been speaking, and now that he was being challenged. 'Is Mick right about that? There's no hiding place, is there?'

Brian said, looking at the floor, 'If I can, you can. You never give anything. And you've got to give or you'll never get any further, and he's right, what's the point?'

Will sat shaking his head, smiling. 'I'm sorry if you feel like that.'

'Not how we feel — how do *you* feel about yourself? Because from where I'm sitting it

216

looks as if you're not that bothered and you fuckin' should be.'

'Oi.'

'All right, cool it. Will?'

'What am I supposed to say?'

'You're addressing what you've done, your urges, what they led you to do, what you felt about that and what you feel now . . . you shouldn't need me to tell you.'

'Wasting the time, that's what, and some of us object to that. You want to waste time, you get out of here first.'

'No need to raise your voice.'

'Listen, I'm not even sure if I've got the right to say anything here . . .'

The rest of them fell silent as Simon spoke. Respect. Respect for a newcomer having the courage to open his mouth, not for a copper. He was not a copper.

'Will . . . as I see it, nobody in here is going to criticise you for telling the truth. I mean, that's why we're all in this. Nobody would have any right to . . . I know I wouldn't. I just think maybe if you had the courage to open up you'd . . . I don't know . . . find it easier and . . . get the point of it. Sorry, I'm not really the right guy to say this, I know . . .'

The man next to him nodded. 'You are the right guy though because we're all the right guy . . . in here you're the same as the rest of us, innit. Come on, mate, else the session'll be over and we've just pussyfooted around — or you have.'

'OK, OK. Sorry.' Will took a breath and for a moment looked as if he was going to dodge again. 'I . . . listen, I'm not making excuses or passing the buck here but there were others in this . . . it got to be more than . . . the way it started out. I'd had feelings about children . . . sex . . . about . . . I got aroused by looking at little children . . . girls . . . I'd go to a beach or a pool or . . . but then it wasn't enough, it wasn't . . . what I wanted. It's so easy online now, you know . . . a couple of minutes, even for someone like me who isn't very up on all the techno stuff . . . I found a couple of sites . . . then another which was more a group. I joined that . . . they send you stuff . . . and you can just . . . go into sort of hidden websites . . . hidden behind legit ones, I mean . . . that was it.'

'What?'

'What was happening . . . what I was doing.'

'You don't get eight years for downloading.'

'You're taking the piss.'

Will's expression was defiant.

The therapist leaned back. 'Tell us what your feelings were when you got into the sites the first time, Will.'

'Excited.'

'Right.'

'This was — what I wanted, where I wanted to be.'

'How long did you stay online — on average?'

'God, I don't know.'

'You must know. Ten minutes? Three hours?'

'No, no. I just — went in here and there . . . then I started talking — chatting — to the others.'

'Who were they?'

'No idea. You don't exactly give out your name, do you?'

'Could have been anybody then? Your best friend even.'

'Not very likely.'

'Why?'

'So you started accessing these sites regularly — every day?'

'No . . . well, not at first . . . then, it got more.'

'So what did you think?'

'How do you mean, what did I think? It's not about thinking, is it?'

'About the sites — what did you think

219

about how they came to exist? About what lay behind the images?'

'Nobody tells you.'

'You're blocking again, Will. You must have realised in a nanosecond that these were real images — not cartoons.'

'Well, yes.'

'Real images of real children being abused. So what did you think about that?'

'I don't remember.'

'What did you feel about it?'

'Nothing . . . it didn't — I didn't . . . just looked at the images. I got off on those.'

'Are you saying you didn't ever think of these images as being real kids?'

'I don't . . . well, yes, I must have done.'

'Did you wish they were real, not just images?'

'Maybe.'

'How many real kids did you sort out then, Will?'

'None.'

'Come on.'

'I said — it was pictures.'

'You went down for more than that.'

'All right . . . after a bit you watch the films and you . . . want to go further.'

'Films?'

'I said so.'

'Pictures and films are two different

things, aren't they?'

'Depends.'

'No, in this context, Will, it doesn't depend
— and you were watching films.'

'After a time.'

'What was the difference?'

'Not a lot.'

'Come on.'

'OK, films were — more . . .'

'What? More what?'

'Real, if you like. Yes.'

'It's a bit like getting blood out of a stone,'
the therapist said. 'You're not engaging with
this, Will. Talk about the films.'

'I can't.'

'Why is that?'

'I can't.'

'How long had you been part of this website and looking and going into the forum
before you got more involved?'

'Months.'

'Two? Six?'

'I don't remember. Quite a few. Then . . .
there was some chat and they were wanting
— some more. Input.'

'And what was that?'

'Help.'

Suddenly, he was not playing, he was
struggling, twisting his hands, his mouth
twitching, moving his head this way and that

as if he had a painful neck. Simon watched him. He had been play-acting and trying to slither away from any real engagement. Now, he was anxious, profoundly uncomfortable.

'I think you're on the brink of something, Will', the therapist said, 'and next time, you're going to take a bigger step forward. Stay with it.'

Simon was working in the pod, doing vegetable prep and swabbing down. It was hot, claustrophobic and noisy but the jokes and banter whirled about, and as with any uninteresting job, he switched off, did it, and thought about other things. Will Fernley.

He waited until after supper and a basketball game in which he scored once, but then retired, his back painfully reminding him that he was a few years older than when he had last played. The team was too good for him. He showered, changed, and knocked on Fernley's door. There was no reply. He waited, knocked again, and opened it.

Will was lying face down on his bed, unmoving. For a split second, he looked as if he was also not breathing, but eventually he grunted.

'Want a coffee?'

'If you like.'

When Simon brought the drinks back he was still lying there.

'Quit feeling sorry for yourself.'

'You fucking wait.'

'Makes me wonder why you're here.'

'Why do you think?'

'Not for the therapy, that's pretty clear. That was a load of bullshit you told me. You've got no interest at all in being here.'

'Yup.'

'So why?'

'Because I got sick of having my head stuck down the loo, sick of being tripped up as I went down the corridor and being punched up in the showers and sick of the screws making snide remarks and treating me like scum. I thought it might be easier in here and it is, because if I'm a nonce then at least I'm among other nonces. And so are you.'

TWENTY-EIGHT

'I'll be as gentle as I can but it will be uncomfortable. It's important that I try and get as many samples as possible.'

'What about the clothes?'

'The lab will test those. Because you took them off and bundled them into a bag rather than wash them there's a very good chance that they can get semen from them and that means they'll have your attacker's DNA. But, of course, positive samples on clothing don't prove there was rape, as I'm sure you understand. Now, just lie as still as you can, Shelley.'

The atmosphere was clinical because of the job the doctor was doing, but it was also calming, accepting, gentle. Shelley felt almost relaxed, for the first time since it had happened. The examination was painful, unpleasant, invasive, embarrassing but nothing more, and it didn't last long.

Far worse was the account she had to give,

in as much detail as she could remember. The counsellor sat with her, the machine recorded silently, there was a glass of water and a cup of tea beside her, plus a box of tissues, none of which prevented her from shaking as she went over it all, from the minute she and Tim had arrived at the dinner and seen Richard Serrailler, to the minute Tim saw her torn dress in the car when they got home. It seemed to take a very long time to recall everything and it was almost more vivid, more affecting, more repulsive than when it had actually happened. Being raped did not fade in the memory — on the contrary, it grew, and it was accompanied by feelings of shame and distress, fear and a strange sense of unreality. It could not have been him, he could not really have been doing that to her, they had not actually been in that place. She would wake up in a minute and the nightmare would begin to loosen its grip. But it did not.

St Catherine's had looked so institutional and forbidding from the outside that she would most probably have gone away without even ringing the bell, if the policewoman had not been with her. The entrance hall, the concrete stairs, the dismal lift reminded her of a cell block. But once inside the third-floor suite, everything was different — fresh pastel paint on the walls, wide windows letting in the light, comfortable sofas and chairs, decent coffee and tea, made freshly, biscuits on a plate. But most of all, there was friendliness and an atmosphere so welcoming that it lifted Shelley's spirits. She was exhausted after giving the lengthy recorded statement and having the physical examination, but talking to the counsellor made her feel not only calmer, but quietly determined.

'Shelley, it shouldn't affect you at all that the man you are accusing has a high public profile locally, and is very well respected. It certainly doesn't affect us. Nor should the fact that his son is a detective chief superintendent. Forget that too. The police are expert at dealing with anything related to one of the force and it won't even come near him. And that's right. If it's hard for you, and women like you, it is actually very hard for relatives of men accused of rape. I know how I'd feel, if it was my father or brother facing prosecution for this. You have to set all that aside and leave other people to deal with it. Focus on yourself — you've had a traumatic experience. You'll take time to recover — maybe longer than you expect. But you will because we're here for you, as long as it takes, OK?'

'So, how long will it take?'

'Forensics will come back in a couple of weeks — depends how stretched they are at the moment. Could be a bit more than that but not usually. Assuming they have a positive result — and I've no reason to suppose that they won't — then the police will pay your attacker a visit and charge him.'

'And that's that? It's all like a moving train and no one can get off it.'

'No. You will be asked if you want to press the charge of rape. You can change your mind at any point, even up to the moment you all go into court for the hearing, assuming it comes to that. You know about the way a case has to be handed over by the police to the CPS?'

'Yes.'

'So, if the CPS decides there's enough evidence to bring the charge of rape, then a date will be set for the court hearing. That could take several months. None of this is going to happen in a hurry. That's just one reason why it's all so stressful and you don't have any choice except to endure it. It's why I said we'll be here to support you all the way — and after it's over, if you still need us, no matter what the outcome.'

'I keep rerunning what happened. I see

hideous images and scenes . . .'

'I understand . . . do you want to talk about them?'

'No. I want to forget them. And I don't think I could tell you — they're muddled, they swirl about . . . it's the atmosphere of nightmares. That sounds daft.'

'No, it doesn't. To be honest, I'd worry if you weren't going over things.'

'God, I hate all this. It's going to sound ridiculous but . . . in a way, everything that's happening now is almost worse . . . and it's going to go on, isn't it?'

'But the difference is, then you were on your own, now you have us and you won't be alone again so long as it lasts.'

TWENTY-NINE

'Anyone seen Austin?'

'Out.'

No one in the CID room looked round.

'How long has he been out?'

No reply.

DS Lois Dancer went to her own desk and sent the DCI — Austin Rolph was acting head of CID in Simon Serrailler's absence — a text message. *Urgent. Important. Call me.*

Three hours later he had not called and Lois had had to leave the building to attend to a case of a missing teenager who turned out not to be missing, and the case of a stolen car which turned out not to have been stolen. He did not call her until she was about to go off shift.

'What is it, Lois? I've been at this car-shunting workshop. Can it wait till the morning?'

'It ought not to. It's not so much urgent but it's pretty sensitive and I'm not sure what to do.'

'Use your intelligence — it's why you're a DS.'

'Yes, but —'

'Tomorrow, Dancer.'

'Bastard,' she muttered, knowing he had already switched her off. The DCI was one who thought that as women aspired to be treated in the same way as men in the force, they should be spoken to in a way no male officer would tolerate.

Rolph was a good copper, an instinctive one with a great record, and he was a decent enough stand-in for Serrailler as head, in the sense that the administration flowed smoothly, but he had no tact and no empathy. He was not a team player, he simply expected to provide the lead and for them to follow, without much question. If they objected or put forward their own ideas or point of view, he would always listen, before ignoring them.

She joined a couple of the others from CID for an hour in the pub, went home and had a Skype call with her sister and family in Vancouver, got her gear ready for her Territorial Army weekend assault course, watched a particularly violent horror film with her husband Lee, then went to bed. And all the time, she thought about the bombshell that was in her notes, the bombshell she had to present to Rolph. She had liked Shelley and more importantly, had believed her story, though she knew nothing about the Super's father, beyond his name and reputation. But that the case was a ticking bomb, whatever the outcome, she had no doubt.

She had only been at Lafferton a couple of years, having transferred from Bevham on promotion, and did not know DCS Serrailler well. They had worked together, he had been approachable and was good at delegating and trusting his juniors, but there was a reserve about him. He would be forgiving of any genuine errors, especially those made by rookie cops, but hard on stupidity, even harder on disloyalty, and he would never dream of calling her 'Dancer'. But clearly, in spite of his apparent openness, he was a very private man who might not cope well with anything like this, so close to home. Given that his whereabouts and the length of time he was likely to be away were unknown, at least to most of them in CID, Lois didn't envy Austin Rolph, to whom she would be handing over the Shelley Pendleton file.

She was in the office well before eight o'clock but it was after eleven by the time Lois saw Rolph drive onto the forecourt.

'Right, DS Dancer, what's all this about? You're like a cat on hot bricks.'

She followed him into his office and set the file down on the desk.

'Can you look at this now. It's tricky.'

'Why?'

'Just look at it — sir.'

The DCI was putting his things down, taking off his jacket, opening his laptop, at the same time as he started reading the first page of Lois's report, and for a few seconds and to her annoyance, he was clearly only paying it cursory attention. And then he let his jacket fall onto the floor and sat down, reading rapidly.

'Why didn't you show this to me straight away?'

Lois simply looked at him.

'Right, OK.'

He sat back and put his hands, folded together, up to his face.

'Has anyone else seen this yet?'

'No.'

'What's the latest with Mrs . . .'

'Shelley Pendleton.' Lois filled him in.

'What was your advice?'

'That she press charges.'

'Right.'

He was silent for a moment, drumming his fingers on the desk. Then he said, 'Nothing's going to happen until forensics report on it, so you leave this one with me and get on with whatever else you've got on.'

'I was going to see Mrs Pendleton.'

'No. Leave this to the St Catherine's lot, it's what they're for. And for the time being, the name of the accused doesn't go further than you, me and the report. File it separately, password protect it and that's that.'

'Sir . . .'

'I'm talking about discretion until we know more. These things always boil down to he says/she says, especially when the two are well known to one another. Right now, you can take someone down to Carter's Buildings — there's a body. About a hundred years old from what I gathered but uniform want a presence.'

Lois went back to the CID room with pent-up anger like heartburn in her chest. 'Discretion'? Cover-up? Where was the difference? She resented Rolph's implication that she was not able to maintain confidentiality and his assumption that Shelley had been exaggerating, and that the sexual encounter had been 'six of one, half a dozen of the other'. He had not talked to her or assessed her state of mind and the shock she was still in. He had not taken her to St Catherine's, white-faced and shaking, but still quietly sure of what she had experienced. And now, because the man was related to a top cop, Rolph wanted to brush the whole thing under the carpet.

Well, that wasn't going to happen. It was her case, she had the details, she was not going to let it dematerialise. Nor, she suspected, would Simon Serrailler want that. Oddball he might be but he was straight and honourable and the last thing he would ever entertain was so much as a hint of a cover-up.

She collected a brand-new, shiny DC and went off to find the hundred-year-old body, filing the Shelley Pendleton case at the back of her mind — pending, not forgotten.

The DCI put in a call to the Bevham Police HQ and asked for a meeting with the Chief Constable that day.

'He's out till after four on the other side of the county. Can I help?'

'No, it's urgent that I see him today.'

'I'll get back to you, Chief Inspector, but I'll need to know something of what it's regarding.'

'Just tell him it's highly confidential and sensitive.'

'I'll do my best,' the Chief's secretary said wearily, 'but I can't promise — he's got one hell of a week.'

Rolph was in the Chief's office at twenty past five, for an appointment at half past, but Kieron Bright was delayed, having been asked to meet a government minister who was visiting the county, and it was well after six before he appeared, briskly apologising.

'I can't give you more than ten minutes, I've got to go home and change and be straight out to a dinner. But I'm sure you can give me a digest in less than that.'

Austin Rolph had not liked the previous Chief, privately because she was a woman but publicly because he felt she was soft. He had hoped for a senior male figure as her successor, and got Bright, considerably younger than him and, as he had quickly decided, too full of himself. But when Bright had appointed him acting head of Lafferton CID in Serrailler's absence, he had changed his mind.

He told him about the rape case in succinct detail, waiting for the other man's startled reaction when Richard Serrailler's name was mentioned. There was none.

'We have a delicate problem, as I'm sure you agree, sir.'

'You could have sent me this stuff by email,' was all the Chief replied.

'Well, hardly, sir, with respect . . . emails aren't totally confidential.'

'Mine are, though my secretary sees them, but that's not my point. Even supposing someone intercepted this one, which is a bit cloak-and-dagger, what precisely is the problem?'

Rolph was caught off guard for a second.

'With respect —'

'What you're thinking is that because the accused happens to be the father of a detective chief superintendent, and also happens to be a prominent local figure and a Freemason, this makes it somehow a special case. Different.'

'No, but —'

'Yes. Are you a Mason?'

'No, sir.'

'Nor am I. But even if we were it would be irrelevant, just as the police connection is irrelevant. I don't know what you were thinking I would say or do — maybe even hoping — but this case proceeds like any other.'

'Sir. But ought you not to warn the Chief Super?'

'If he were around, he would be told, and by you, or by DS Dancer, as a matter of courtesy. But he isn't. He'll have to find out when he gets back.'

'From . . . ?'

'Time I left. Incidentally, to be clear — I don't believe in cover-ups and on my watch the phrase "special treatment" isn't part of the language.'

THIRTY

In the market at Cahors they had bought olives, four different cheeses, fresh bread, oil, pâté, salami, farm eggs, fruit, and two small zesty lemon tarts from the patisserie in the side street. Now, they sat at a cafe table watching the throngs around every stall and the groups of old men shaking hands before sitting down to their mid-morning pastis and tiny glasses of rosé. The sun was bright. It would be much hotter by lunchtime.

'Bliss,' Judith said.

Richard nodded, and raised his *café crème* to her. 'Why put up with an English summer? Shall we just stay as long as we feel like it?'

The South-West, like everywhere else in France, was suffering badly from the recession and a poor spring and early summer which had deterred visitors. The area was half empty, though the morning market looked as busy as ever. The small hotel they had stayed in for a couple of nights on arriving had directed them to a gîte owned by the proprietor's son. Usually, it was booked solidly between April and October. Now, in June, there had been a rash of cancellations. It was small, airy, white-painted, pale-blue-curtained, with a stretch of garden and a pool, shady trees and a terrace. They had taken it on the spot.

Richard looked across the table. 'Better here than in the Dordogne. Haven't seen an English car other than our own.'

'Everything changes. France was the land of eternal sunshine and cheap property to convert. Cheap food and drink, good restaurants, and every village had a cafe. Now? Expensive food, most villages haven't a cafe or a shop, restaurants are poor . . . don't they know any meat but duck?'

'And the weather has only just bucked up. Do we still love France?'

'Of course, but I could never live here.'

'Expats? No.' He suddenly patted the pocket of his linen jacket, took out his phone and checked the screen.

'Is there any signal here?'

'Not bad. None to speak of at the gîte.'

'Have you sent a message to Cat? She'd probably like to know where we are and what we're doing . . . and that we're both fine.'

'Why wouldn't we both be fine? You're not likely to suffer any after-effects of that damned bug, you know.'

'No.' Judith looked at him for a long moment. But it was all right. It was as if a switch had been thrown and he was again the Richard she had loved and married, occasionally brusque, occasionally silent, but otherwise good company, funny. And loving.

There was no point in wasting a precious holiday in the French sun wondering about the other Richard.

'Have you brought your phone?'

'It's in my bag. Not sure if there's any battery life though, I do tend to forget about it. Why?'

'No particular reason. But you're right — being permanently available is a bad thing. People become surgically joined to these damn things.'

'Don't switch yours off as well, Richard. There are always the children.'

'The children.'

'Oh, I know — not one of them under forty. Still . . . you haven't heard from Simon?'

'Don't expect to. Simon never bothers to

contact me — and especially not when he's gone underground.'

He got up and held out his hand to her. 'Let's stroll into the covered market and buy one of those fresh pizzas and some salad. Nice simple food and a good bottle of St-Emilion.'

Judith took his hand.

She woke to find the white muslin curtain at the bedroom window blowing gently into the room on a faint breeze. It was half past six and the afternoon had been hot. They had swum, eaten, gone to bed, slept. Now, she was on her own. She went to the window. Richard was sitting in a deckchair in the shade of the terrace reading. His phone was on the small table beside him.

She had not realised how worried he must be about Simon, though she was fully aware that he would never admit to it or show it, but he was clearly anxious for some news, even just a quick 'I'm fine'.

She made citron *pressé* with ice and went outside. Richard glanced up and closed his book over his forefinger to keep the place. The gîte had several shelves of paperbacks left by previous visitors, mainly in English, and he had found *Captain Corelli's Mandolin*, a novel he had enjoyed greatly the first time round. Cat and Judith had loved it too, Simon had not.

'Any news darling?'

'What do you mean, any news? What about?'

'Sorry, don't bark at me. I was just wondering.'

'I don't like being interrogated.'

'Richard . . .' She handed him the drink. 'Enjoy this. Don't let's spoil the day.'

He frowned but then raised his glass to her. 'Quite right. I could stay here for a long time.'

'While the weather lasts. I think I'll swim again in a little while.'

She closed her eyes and turned her face to the late-afternoon sun. Happy. Yes. Probably. More than for some months, certainly.

Let this last. Let it last.

She shivered slightly.

THIRTY-ONE

Walking to village.

He put the envelope on the kitchen table. It was still early, but the text had come through half an hour ago. Judith was still asleep and he moved about quietly, without opening the shutters, anxious to be down the slope and away long before she woke.

It would be hot later but now the sky was pale with a haze on the horizon. Richard struck across the track which formed part of the Santiago di Compostela route and saw a party of pilgrims a little way ahead, backpacks, faded shorts, heavy boots, cotton hats. As he neared them, he saw the scallop shell of the pilgrim hanging from each backpack.

'Bonjour. Bonjour. Bonjour.'

He passed them, raising his hand, then went off the track into an area of scrub and gorse and stopped beside a single tree. From here he looked out over the fields towards the village, far below. It was the nearest point for a good mobile phone signal.

The text had read: *Dr Richard Serrailler, please contact Lafferton Police Station as soon as possible.*

Shelley Pendleton had reported him then. It was just conceivable that the text was about Simon and his secrets but he could not risk calling in to find out.

Well, he would simply not reply. He would switch his phone off and ignore it all, though he knew this was not sensible, was the action of a man in a panic and with something to hide.

He checked the time the text had come in. Allowing for slow communications and the hour's time difference, it was perhaps not too late to send an apparent auto-reply — though he did not know if mobiles, like computers, could be set to do such a thing.

Worth the risk.

Dr Richard Serrailler is abroad on holiday. Messages will not be picked up at this time.

He pressed 'Send', then stood looking down the valley. The sun was up now. The little file of pilgrims was wending its way down the track and onwards, onwards, to Santiago de Compostela. He wished he could join them.

THIRTY-TWO

Tim was a good cook. She was a lousy cook. Tim was generous, too, more than happy to get in from a late appointment showing spoiled clients round a mansion thirty miles away, drive back in terrible traffic, and immediately prepare supper including a starter. Tonight, he had made a dish of cold prawns, smoked salmon and gem lettuce with his own recipe French dressing, a chicken breast curry with almonds, and brought out some of the marmalade ice cream he had concocted the previous weekend. Shelley had managed most of the fish, by dint of taking very small pieces into her mouth and washing them down with her wine, but when he had set down the curry, one of her favourite dishes, her throat seemed to have closed and been stitched up and she could not swallow any of it. Tim was easygoing, did not take offence, looked sympathetic.

'You haven't picked up that damn tummy bug everyone and his wife have had? Poor Shell — if so, go to bed, I'll bring you some iced water and you can just try and sleep it off.'

It was not a bug. Her stomach was as it had been for the past nine days — churning, nauseous, unable to digest food, but not because of any virus.

'I'm sorry — it's always so delicious. You are good.'

'Go on — bed.'

'No . . . Tim, I haven't got a bug.'

He put the plates together and took them into the kitchen. Then he sat down at the table again.

'Tell me what's wrong.'

'You know.'

'This stuff about Richard Serrailler?'

'Stuff. Yes, if you like, call it "stuff". He raped me.'

'Darling, you know what I —'

' "Darling, you know what I" . . . You know what I said, Tim. He raped me. Not possibly, not maybe I was drunk, not perhaps it was consensual sex. Rape!'

Tim reached out and offered to refill her wine glass but she put her hand over it.

'What's wrong with you that for some reason you can't — won't — believe me? I know there are men who stand up for their mates when the mates have had "a bit of you know what" where they shouldn't, but you are not that kind of man . . . I have never, ever said this sort of thing before, have I?'

'Of course not.'

'No. So why would I suddenly invent a story about being raped in a hotel cloakroom?'

'I didn't say you had.'

'More or less. You said I was imagining it, you said I'd had too many glasses of wine and maybe invited it . . . you said . . .'

'No, no, Shelley, I didn't. It's only that — well, "rape." . . . it's a violent word.'

'It was a violent act. I felt like a tart in an alleyway and I am not. I am so not. And even if I had been, tarts can be raped too, did you know that?'

'Of course they can't.'

'Tim, they can. They can. Just because of what they do —'

'Precisely because of what they do.'

'If you'd heard what . . .'

'What? Heard what? When?'

She looked at her hand, moving about on the edge of the table, twitching, not in her control.

'Shelley, tell me. If you want me to take

this seriously, you can't just sit there.'

She sat there. Tim looked distraught but she felt removed from it, locked in her resolve not to be dismissed, patronised, disbelieved or talked out of what she knew was the truth.

'Listen, if you say that is what happened then I believe you, of course I do. I'll have a word with Serrailler — well, obviously —'

'Excuse me, you will what? "Have a word"? What the hell does that mean? "Listen, old boy, I hear things got a bit out of hand the other night, you know what I mean — Shelley's a bit upset, to be frank, so I thought I'd have a word, between ourselves, Mason to Mason." '

'Don't joke about it.'

'Well it sounded like a joke to me. "Have a word." '

'Well, what else can I do? It's over with but he shouldn't just walk away without getting some sort of reprimand.'

'Oh, don't worry, he isn't going to. He's not walking anywhere.'

'What do you mean? Shelley, you mustn't go to the police. I said this before. You'll only show yourself up, make yourself look a fool. They're not very nice to women who cry rape, you know.'

'Actually, they were very nice. Extremely

nice. Sympathetic and understanding and entirely . . .'

Tim's eyes widened. 'Tell me I have this wrong.'

'You don't.'

He got up and walked round and round the room, banging his right fist into his left palm. 'I don't believe this. I don't believe it. What am I going to do?'

'You?'

'Yes, me. You know this will be all over Lafferton, don't you?' He stopped beside her and bent down, leaning his arms on the table, his face close to hers. Have you thought what effect this could have on my career? On Richard's reputation? Has it crossed your mind in your headlong pursuit of revenge —'

She stood up so fast she knocked the chair over and it caught him on the shin.

'This has nothing to do with revenge, this has everything to do with a man being brought to book for raping a woman. That's all and if it gets headlines on the front page not only don't I care, I'll be glad, because men like that think they're immune — you'll "have a word" and that's it, "naughty boy, but never mind, it won't go any further". But it is going further. It already has.'

THIRTY-THREE

Simon leaned back and closed his eyes. His hands were damp, and he could feel his hair flat with sweat. It was warm — a dozen men packed into a small room and the only window locked. Emotions were always high in the group and he had relied on his own tension at concentrating on his story and on telling it with conviction to make him blend with the others. He had the basis of the legend which he and Jed had worked on so carefully. 'When you get to it, the detail will take care of itself,' Jed had said, 'but the trick will be to remember that detail afterwards. Try not to give so much that it isn't possible.'

He had told them about Johnno Miles's attraction to small girls, from the time he was a teenager, and how he had at first been puzzled by it, then perturbed, how he could never talk to anyone at all but had to keep the secret locked up inside himself, which caused him great stress and anxiety. He had told them how he had learned there were thousands of others like him out there, and how he had started to make contact, but very warily. And then the Internet had come to help him, as it had helped them all, and opened an Aladdin's cave of websites, forums, secret meeting places online. Shared information and assistance had converted him from a solitary, troubled paedophile, into an active, even aggressive one. He had told them that he had begun to believe children could be groomed to enjoy abuse, that sex with children had been a part, often an accepted part, of life in past civilisations and that as long as you stuck to certain rules, there ought to be no shame in it.

He told them how he had joined groups of like-minded men. He told how he had converted thought and desire to action. He told about the first time he had had misgivings, because of the reaction of the child, and from there how he had tried to control his behaviour and failed, how he had started to ask himself if he had to stay as he was, missing out of normal adult relationships and even marriage and a family.

He had told his story so well that he found himself shaking, and having to stop and take deep breaths before going on. He had started to sweat and a couple of times the therapist had suggested he take a break, have a glass of water. Adrian had patted him on the shoulder.

He felt drained and exhausted but he could not relax. He had to be wary, watch himself, remind himself all the time except when he was alone in his room that he was Johnno Miles. He was beginning to understand Johnno's complex personality, his motivation and, above all, his self-deception.

He felt as if he had sat there with his eyes closed for a very long time. The room had gone quiet as they digested his story and thought out their responses.

'Did you honestly believe all that about kids enjoying the abuse? Did you? Let's face it, what we've done is bad in every way but pretending it's OK is like — like pretending women enjoy being raped. I know because that's what I told myself.'

'I don't believe it now,' Simon said. 'I just went through that stage. And it is a point of view out there, there's plenty of guys can argue from history — ancient Greece. You know.'

'No, mate, I don't, I didn't go to your posh school.'

'Will did.'

A laugh.

Will's face reddened.

'You don't think there's a bit of you that still likes to believe kids are enjoying it?'

'No. I saw enough — I've . . . no.'

'What got to you, Johnno?'

'It all got to me.'

'Must have been something, some kid, some time . . . when you woke up to it. You with me?'

'Yes.'

'When was it?'

'When . . . once when I looked at . . . when I just thought, I was six years old again and it was happening to me. Remembering — what it felt like.'

'You ever talked about any of that, Johnno?'

'No. I can't.'

'You got to.'

'I can't.'

'We've all had to face up to remembering stuff. Nothing unusual about you.'

Simon stayed silent, head down, looking at the scuffed blue floor.

'There's something I want to say to you.' Brian.

Simon raised his head. 'Sure.'

'No offence and all that.'

'No, of course not.'

'All right — everything you just said . . .

this story you told us . . . I don't know . . . you're covering something up, aren't you?'

His stomach lurched but his head remained completely clear and as he reacted he was working out his strategy.

Someone else jumped in. 'You only just started this therapy, and you've gone straight into what's the hardest bit, in my view, and that's working out what they felt — and then what you feel about what they felt. That's a bloody great leap into the deep end and respect for that.'

'Thanks. Thanks . . . I . . . trouble is, for me it isn't the deep end, well, not the deepest. I — I don't feel out of my depth, if that makes sense.'

'And you've got to. You've got to feel yourself drowning and panicking.'

'I know. That's . . .'

'Scary.'

'Very.'

Brian leaned forward and looked at him. 'OK, maybe I was being a bit hard, but I just got a feeling you'd rehearsed all that, got it off pat, knew what you were going to say, and you said it, but it all felt a bit like you were skating over the surface, like you hadn't had a shock yet.'

Simon relaxed. 'Right.'

'You wait till you get to the play-acting.

That's when it strips you down to nothing.'

'I'm not sure how I'll take it.'

'You'll sweat blood, mate, but you'll get nowhere till you do. I found that out.'

'Didn't notice you sweating anything. Stop making out you're sorted when you know what happened last time, big-head.'

'All right, cool it, Pat. This isn't a competition.'

'Never said it was.'

Simon leaned back, the pressure off him.

An hour later, after a WCM about job assignments and some complaints about the plumbing and the bad taste in the last lot of tea, they were outside. A five-a-side football game had been started but it was too hot for the play to become very energetic. Those who were looking after the kitchen garden were already out there, harvesting potatoes and beans. There was nothing now until pod duties started at four. He lay on the grass. The place was set on a slight rise, from where he could look towards a circle of trees. Otherwise, this was flat land, still scarred by its past as a wartime airfield. There was brown dust and chalk dust, broken-up strips of concrete. Nothing grew for miles beyond the perimeter fence.

'Nowhere to hide,' Will said, dropping

down beside him. 'You OK after that grilling?'

'I can look after myself.'

'Sure you can.' Will was sitting up. 'Prison camp.'

'Must be a bit like it. Worse food then.'

'I miss a good steak.'

'Fresh salmon. Crab. Mussels.'

'You could hike from here, get some, have a swim, walk back.'

'Bike.'

'Rather walk. Or ride. You ride?'

'Horse? Not bloody likely.'

'Funny that.'

'What?'

Will shrugged. 'Just have assumed.'

Simon picked it up quickly. 'Oh God, did all that bloody pony stuff as a kid and then had a bad fall at a fence. By the time I was out of hospital the fear was rooted.'

'Surprised they didn't just bung you back on.'

'They tried. I was no pushover when I was ten.'

'Did you know the Gregorys? Lived at Barkford? The Cheney-Knowles lot? Six girls then David? You must have — all those bloody sisters . . .'

Simon hesitated just long enough. 'Rings a bell . . .'

'The dad was killed flying a small plane over to Paris for lunch with his mistress.'

'Nope, don't think I do then. Why?'

'Oh, you know . . . mutual acquaintances.'

'They close friends?'

'Kind of. Knew them when we were kids. Met up again in London — as you do. Ten, twelve years ago. Through Andrew Morson.'

'Right.'

At last? Will had been cagey about his past, except in a general way, mentions of the odd thing to do with school, Oxford. No names.

'Andrew. Barrister. Top man.'

'That's where I've heard the name then. Andrew Morson, QC.'

Will gave an odd laugh.

They sat up and watched the game without much interest. The football standard was usually high but the best players spurned five-a-side knockabouts.

Simon watched on. Waited. Nothing.

'Was he your brief?'

'What? Oh, Andrew? No.'

Nothing.

Nothing until the bell rang for the pod team to go in to work.

There was no official lights-out time but not many stayed up beyond midnight. The games and recreation rooms were locked at eleven. Simon was exhausted at the end of every day, mainly because of the stress of keeping up his role, never relaxing his guard. Work in the pod was tiring, with the constant heat from the cookers, steamers, dishwashers.

'You awake?'

'What is it?'

'Can I come in?'

He sighed. 'OK.'

Will slipped in, barely opening the door. The security light from the corridor was only a few feet away, so that Simon could make him out in the yellowish glow.

'I've got a joint.'

'Don't be so fucking stupid, Will.'

'Oh, come on. Don't tell me.'

'Whatever, if you smoke a joint in here and they find out, which they will, you're out, feet don't touch the ground.'

'So?'

'What are you messing about for? You told me how long you'd waited to get in here and you want to blow it?'

Will did not move.

'Go on.'

'To tell you the truth, I wouldn't give a fuck if it got me out. I can't hack it, Johnno. Thought I could. Can't.'

'You'd rather be back in Wandsworth? You'd rather be having to watch out every time you go for a shower in case they're waiting to pin you to the wall and break your nose while two of them keep guard? You'd rather —'

'Shut up.'

'I don't get you.'

'No, I wouldn't rather.'

'So, what are you bringing a joint in here for? Where did you get it anyway?'

'Easy when you know.'

'Bloody stupid.'

'Are you going to snitch?'

Simon laughed. 'Snitch! Seriously, stop playing silly buggers and get to bed.'

Seconds later, Will had jumped him and they were wrestling on the floor, trying not to make a noise, laughing as they would have laughed if they had known one another as boys and teenagers, muckers and mates, same background and mores, same life-styles. Simon threw him over eventually and had him pinned down.

'Bloody hell,' Will said, 'you've got me in a vice. Where'd you learn that?'

Simon let him go and they both struggled up, winded, calming down.

'God, what are we doing in this dump?' Will said.

'Christ knows.'

'I need a drink.'

'Bad luck. Can't even make a cup of tea at this time of night.'

'Good behaviour for six months gets you a kettle in your room. You have to buy it yourself of course.'

Simon swore.

'Can I trust you?'

'What with? Your sister, sure.'

'A plan.'

'What sort of plan?'

'Shut up . . .'

Footsteps. They didn't usually do night patrols here.

'Shit.'

If Will's room was found empty the alarms would go off.

Footsteps. A long silence. The men had held their breath and now exhaled.

'Jeez. You get back while it's clear.'

'Right. Just wanted to ask if you kept secrets.'

'Depends what, but for Christ's sake, Will . . .'

'Going.'

He slipped out of the door.

THIRTY-FOUR

'Need to talk,' Will said, passing with a trolley of crockery steaming hot from the dishwasher.

'Now what?'

'Plans.'

Simon shrugged and poured a second lot of potatoes down the funnel into the peeler. It was the hottest day of the year and the temperature inside the pod was well beyond reasonable levels. Jokes went round about trade unions and health and safety demanding a walkout. The cooler fans made no impression, merely swirled the hot air about.

He wiped his brow with his sleeve. The cotton cap he had to wear was soaking wet round the band. He glanced up. Will Fernley was hauling out a second load of crockery. It was surprising. Everyone worked well in here, it was as professional as any other institutional kitchen, the grumbling was cheerful enough, the banter and jokes flew.

If people walked in from the outside world now and were asked to guess what these men had in common, not one would get it right. Prepping veg, cracking eggs, boiling water, cutting meat, opening huge cans, swabbing down, loading and unloading machines — and every one a man who had abused children, raped, committed murder, in here to try and master their urges.

It occurred to him that they were courageous. That maybe it was easier to stay in mainstream prison, keep your head down and the lid clamped on your inner imaginings and memories, get on with it day to day. The relative freedom they had here was more than balanced by the pain of digging down into their own souls and bringing up appalling thoughts and fantasies, by the shame of recounting in every detail the crimes they had committed, and of then putting themselves into the hearts and minds and bodies of their victims.

He was play-acting, and, at moments, ashamed of the fact. He was deceiving men who were trying to be honest, whatever the horrendous nature of their crimes, and it felt dirty. Living in close proximity to them was making him search his own conscience, though in a very different way.

They finished serving the evening meal,

cleaned up, ate their own. Tomorrow, a different pod crew would take over and he would not be back in here for a week. He would be on grounds duty — mowing and rolling and sweeping up. He would also have three sessions in the library. He tried to get Will to open up without appearing to do so. Will, tight as a clam, rarely obliged. He had mentioned one name only.

Andrew Morson, QC.

He got a plastic cup of cold water and took it outside. The grass on the bank was yellowing and sparse. No one was playing football. Everyone sat or lay about, exhausted by the heat, shirts off.

There was a low whistle. Will was sitting some yards away from the rest, close to the perimeter wire of the pitch. After a minute, Simon went to join him, in no hurry, wandering in the other direction before doubling back. Nobody took any notice. It was half past seven and still stifling, a haze filming over the sky.

Will said nothing except 'Ice-cold lager'.

Simon groaned.

'I'm serious.'

'Ice-cold beer? Why torture yourself?'

'I might get it.'

'Shouldn't think even the governor has a stash.'

'Outside.'

Simon looked at him. Said nothing.

'Told you, Johnno. I've had it. Doesn't work, doesn't help, I can't see the point.'

'Sun's got to you.'

'No.'

'Don't follow you.'

'Come on, yes you do.'

Serrailler thought fast while lying back down and closing his eyes. 'Don't be stupid. If you made a move they'd have you in solitary, you'd have all your paroles cancelled for good, you'd be serving your full time —'

'Assuming I was caught. But I wouldn't be.'

'Right.'

'You think I'm joking,' Will said.

'No. Actually, no, I don't. Just wondering if you've thought this all the way through. I mean, how often do guys even make the attempt? And how many of them get near succeeding?'

'Ocean's Eleven.'

'Oh, it's been tried, it's been tried . . .' Serrailler quoted the film.

'One guy actually tasted fresh oxygen . . .' They laughed.

'Forget it, Will.'

'Doesn't involve breaking through the security of three casino banks either.'

'Go on then, make me laugh.'

'You kidding? Why would I tell you?'

'Thought you couldn't wait.'

Will chewed a grass blade.

Simon thought quickly. If Will was serious about trying to get out of Stitchford, his chances of succeeding were almost zero. It was the 'almost' that was a worry. One thing was for sure — he had to deal with this on his own. He couldn't ask for advice, and getting a message to the governor would mean, everything else apart, an end to his chances of finding out more information from Fernley about others in his ring. Diversion, then, for the moment.

'What was that about that QC — what was his name, Anthony Morson?'

'Andrew. You said you didn't know him.'

'I don't. Just wondering.'

'Why now?'

Simon shrugged. 'Came to mind for some reason. Forget it. Think I'm going in. Test match highlights.'

He got up. Will got up. The others were still idle in the last of the evening sun. They walked back slowly, amiable, relaxed. And yet, this is where we are, Simon thought, as they went inside.

At his door, Will said, 'I'm not joking.'

Simon waited.

'It's all worked out.'

'Listen, Will —'

'Not in the corridor . . .'

They went into his room. Some of the men had tried to make theirs homely. Will's was as bare as when he had arrived. He had a small shelf of books but nothing else, not a family photograph or a calendar. He was meticulously tidy. The books were arranged spine exactly to spine and size-coordinated along the row.

Simon said, 'Listen, I still reckon you're taking the piss, but if you're not, think hard about this — how many men have ever escaped from any prison and stayed out for longer than a day. You can count them on one hand. What are you trying to prove?'

'Nothing at all. Just trying to get out of here. The first thing is —'

Simon held up his hand. 'I don't want to know. Then I can't tell anyone else, can I?'

'And would you?'

'Might have to if I was questioned hard enough.'

'The only reason I was going to tell you . . .'

'What?'

'In case you felt like coming with me.'

THIRTY-FIVE

'Tim?'

'I don't believe this.'

'Are you on your own?'

'I'm sorry?'

'Is Shelley with you?'

'As it happens, no, she's not, but if she were it would make no difference. I'm not prepared to have a conversation with you.'

'Listen, Tim . . . I'm in France, and it's a bugger of a job to get a decent signal. I can't waste it arguing. I need to speak to you.'

'Apparently you are.'

'Will you hear me out?'

Tim hesitated. He was angry and insulted, but he felt he should at least hear Richard Serrailler's side of the story. They had known one another for a long time.

'Tim?'

'Go on.'

'Has Shelley said anything to you about the night we were at the ladies' dinner?'

'She has.'

'I have absolutely no right to ask this but would you tell me what she told you?'

Tim was silent.

'She wasn't herself. That's entirely understandable. She may well have been confused or even incoherent.'

'You mean "drunk"?'

'No, no. We'd all had the usual quantity. I wasn't entirely sober and I dare say nor were you.'

'I was driving. So I was, actually.'

'Listen, whatever Shelley has said —'

'She told me that you'd raped her.'

Richard spluttered at the other end of the phone. 'For heaven's sake! My dear Tim . . . well, I'm quite certain you don't believe that.'

'Why shouldn't I? My wife isn't in the habit of lying and why would she lie about something as serious as this?'

'Tim, that is an extreme — actually, it's probably a libellous accusation. Of course I didn't rape her — what do you take me for?'

'To be honest, Richard, I'm not entirely sure. There are words but I wouldn't care to use them.'

'That's understandable, but as descriptions, do these words include "rapist"?'

Tim sighed. 'Well — no. It would never

have crossed my mind but once Shelley had
—'

'Rapists are men who attack women not known to them. They are violent, and they do untold hurt and harm. They deserve everything the law can throw at them.'

'Well, of course, but you attacked my wife, and whether or not you're a stranger to her makes no odds.'

'I wish we could talk about all this face-to-face, but there it is, I'm in France and we can't.'

'So why are you ringing me now? Why not leave it till you come back?'

'I don't know when we'll be back, and I need to talk to you.'

'But why?'

'I need to put the record straight. We've been friends for too long to let something fester.'

'All right, Richard. I suppose the least I can do is to hear your side.'

'Thank you. I'm extremely grateful to you, Tim. And this isn't easy and you won't like what I am going to say but it will be the truth . . .'

He paused but Tim said nothing.

'As I said, I'd had a few glasses — we all had. And Shelley had been flirting with me since the start of the evening — no, please don't interrupt. Flirting — there's no shame in that, it isn't a crime, she's a very attractive woman and we've often been flirtatious with one another — in public, always in public, you understand. I can't believe you've never noticed.'

'Well, yes. I have. And to be fair, it isn't only you she's flirted with. I'm afraid it's just something she's prone to do when she's had a glass of wine and it's wholly innocent of any further intent, as you should well know. Are you suggesting that my wife led you on and that when you raped her it was somehow her fault and that she invited it?'

'There does come a moment when innocent public flirting moves up a gear.'

'Does there?'

'Heavens, not always — not usually — please don't misunderstand me, Tim. But on that evening, Shelley was sending me unmistakable signals across the tables. Listen, I'm very sorry to have to tell you this —'

'Just go on — but I warn you I'm pretty bloody angry.'

'And there came the moment when we'd finished eating, and before the coffee and liqueurs, when we had a break . . . well, you know all this. It was then that Shelley gave me a look and started to go out of the room.

271

She gave me another, she turned round as she got to the door, and she didn't need to ask me to follow her, the meaning was perfectly clear. By then, of course, I was nicely mellow . . . Shelley is attractive, and between us — this is very private, Tim, and it goes no further please . . .'

Silence.

'Tim?'

'Just go on.'

'My marriage hasn't been — shall we say, fulfilled, for some time. These things take their toll. So, that was that. I very foolishly allowed myself to be misled by following Shelley down the stairs and into the ladies' powder room. It's that sort of rather louche hotel in its furnishings, have you noticed? I'm never sure why we have our dinners there — all that plush and gilding, curtains like a tart's boudoir. Anyway — so I followed her, there was a sofa — chaise longue type of thing — and Shelley sat down on it . . . and . . . do I need to continue? This is difficult and embarrassing.'

'I think you do, yes.'

Richard sighed. 'Shelley made it clear that she was — how shall I put it? — wanting me to . . . dear God, I feel appalled now I'm recounting it in the cold light. And so — I'm afraid I succumbed.'

272

'You had sex on this chaise longue — is that what you are telling me?'

'It is.'

'And this was my wife's idea?'

'Listen, I wouldn't want to put it all onto her, of course not, it takes two, and I readily admit that I didn't hesitate. Yes, as you put it, we had sex, and then Shelley rushed out . . . we'd put a chair against the door handle but people were coming down the stairs and she fled. I had to — this will sound like a French farce — I had to hide behind a rail of coats, then dash out of the door as soon as I could. No one spotted me, and by the time I got back to the banqueting hall, she was nowhere to be seen. I wanted to talk to her . . . but she'd gone. You had both gone. I left shortly afterwards.'

He drew in his breath and let it out slowly.

'I'm pretty damned ashamed of myself, Tim. I had to ring you to square things . . . to confess, and to ask you not to let this go any further. To be frank, the reason we've come to France is to try and repair the breaches in our marriage. Judith hasn't been at all well either. So you can imagine, it's a delicate situation and the very last thing either of us needs is to have this — or a distorted version of this — get out. I'm sure

I speak for you as well. What possible good could it do? None. But it could do a great deal of harm, to you, to me — and of course most of all to your wife.'

'Why to her most of all?'

'I should have thought that was obvious. I'm very sorry indeed if she's at all upset.'

'Richard, Shelley is my wife, I love her, and we are very happy and there is nothing whatsoever wrong with our marriage in that direction. You're telling me that you had consensual sex after she led you on, she's telling me that you raped her. So, who do I believe? How do you think it feels to be in the middle of all this? We've been friends for a long time, Richard, but not any more, whatever the truth of the matter. Why would I believe you rather than my wife?'

'You're trying to be loyal, of course, and I entirely understand that. But I can assure you, Tim —'

'I don't rate your assurances very highly, to be frank.'

'Tim, isn't it best left there? No point in making this out to be life-threatening, and let me tell you that the very last thing I want, especially at the moment, is for Judith to hear about any of this.'

'That is one thing you may rely on.'

'Has Shelley talked to anyone other than

you? Do you know?'

Tim hesitated. Was there any point in telling him that she had talked to the police? No. There was no point, because he would persuade Shelley to withdraw her statement. On reflection, he didn't blame her for going to the police, but if a case did come to court, he believed that she would suffer far more than she had already. Richard had gone off to France, which made Tim see that the best possible thing was to take her away somewhere, bring his holiday forward. They could well afford it. When they got back, the whole thing would have receded and she could get on with life. He owed it to her to cut off all connection with Richard and, when they had to meet, to ignore him.

That should be enough. In a few days, he would take her to the police so that she could withdraw her statement and that would be that.

THIRTY-SIX

Five small children, each of whom had won a school prize, were slowly and, with endless changes of mind, choosing books at the far end of the shop when Rupert Barr came in and began to browse. Rachel smiled but was then called down to help a girl unable to decide between *Room on the Broom* and *The Tiger Who Came to Tea.*

It was another quarter of an hour before they had been chivvied into making final selections and taken them to the counter. Rupert glanced over occasionally, marvelling at her patience and attentiveness.

'I'm sorry,' she said, when the children had eventually gone out of the shop, like a flock of little chattering birds, 'but you can't hurry important decisions. Can I help or are you happy browsing?'

He took a piece of paper out of his wallet. 'I have numerous family birthdays in the next month and I usually buy books unless

someone hints otherwise, and your professional advice would be golden.'

Rachel laughed. 'You may remember that
I'm only a stand-in and tomorrow is my last
day. I can try but I'm no professional.'

'You could become one.'

'I'd like to. The trouble is, I make grand
plans for this shop while I'm here but I
don't think Emma is up for any of them.'

'So, how is business?'

'So-so.'

'But it might be so much better if you had
your way?'

She smiled as he handed her his list.
'Which ones do you need help with?'

'All of them . . . shall we just start at the
top?'

The first two were men, both over seventy,
one easily satisfied with biography and
memoirs, and the other with anything mili-
tary.

'Has to be new, though, otherwise he'll
have got it.'

Rachel went down the list and from shelf
to shelf, offering books, discussing them,
having a sudden clever idea, failing to find
anything about Italian Renaissance painting
but hitting on the perfect book of poetry,
among the very small selection in stock, for
someone who would only read things that

rhymed.

'You're a genius. Now for the children? Will this be harder or easier?'

'The trouble is, we don't have enough — it isn't Emma's real interest and she tends to buy the old classics or a few the publishers' reps push onto her. We could do so much more with this end of the shop to entice the children. They're the readers of the future and they deserve it.' She blushed. 'Rant over, sorry . . . Now, let's look for — oh, groan, a book for a twelve-year-old boy.'

The completed selection was on the counter and Rachel was starting to add up when Rupert said, 'That rant of yours.'

'Sorry . . .'

'No, you were spot on. You could turn this shop right round and make it buzz, without question.'

'Give me a chance to try. That's a hundred and forty pounds.'

He set down his card. 'Would you have dinner with me to discuss it?'

Rachel gave him a panicky look. He smiled, before glancing round. But there was no one else in the shop.

'To set your mind at rest, I have a partner and he happens to be in Beijing on business but even if he weren't I would be inviting you to dinner.'

Rachel felt both relieved and rather put out. But she was intrigued at what he might say about the bookshop. She had also not been out to dinner for some time and it seemed likely that Rupert Barr, personable and interesting, would make good company.

A message box flashed up in the bottom corner of a laptop. It was an older make, a Lenovo T420, unusual in the ownership of someone who had the taste, the money and the need for far more up-to-date and sophisticated hardware. But that was elsewhere, the on display, fastest available desktop, an iPad nearby, iPhone on the coffee table. The T420 was kept for one purpose and wiped clean immediately after every use.

'Blind Runner' flashed again.

He typed.

'Log in please.'

There was a pause, then a long series of encrypted letters and numbers.

'Logged in.'

Then, *'Good evening, Blind Runner.'*

'Who is that?'

'Green Hovercraft.'

'Confirm.'

Hieroglyphics. A scroll of numbers.

'Confirmed.'

The screen went blank for a split second,

then came on again with a slightly different background, as if a light had been switched off in one room and on in another.

'*Everything OK?*'

'*Bit concerned about radio silence.*'

'*You got the round robin?*'

'*Yes, but that was a couple of weeks ago.*'

'*If everything is still quiet at the end of this week we'll go online again. Leave it to me. Better safe.*'

'*OK, but the membership fee is pretty high for a non-service.*'

'*You can opt out any time.*'

'*Don't want to opt out, just want some action.*'

'*When I'm happy with security.*'

'*OK.*'

'*New password details will follow your log-out as usual, BR.*'

'*Ciao.*'

The T420 screen went black. Nothing else flashed up. After five minutes, it was closed down, and returned to its place of concealment.

Thirty-Seven

The child's eardrum was bright pink.

'Has Mia been swimming recently?' Cat asked.

'Tuesday — she's just started.'

'Surprise, surprise. I get a steady stream of children with ear infections after they've been swimming. But this will clear up on its own. Give her some Calpol if it hurts — she doesn't seem unwell in herself and the other ear is quite clear, but if she starts to run a temperature or won't eat, bring her back. All right?'

'Well, no, not really . . . Dr Sparks always gives her antibiotics for anything like this. Can't she have some penicillin?'

'She really doesn't need it at this point and we try not to give young children antibiotics for minor infections — the body deals with them very efficiently.'

The mother sighed and showed no signs of leaving. 'I suppose this is all about cutting costs like everything else. We used to ring and a doctor would visit but not any more.'

'Mrs —' Cat glanced at the computer screen.

'Browning. And the doctor always used to know you — know your name and everything. Not any more.'

'I understand. The trouble is I'm just a locum, filling in for Dr Sparks while she's ill, so I don't know all the patients. I'm sorry. But as I said —'

'Could I just have a prescription for the penicillin, give it to her if she needs it? Save us having to come back.'

'I really don't think she'll need it, and it isn't a question of money, it's because too many antibiotics given for minor things mean they won't work if they're ever needed for something serious.'

'There are plenty of different ones, aren't there?'

'It's the same principle, Mrs Browning. Now, Mia will be fine — but come back at once if you are worried, and if you do, tell the receptionist that I said you were to have a quick-access appointment the same day.'

She could read everything into the woman's back as she went out, pushing the child in front of her. How many times did it happen a day? She didn't blame the mother. The rot had started thirty years ago, she thought, pressing the buzzer for the next patient. We thought everything needed antibiotics and nobody thought of tomorrow — which is now today.

'Mr Leeming? Good morning, I'm Dr Deerbon. Come in and take a seat.'

'Where's the other doctor? I don't like seeing someone new every time I come.'

Another day in the life of a locum, Cat thought, smiling her sweetest smile at yet another grumpy and dissatisfied patient.

She had started doing locum surgeries a few months earlier, when her finances had taken a further nose-dive and her role at the hospice had been downgraded. There was nothing else she could do, there was plenty of locum work, and she took everything she could get. It was well paid, but it was also very unsatisfying. She understood the complaints of a patient like this one, with chronic problems. He wanted, and was entitled to have, an ongoing relationship with one GP, though he could not be guaranteed to see that doctor in an emergency. With a locum, he had to start again, detailing his symptoms and the history of his illness, waiting as Cat tried to absorb a screenful of complex notes. Most of the patients in these surgeries had minor complaints. She was happy to see them, even if a good number could have treated themselves, but she had no relationship with them, did not know their families, their personal and domestic problems, all of which helped to form a full picture of human beings in need of medical care. Once . . .

She shook her head now. Stop harking back to the good old days of general practice, she had to tell herself half a dozen times a day. Things have changed and they're not going to change back. Get over it.

Perhaps one patient in fifty she saw now had something serious or unusual, and therefore interesting and perhaps challenging. But in that case, she would hand them over to one of the permanent partners in whichever practice she was working that day, and hear no more. It was frustrating and she enjoyed her job a great deal less than she used to, but it was a job, she was never short of requests to take a surgery for a day or a week, in Lafferton and further afield. Bevham, where she was today, had a particular shortage.

In the corridor on her way out, she bumped into one of the senior partners.

'I can't tell you how grateful we are, Cat

— it was becoming impossible, with one on maternity leave and one ill. You're a godsend. How are you finding us?'

'It's a lovely practice to work in — very efficient support staff too.'

'Any buts?'

'Only the usual every locum complains about. But no, not really. I'd rather work here than in some others I won't name. Only one thing concerns me, and as it's fast becoming the situation everywhere, there's no point in bothering about it.'

'What?'

'This is a large practice, even with two doctors off. So like all large practices, you tell patients they can book in with anyone, they don't have to wait to see their own GP. And you only take appointments for up to a fortnight ahead, which means —'

'I know. The most popular doctors are always booked up. But there's been a lot of research on this and people really don't mind seeing any doctor if that means they can get an appointment quickly.'

'Sometimes. If your child has raging tonsillitis it doesn't matter who you see, but if you're, say, a cancer patient with ongoing problems, it makes a huge difference to your morale and confidence if you can see your own doctor every time.'

Clare Boyle leaned against the wall. She wore her spectacles on a cord round her neck and had a permanently distant expression. Perhaps it was just her bad sight, Cat always thought, but it made her seem haughty. She could be quick-tempered with the reception staff too.

'You've spent most of your time as the old-fashioned sort of GP, night calls and all. Those days are gone. With everyone's notes accessible on the computer system —'

'Clare, sorry, another time, I've got to meet my daughter from the bus.'

She fled. The computer system was fine but it did not give seriously ill and anxious people a personal consultation and reassurance. She would fight for the principle that a good doctor can often heal simply by being there and listening. Well, so be it, she was only a locum. She worked the surgeries she was offered and went home. Which was part of the problem, on both sides. Now, when she clocked off, she never left feeling satisfied that she had made a difference.

She was not in fact meeting Hannah from any bus, Hannah was staying with a friend as she always did on Tuesday, while Cat went to St Michael's Singers practice. When Richard and Judith were at home, Felix

286

went to them at Hallam House, but now, and for however many weeks they were in France, Sam would babysit. He took his role as babysitter so seriously and responsibly that she sometimes wondered what she wasn't being told. When she got back, he was always in bed reading, the kitchen had been tidied and the dishwasher loaded, Wookie and Mephisto fed. Sam earned his money.

She had a couple of hours in which to go through the score for tonight's practice. The Delius, which she disliked, was not giving them many problems but a work by Peter Maxwell Davies certainly was. Most of them were up to the challenge but she doubted if she was — it would have to be a case of clinging on for dear life to the person standing next to her.

Not long after Cat got in, Felix was dropped off by the family with whom she shared school lifts. Sam walked from the bus stop a little later. Felix was allowed toast and Marmite and half an hour of television before 'homework', Sam the same, plus a mug of tea, but then he hung about, first wandering in and out of the kitchen, then going up to his room and coming down again and finally, swivelling round on one of the counter stools. Cat looked up twice from her score. He went on swivelling, then stopped and smiled at her sweetly.

'What do you want, Sam?'

'Nothing. Just, you know, being here.'

'Right.'

'Hanging.'

'Fine.'

'What time are you going out?'

'Twenty past six. As ever.'

'Cool.'

'Do stop that. Stay here by all means, be my guest, but do not swivel.'

'Gotcha. Mum?'

So there was something.

'Here I am.'

'When's Uncle Si coming back?'

'I've no more idea than you have — nor where he is or what he's doing.'

'Truly?'

'Absolutely.'

'Don't you think it seems odd?'

'Not really. It'll be something to do with SIFT, I suppose.'

'Only he usually sends a message to one of us. At some point. From somewhere.'

'Police for you. You know how it is, Sambo.'

'Do I?'

Cat put down the pencil with which she

was marking her score. 'Are you worried?'

'Are you?'

'Yes, a bit, I always am when he disappears, but worrying doesn't help and chances are that he'll just pop up again, say nothing, and carry on as if nothing's happened. God knows what some of these jobs are about, but it's what Simon loves, it's his life, always has been. We can't stop it.'

'Maybe he ought to think a bit more about — you know. Us. And Rachel.'

'He does think. But the job always comes first.'

'Time he married her.'

She hid her surprise. Sam had never made such a remark — she hadn't thought he had registered Rachel much, though he had always appeared to like her when they met, which wasn't often. It occurred to her that her son was in many ways as deep a pool as her brother.

'You'd better get going.' Sam swung off the stool. 'I'll start Felix's supper.'

'Make him finish —'

'His omelette and drink his milk and do his teeth and wee and . . .' He pushed her gently from behind. 'Go.'

'You're taller than me now, Sam, did you know that?'

'Have you only just noticed? I've been

taller for months . . . years even. Decades. Centuries . . .' Gradually, he shunted her out of the kitchen into the hall.

'OK, little bro, I'm coming to get you . . .'

Squeals from the den.

Just after nine, Felix was asleep and Sam had done most of his homework. He had to finish an essay, which was already late, on manifestations of evil in *Macbeth,* but decided it could wait another day, until he had fine-tuned his excuses, giving him an hour before his mother would be home. He opened up the file on his laptop called 'Geography — Maps and Charts' and began to scroll down the individual entries for guns, with detailed specifications and a photograph beside each one.

Glock 17 pistol
Glock 26 pistol
Walther P99 pistol
SIG Sauer P226 pistol
Heckler & Koch USP
Heckler & Koch MP5
Heckler & Koch G36 variants[4]
LMT Defender AR-15 variants
Heckler & Koch G3
Remington 870 shotgun

SIG 550 (553 variant)
HK417 marksmen Rifle

He knew most of them by heart now, but
he liked to test himself on the detail, and
make comparisons. He became so absorbed
that when the car headlights flashed into
the drive, he had to make a leap to close
down and head fast for the bathroom and
his toothbrush.

■ ■ ■ ■

PART THREE

■ ■ ■ ■

THIRTY-EIGHT

First shift started at half past five and went on until after lunch, with a half-hour breakfast at eight. It was a popular shift. The rest of the day was free, there were perks like extra snacks and hot drinks, there was good camaraderie, and because there were never quite enough hands, they were kept too busy to be bored. No time for brooding.

'You're with me,' Will said. 'Back stores.'

The supplies started arriving from six — milk first, whatever dry goods were ordered, vegetables and bread last. A row of sack trucks stood by the open hangar, the vans and lorries backed up right to the platform. Some of the work was unloading from the forklift, some was wheeling off the trucks. If you started off finding the lifting near impossible, by the end of a few weeks you had strengthened so much you could take double.

But there was not much breath left over

for chat. Simon and Will worked steadily, passing this, moving that, crossing over to take a different side. There was constant noise from engines reversing, the whine of the lifting gear, the clatter of the trolleys, an occasional thud as something dropped. From behind the stores, the kitchen noise was just as loud.

When they started, there was a chill in the air. An hour later, they were sweating with effort, and the sun was up.

'Great,' Will said.

'What?'

'Going to be a fine day.'

Serrailler shrugged, taking down a sack of carrots.

'Just right.'

'What for?'

Will put his finger to the side of his nose but then swung round to grab a swaying crate before it hit the side wall.

They worked on. It was a heavy morning. The domestic supplies normally came in to a different side but there had been problems with the ramp, and everything was diverted. After the carrots, potatoes and boxes of catering-size tins of tomatoes and sacks of flour, they had to deal with cartons of bleach, floor cleaner, scouring pads, toilet rolls. Simon wiped the back of his arm

across his forehead every so often. He and
Will had taken off their shirts and tied them
round their waists.

'Galley slaves,' the last driver shouted, getting into his cab. Will chucked an onion,
which missed the driver, hit his wing mirror.

'Shit.'

But lorry mirrors were built to stay put.
The vehicle went on reversing slowly out.

With luck, they'd have a few minutes
before the bread van. Will moved to the
back of the store, beckoning Simon to follow. The machines banged and whirred
from the kitchens behind them but no one
else was nearby.

'Get your shirt back on. You'll need it.'

His voice sounded odd, tense, almost excited.

'What's up?'

'This is it. I've got it worked out.'

'What?'

'Getting out. This is it.'

'Don't be —'

'Shut up and listen. Are you in with me or
out? If you're out, that's your choice, but I
need to know.'

Serrailler's mind whirred. Whatever plan
Will had made, he had not said another
word about it. Until now. His instinct told

him not to ask, but he had to make a fast decision. If Will Fernley went on his own, that was that, his own reason for being in here would have gone without his being in possession of any information. When Will was caught, which he would be, sooner or later, he wouldn't be back to Stitchford.

But if Simon managed to stick to Will for long enough, there was a slight chance that he might strike lucky and find out something vital.

'Johnno?'

He almost failed to recognise his false name, hesitating before glancing round. But Will didn't appear to have noticed. Simon's adrenalin was punching round his system, he was on a high, wound up, going over and over his calculations, the sequence of events, their speed. It would have to be quick.

'I'm in.'

'OK.' Will did not show any emotion, merely nodded. 'Now listen hard.'

They were squatting on the dusty floor at the back of the loading bay, Will talking fast and low, as if in bullet points, close to Simon's ear.

Will had been a Guards officer and the training showed. In any other situation, Serrailler would have been confident of his abilities. This was different. In the very short term, the scheme might succeed. In the longer, it was guaranteed to fail, but taking careful stock of the plan as Fernley put it to him, he saw that almost nothing had been left to chance. He made no comment, asked no questions, because he judged it better to stay silent, but in fact there was little he could criticise. It was the maddest of mad schemes, and yet it had been thought through comprehensively and coolly.

They might be on the run for days, during which time they would be totally dependent on one another and as close as they could be.

'Got it?'

'Got it.'

'It should work.'

'Livin' on a prayer.'

Will shook his head.

He went to look out of the open doors. Nobody was about. The pod was noisier than ever as the peeling and chopping machines came on. Will had timed everything.

Three minutes later, he signalled. Simon moved to stand beside him in the shadow of the overhang.

The bread van slowed at the security post and the driver lifted his hand. The guard raised the bar for him to drive through, he came up at the statutory five miles an hour and then turned left at the top, and reversed slowly up to the store, the warning beeper sounding before the robotic voice took over.

'*This vehicle is reversing. This vehicle is reversing. This vehicle . . .*'

The bread van was smaller than some of the trucks and took up less of the opening, but once it had backed right into the bay and touched the loading ramp, the daylight was pretty much blocked out.

'Morning,' Will said.

Some of the guys were friendly, some not, some cheerful, some not, some treated the men on work shift like normal human beings, a few didn't. The bread man didn't. He was small, sour and morose and barely gave any of them the time of day.

The van doors were opened onto the stacked trays. Will jumped in first, Simon stood on the tailgate. The delivery man had gone to get his load ticked off. They worked fast and in silence, their rhythm well established, barely glancing at one another, as the trays were rolled out and slid onto the ramp. Bread came in only once a week — two-thirds of it going into the freezers. Will kept one eye on the back of the hangar, until the driver appeared, carrying his signed docket. Will had been whistling 'John

Brown's Body', in time with his unloading movements, but as he saw the man, changed the tune abruptly to 'Lili Marlene'.

Simon leaned over the tailgate of the van and shouted, 'Something wrong up here, mate — this isn't moving smoothly. Can you jump up and take a look?'

The man stopped. 'Nothing wrong with it last load.'

'Right, well, there is now and it could shunt down suddenly and catch someone below.'

Grumbling, stuffing the chit in his pocket, the van driver started to haul himself up beside Simon. As he was doing so, Simon stepped forward and trod lightly on the man's thumb, not enough to do damage, but enough to distract him. The driver swore under his breath and went on swearing, holding his hand, shaking it, mouthing more obscenities. He did not notice that Will had slipped off the far side of the tailgate and run round in the shadow of the wall.

Simon heard Will jump up into the cab, and immediately pushed the van driver down to the floor hard, hauled the doors shut and dropped the bar across. Will had started the engine and was swinging the bread van round and then going forward.

He hooted as he made for the security gate. This was the moment when it could all go wrong before it had started, but the guard on duty must have lifted the barrier without bothering to check the driver and van which he had let in fifteen minutes earlier and which had been in his sights the whole time. Simon had his hand over the bread man's face as he felt the van swing out of the main gates, and turn left. Will accelerated and they were moving quickly and smoothly down the road.

The man had been spluttering and groaning underneath Simon's hand, but now, terrified, he went silent and limp. Serrailler leaned forward. 'Now listen. You're not going to get hurt if you do exactly as you're told. If you don't . . .'

The man nodded.

'OK. You've got a watch. When we stop, you lie right there, and you don't move a muscle and you don't speak — for an hour by the dial. If you do, if you try to get out, if you try to raise the alarm by banging on those doors, you're a dead man. I've got a tracker which will tell me exactly what's going on — it's placed where you'll never find it and even if you did you couldn't disable it. If that goes off, I'll know and I've got lads on the other end who'll be only too delighted to come and find you, get it?'

A sound in the driver's throat, like a sob.

'After an hour, we're long gone and out of reach, so you can make whatever din you want.'

A slight pause. Simon lifted his hand. The man's eyes were wide with fear, shifting from Serrailler to the van sides, roof, floor, and back.

'I don't suppose this van carries an alarm — not for bloody bread.'

Shake of the head.

'There you are then. No, lie there, don't say anything, don't stir.'

Simon's hand moved as if to his inner pocket. The man drummed a foot on the floor, shaking his head to and fro in panic. Simon moved his hand away from the pocket. Now that the driver believed at least one of them carried a gun, the driver would hardly dare to breathe.

It was uncomfortable in the back of the van, and because he didn't know the area, Simon had no sense of the direction in which they were heading. They bumped and bounced, swung and lurched, for what seemed like an hour. And then they slowed finally, and stopped. The engine died.

'Out, Johnno.' Will had opened one of the rear doors a few inches only. He looked at the driver on the floor. Simon nodded. The man did not stir.

The next minute the doors were shut and locked and Will had pocketed the keys.

'Maybe chuck them somewhere they can be found?'

'What for?'

'Look, we want to get away and stay away — we don't want a death on our hands.'

Will snorted, 'He's not going to die. They'll find the van before long and crowbar it open. Worst that'll happen, he'll pee all over the floor. OK, now we move.'

'Where the hell are we anyway?'

'Middle of nowhere, west of the back of beyond.'

Simon looked round. They were on a lane which swerved sharply just ahead. To the right, there was a verge and a ditch but no hedge, and beyond, nothing for miles. It was flat field after flat field, with what looked like abandoned farm units just visible. Nothing else. No building, no traffic, no trees. Just a vast sky, silver blue but with puffs of cumulus on the horizon.

'We'll be seen for miles,' he said. 'We're sitting ducks, Will.'

'Not the way I'm going.'

'Food?'

'Bar of chocolate in my pocket.'

'Drink?'

'No, but farmyards have taps.'

'Tell me where you're planning for us to end up. Give me something to hope for.'

'You'll find out.'

'No, sod it, Will, I came with you, I've got a right to know.'

'Andrew's.'

'Andrew . . .'

'Morson.'

'QC?'

'Yup.'

'And does Andrew know he's having the pleasure?'

'He does. He isn't there, never is midweek, but we'll be looked after royally. He's left instructions.'

'Who with?'

'Housekeeper. Who gets paid fat chunks of cash as a reward when she keeps her mouth shut.'

'Shit.'

'We should move. You all right?'

'Never better.'

Will turned through a gap in the hedge, Simon following. The field ahead was flat, but crossed by a deep ditch, like the water-ways of the Fens. They made their way to it and Will dropped down, so that nothing of him was visible, Simon after him. There was

305

barely a trickle of water in the bottom, but the vegetation had grown thickly, narrowing their route so that they had to walk single file. They went on steadily, not speaking, saving their energy.

At one point, the drone of an aircraft made Will drop onto his stomach. Serrailler did the same. They waited, but the plane was over to the west and the sound of its engines faded quickly. They waited a couple of minutes more, then went on. It was tedious and, as the sun rose higher, steamy and close. The ditch smelled of damp greenery and earth and they began to sweat inside their thick shirts until the cotton stuck to them. Simon saw the dark patches on Will's back. All they could see over the bank was flatness, acre upon acre, mile after mile, broken only by the dykes and a few spindly trees, a half-yard of stunted hedge. Far on the horizon, a single ugly house. To the south, a distant church spire, blending into the paleness of the sky. There was little sound. No major road anywhere near, no habitation.

'How long does this go on?'

'A mile or so yet.'

Serrailler swore.

'You're out, aren't you?'

'Yes, OK. So, after the scenic part, where?'

Will did not reply, just turned and started the slow walk along the bottom of the dyke.

It was ten o'clock when they stopped again, and now there was some noise of machinery in the fields to the east.

'We've got to drink something. We'll dehydrate.'

'Another mile and a half, there's a petrol station. I'll go in and get bottles and food.'

'What with?'

'The money in my trouser pocket, Johnno — did you think I'd come away empty-handed?'

'Thought of everything, haven't you?'

'Hope so.'

'How long have you been planning this?'

'Pretty much from day one.'

'You didn't give the place a chance.'

'Nope. Never meant to.'

Simon was silent.

'Come on.'

They moved off again. The sun shone. At one point, they disturbed a huge flock of seagulls. Simon stopped dead.

'Shit. Someone's going to wonder what set them up, aren't they?'

'Who?'

'Farmer? Dog walker?'

Will leaned on the side of the dyke, wiping the sweat from his forehead on his shirtsleeve.

'I'm not worried,' he said, 'about farmers or walkers or traffic in the lane. Only one thing is going to spot us, and that's a helicopter. Surprised they haven't got them up and buzzing all over here by now.'

THIRTY-NINE

'Keep your voice down, Shelley.'

'Sorry . . . we shouldn't be talking about this in a bar anyway.'

'Well, we are, and if we speak in normal voices nobody will hear. There wasn't any need to screech at me. All I said was —'

'I heard what you said.'

'If you let me finish . . . that he's apologised, he's said you'd both had too much to drink.'

Shelley set her glass down and looked across at the man she had discovered she hardly knew, after seventeen years.

'Who do you believe, Tim? I need to hear you say it.'

Tim sighed. He looked wretched, she saw that, looked as if he wished he were a million miles away.

'I wish none of it had happened,' he said.

'*You* wish? And stop telling me not to raise my voice because if you do it once more I'll stand on this table and shout. I was not drunk that night. I'd had one glass of champagne and two of white wine by the time I went down to that ladies' cloakroom and no way would that quantity make me drunk, just pleasantly relaxed. If Richard Serrailler told you I was drunk —'

'No, he didn't, not in so many words.'

'What, she'd had a few? Had a bit of a skinful? Had enough to say yes? Whatever he said he's lying. I was not drunk. I did not say yes. I did not indicate yes. I did not say, do, imply anything which would have led anyone to believe I was happy to let them . . . that I was up for it . . . however he put it . . . you put it . . . I hate it that he had the gall to ring you and try and fix it between you — get the little woman to see sense: Tim, apologise from me but I can assure you . . . Ach.' She finished off her glass of wine — the first she had had that evening. 'How bloody dare he.'

'Shelley . . .'

'And what did you say? Reassure him you believed him and not your wife?'

'No, on the contrary. The one thing I did say was that I knew you'd think better of pressing charges against him.'

'You did? And what made you sure of that?'

'Come on, you must see that now the dust has settled . . .'

'It hasn't.'

'I honestly want you to think about this hard, which I'm not sure you have. Maybe you don't understand the full implications of going ahead with a case that could come to court. Do you want your name dragged through the dirt?'

'No, but I want his.'

'Now you're being stupid. You're not thinking it through. Your name would be everywhere . . . and everything that happened, every detail . . . how do you think friends and colleagues and neighbours will find that?'

'To be honest, I don't give a toss. How they find it is their problem, not mine.'

'But it will be yours and you know perfectly well what people will say.'

'No, tell me.'

Tim shook his head wearily and drank his pint.

'Do you mean they'll say there's no smoke without fire?'

'Look . . . let's leave it. Try and enjoy an evening without going back over this again, can't we?'

'So long as you accept that I'm not giving up on it and I am pressing charges. No way is that man going to walk off into the sunset and think a friendly word in the ear of another Freemason —'

'This has nothing to do with Freemasonry.'

'The "word in your ear, old boy" thing? I think it has.'

'I'm not arguing with you any more.'

'Fine. I'd like another glass please.'

Tim got up. 'They do hot roast beef sandwiches. Fancy one?'

'No thanks, but you go for it.'

'I don't want to eat on my own.'

They looked at one another. Shelley felt her eyes filling. As well as everything else it had done, the rape had brought them to this hostility and coldness and endless bickering. She loved Tim. He loved her. They were happy — had been happy, until Richard had destroyed that too.

'All right . . . two hot roast beef.'

Tim smiled.

She wouldn't change her mind. The support she had been given, the advice, the understanding, the determination to be with her all the way, the expertise, all of it, had made her quite sure that she was right and would go through with it. And win. If there was any justice, surely to God the truth was all she need stick to. Whatever Tim had

agreed to, however Richard Serrailler had
made him see it, made no difference at all.
The worst was just that she wanted it over
and done with, and it wouldn't be . . . the
law was nothing if not protracted.

Tim came back with their drinks.

'Feel better?'

He looked so anxious, so desperate for her
to say yes, she did, and yes, she had been
wrong, and yes, of course she would drop
the case.

'Yes. Thank you, darling.'

FORTY

'Excuse me, but is that Dr Deerbon?'

'It is, yes.'

She was settling down to read the latest choice for her book group, with a glass of wine.

'I don't suppose you'll remember me — my name's Jack Dacre, you only saw me a couple of times over the years but my mother was your patient . . .'

'Yes — Elaine, is it? I do remember her. How is she?'

'Not good, Doc, very poorly in fact, and it's why I've rung you and I hope you don't mind. We've been at our wits' end knowing what to do for the best.'

'Jack, you're welcome to talk to me but I'm not your mother's doctor now, so I can only give you general medical advice.'

'But I think you are — I know you've done some sessions at her practice — Granham Road Surgery? She sees Dr Marriott, but she's been away having a baby, so Mother hasn't got attached to any other doctor in particular.'

'That makes all the difference. I only do locum surgeries for Granham Road but as it happens I have done several in the past couple of months, some for Dr Marriott. So tell me what's wrong.'

'My mother has cancer. She's at home — they sent her out of Bevham General because apparently they can't do any more there, and in any case, she said all along that she wanted to come home to die. She knows she hasn't got much time.'

'I understand. I'm so sorry. How long has she been out of hospital?'

'Four days. She doesn't seem too bad in herself — she gets up when she can, even if it's just to sit in a chair, and she comes down in the evening if she can make the stairs. The real problem is that she's distressed in her mind. Then tonight, she suddenly said she wanted to talk to you. She said she'd have gone into the hospice only it's closed . . .'

'Not exactly — it has day-care patients.'

'She's past just going in and out for a day.'

'I see. The nurses from the hospice would come out to see her — does she know that? It's part of what's done now there are no beds at Imogen House. It's called hospice at home.'

'My mother said you were the hospice doctor.'

'I am — but I'm not working there so much at the moment.'

'Oh. It's all a bit complicated, isn't it? I'm sorry to have bothered you then, Doctor.'

He sounded exhausted and flat, as if a final door had closed in his face.

'No, no, it's fine. Remind me where your mother lives — of course I'll go and see her.'

'Dr Deerbon, she said you would. I am so grateful to you, I'm so grateful.' Now he was struggling to hold back tears.

It was mid-afternoon before she turned into St Luke's Drive, remembering the road only vaguely — the GP practice she and Chris had run had been on the other side of Lafferton so not many patients had lived here.

'I can't tell you how grateful I am to you,' Jack Dacre said, leading her into the quiet sitting room overlooking a long garden. 'She hasn't been sleeping well but when Angie went in to her last night, she said knowing that you would come was such a relief that she went out on a cloud and didn't wake until after seven.'

'Are you staying here?'

316

'One of us sleeps here every night but we only live a dozen houses down so we come in and out . . . Angie works part-time so she can be here quite a bit, and our daughter Lou — she's in the sixth form — she's pretty capable.'

'Lots of family support then. That's so important and many people just don't have it nowadays, for one reason or another. It'll make a lot of difference to her.'

'I hope so. We know they can't cure her but I was afraid she was going to die in Bevham General — she went right down, didn't eat, seemed to shrink into herself, if you follow me. It was as though she was giving up.'

'She would have been very depressed . . . realising that you're not going to get better and that you might end your days on a busy hospital ward is a pretty bleak prospect.'

'That's where the hospice should have come in . . . Well, anyway, she's up and dressed and in the chair. She's had some soup and toast — not a lot but as long as she eats something, we try not to fuss her.'

The wall between the second and third bedrooms of the house had been removed, making one light, spacious room, with a wardrobe and chests of drawers built in around and above the bed, and one end, also overlooking the garden, made into a sitting area. A bracket had been fitted outside the window with three bird feeders attached, and as they went into the room, there was a flurry of wings as blue tits, chaffinches and a robin scattered away in momentary fright.

The minute Cat looked at Elaine Dacre, she remembered her — a pretty woman with hair that had started to regrow after chemotherapy, and now formed a fluffy grey cap. It made her blue eyes look larger and more vivid. She was very thin now, and her skin had a tinge as if a suntan was wearing off. Her hand, as she held it out to Cat, had long fingers and Cat felt the bones moving beneath the flesh, like those of a bird. She was dressed in a silky blue shirt and loose trousers, wore make-up, including a bright lipstick, and a pair of shoes were beside the small armchair on which she sat with her legs up. The room was warm but a woollen shawl was beside her, two cushions at her back.

Cat sat on a stool which was drawn up close to the armchair, and took the fragile hand again between both of her own. Elaine Dacre gripped it tightly in response and her eyes filled with tears.

'Shall I make you some tea?' her son said,

relief softening his anxious expression as he stood in the doorway.

'I would love a cup of tea more than anything, I haven't had one since breakfast, thank you.'

'And there's some lemon drizzle cake left, isn't there?' Elaine Dacre looked at her son with tenderness.

When the tea came, and the cake, cut in neat slices, Jack left to do the supermarket shopping. Cat listened to his mother's lengthy praise of her family and how wonderfully well they were taking care of her, discussed the granddaughter's future, and then Cat's children and Lafferton events. The chat went on for twenty minutes or more and she knew better than to do anything other than take her cue from Elaine.

The house was quiet. The birds had returned to the feeders. A boy in the yard next door mended a bicycle wheel.

Elaine set down her cup. She had said twice how grateful she was that Cat had troubled to come. Now, she looked at her again.

'Do you know what the worst is?'

'The worst' was different for every terminally sick patient, Cat had discovered years ago, though there were only so many variations — the pain, losing control of faculties, leaving partners and children or not seeing grandchildren grow up, loneliness, sense of disbelief, fear of the dying process . . .

'Tell me.'

'Nobody will talk about it. Or at least, they will, but only in a roundabout way, not *really* talk —'

'About dying?'

'Dying. Death . . . all of it. Jack and Angie won't talk, they swerve away and ask if I couldn't manage a bit more of this or that to eat. I can see the panic in their eyes. The doctors in oncology know what they're doing but they would only talk about it in terms of prognosis and statistics.'

'One of the points of the hospice movement has always been to provide a place where people can talk about everything to do with their situation. It's what the staff are trained to do.'

Elaine shook her head, smiling.

'Of course, nobody will start talking about death and dying if a patient clearly doesn't want to . . . that would be intrusive and even unkind . . . though some things do have to be said — gone are the days when it was thought better not to mention the C-word, always to pretend someone was improving.'

'I want to talk. I have had so many questions, so many thoughts whizzing round and round inside my head, a confusion of fears and feelings . . . and I want to say things, tell things. But it does seem to embarrass people — I find myself being very careful not to mention death and dying to visitors — and doctors and nurses — in case I embarrass or upset them.' She laughed.

'You're going through and facing the most important time anyone faces, other than their own birth — only you had far less control over that and you don't remember anything about it, and couldn't prepare for it. Death is different. Or it can be. I really believe that. People say they'd like to die suddenly and not know anything about it but I've always thought that was a lost opportunity.'

'Yes . . . oh yes!' Elaine put her hand over Cat's again. 'I knew you were the one person I could be sure wouldn't dodge and dissemble and change the subject.'

'I hope not. Listen, I have to collect my son from school soon but I'll come again with pleasure if you want to go on talking . . . if I dash off it isn't that I'm trying to escape the D-word.'

Elaine rested her head back and closed her eyes for a moment. When she opened them again, they were brighter, more full of life, and the strain and anxiety in her expression had eased.

'I want to tell you about something that happened — I've tried to tell other people but they've either looked embarrassed and changed the subject hastily — the usual — or they've been a bit scornful and disbelieving. I can't mention it to Jack or Angie, they just say I was under powerful drugs and I should forget all about it.'

She had moved to look straight at Cat.

'Tell me.'

'My grandmother — that was my mother's mother — lived with us for her last couple of years — she had heart problems and she couldn't manage on her own. She was very special — warm, giving, loving, uncomplaining, always grateful for everything — she had lots of friends and they all came to see her even when she'd moved right away from her old home area. But when she was eighty-six, and I was fourteen, she was very ill — no one ever told me what was wrong. I know it was only partly her heart condition, but you know how it used to be — lips sealed or people whispering in corners. They thought I shouldn't know anything. One evening, my mother had sent for the doctor and he came downstairs and said Nanoo — I always called her Nanoo — was, as he said it, "on her way". My mother was upset and she said I shouldn't go up and see her, but I can remember feeling I'd fight everyone rather than not be with Nanoo when she might need me. The district nurse came and she had oxygen. And then I did go to my bedroom, because it was after midnight, and I was falling asleep. I woke up at half past two. I looked at my bedside clock. And I had a very strange feeling . . . it was as if someone else was in the room and they were talking to me, but I couldn't make out the words. I felt very calm and I felt something else too — it's hard to describe it but it was just an extraordinary peacefulness. The house felt different. Everything felt different. The best way I can describe it is . . . it was as if something that had been difficult and hurtful and upsetting had been dealt with at last, and it was all right now. I also knew I had to go to Nanoo. It was such an urgent thing — the feeling that I couldn't do anything else but go to her. I got out of bed and put on my dressing gown. I went to her bedroom — the bedside lamp was on very low, and the nurse was sitting beside Nanoo's bed. When I opened the door she looked round and said, "It's all right, you come in, Elaine. Your gran's been talking about you. I think she wants to see you."

'She was one of the few nurses I've ever

known who just accepted that my grandmother was dying and that I could see her, there was no problem about that. She didn't think I should be kept away. She was a lovely woman, from West Africa, and I think they are often more open about death. The Irish are too, or they used to be. Anyway, she just talked to me about it so easily. I wished I could have her nursing me when I was in the hospital. I even dreamed about her once or twice. Anyway, Nanoo was looking very still and breathing quite slowly. Her face was so full of strain and worry and — I don't know, as if everything in her life that had ever been a problem or gone wrong was piled on top of her now. I remember being very upset and touching her hand and holding it but she went on breathing slowly and I didn't think she knew I was there. The nurse said she would call my mother soon. "Your gran's not going to be with us much longer," she whispered and she took my hand and held it. "You understand what's happening, don't you, Elaine?"

'I did. I felt strange — as if I was there and not there, sad and not sad. It was very muddled and emotional. We just stayed like that for a while, me holding Nanoo's left hand, the nurse holding her right, and then, as if she just knew now was the moment, the nurse got up and went out quickly, and a minute later, my mother was there with her, pulling her dressing gown on. It was November, it was quite cold — we didn't have warm bedrooms then — but the nurse had a one-bar heater on. My mother looked at me, and I thought she was going to tell me to go back to bed, but she didn't. We were waiting, and I knew my mother was standing a bit away from the bed because she was frightened — anything to do with death and dying really bothered her, she couldn't deal with it. And then the most extraordinary thing happened — my grandmother started and her eyes opened wide . . . she was trying to sit upright but of course she was too weak. She didn't look at any of us, she looked ahead — not blankly, she was looking at something. Then she gave a big sigh — as if everything was suddenly all right, everything was as it should be. And then she turned her head and looked straight at me with such a long, loving look, such a sweet, loving look . . .'

Elaine had tears running down her cheeks now but Cat did not stir or speak.

'And then she just lay back and took one breath and that was it. No more breaths. The room was absolutely silent and still, and I felt that we were in a sort of bubble, a timeless bubble, not related to anything else . . . and then I heard my mother draw in a breath. Because there was a light — it hovered just over my grandmother, it reflected on the wall — it was a dim light, and blue, the most intense blue, and so beautiful. My grandmother's face was beautiful too . . . it seemed to have changed in just those few seconds and she was a girl, or a young woman again, and every worry and pain line had gone — they were just smoothed out. We all three of us stayed still and I don't know how long it was but it felt as if it was out of time and just going on and on. And then the light faded away very quickly and my grandmother was dead and my mother was making funny little sobbing sounds. And that was it. And it was as if, when I'd woken up in my bed earlier, I was going through what would happen . . . I remember lying in bed feeling so peaceful and so happy for Nanoo and somehow just accepting — and although I didn't actually see it again, the light seemed to be still there somehow, all round me. It stayed with me for days — until her funeral. They were all for my not going to that but I was furious and I made such a fuss they let me . . . I said Nanoo especially wanted me to go, so in the end, they let me. The blue light was round me at her burial, but after that it seemed to dissolve away and I never had it round me again. And that is as true as the truth can ever be, Doctor, and if you think I'm mad and deranged or whatever, it doesn't make a spot of difference. It never has. I've just lived with it for the rest of my life. I've never told anyone. I tried to tell Neil — my husband — and then Jack and Angie, but they didn't want to know. My mother never referred to it. I didn't try to talk to anyone about it, but I read some article in the paper about a woman who had had a similar experience — not the same, but like enough to make me know at once. The nurse prepared my grandmother, but then the doctor came to do the certification, and of course the undertaker, and all of that took over and I never saw that nurse again. I wanted to so much. I badly wanted to talk to her but I didn't know how I could get in touch with her, so that was it. But it's true, Doctor, whatever you think of me — as true as anything I know.'

'Why would I "think" anything of you? Of course it's true. I've known this — almost every doctor and nurse will have experienced something of this sort when they've been with dying patients, and there's plenty of research about it done by highly regarded medics come to that. It is certainly not hallucination and not the result of overwrought imagination — these experiences are often dismissed as being nothing more than the result of high doses of morphine but in fact drug-induced hallucinations are quite different. So you're certainly not alone, far from it. And thank you for telling me, Elaine. How do you feel now, after talking about it?'

'Every time I remember it — actually, I don't even have to do that, it's with me all the time. It has always been there — part of me, if that doesn't sound strange. When I do think of it deliberately, I feel — reassured? Helped? Yes. I'm not afraid of death though I don't want to die in agony, of course I don't, I don't like to imagine the physical process. But I'm not afraid of dying because I was there with Nanoo and it was — good. A positive thing, even though I missed her so much because I loved her. But I always knew everything was all right.'

Elaine fell silent for a moment. 'Why does everyone try to change the subject, do you think?'

'Fear. The old embarrassment?'

'I think there's more to it. When people had a faith, they accepted death — it was part of the whole business, if you know what

I mean. But now everyone is afraid to look stupid, gullible, they believe death is the end, so anyone who starts to talk about an afterlife, or anything spiritual, is automatically deluded or deranged, or indulging in fairy tales. And if you think death is a big black nothing, you probably prefer not to discuss it, I suppose. People have their own beliefs but it isn't right to dismiss everyone who has other opinions, is it?'

'No, absolutely not. Respect other people's experiences and feelings and views, however different they are. My mother was a doctor, and not any sort of believer, but she always said it was her job to listen and not pass judgement, not dismiss anything. She was right. It's arrogance to do otherwise.'

'I'm very lucky to have you here to talk to.'

'I so often wish I could go into med schools and hospitals and explain about listening. All doctors need to listen more. Lack of time the excuse of course, but people waste plenty of it on stuff that doesn't matter a jot.'

'The worst is when you're treated like a child. "Now, now, let's not talk about nasty things." '

'But don't you think people try to change the subject and chivvy you into being bright

and chirpy because it makes *them* feel better — never mind how you feel?'

'You see, I keep wanting to talk to Jack
about my will . . . it's nothing complicated,
there are just one or two things I'd like to
be given to certain friends, you know,
sentimental things — but he shuts me up,
every single time, he goes all chirpy and
makes jokes, anything to avoid facing the
conversation. It's made me very sad sometimes and then I've been angry — I
shouldn't be angry, I know, they can't help
it.'

'Can't they? What are they afraid of, do
you think?'

Elaine sighed and rested her head back.

Cat got up. 'I have to go. But I'll pop in
again soon. And thank you.'

'What for?'

'You've made me realise something I sort
of knew but hadn't quite worked out — how
important all this is and what I want to try
and do about it, even if it can only be in a
limited way. So yes, thank you, Elaine.'

Cat bent down and hugged the woman
gently, noticing how little there was of her
body to grasp. She would come back, and
soon. She had learned the lesson about putting things off and then to regretting it.

'If there's anything you need or if you

want to have a word on the phone, please ring. I'm at home most evenings, other than Tuesdays which is my choir practice or you can leave a message for me at the surgery. I want to make sure everything's covered so that you're as comfortable as you can be and I'll organise one of the hospice nurses to come in as well, if you think that would be a good idea. I know them all, I'll make sure they're properly briefed — no sing-along and no bingo.'

Elaine smiled. The colour was touching her cheeks again, and her eyes were lively. Something so simple, Cat thought as she left, and look at the difference it makes.

The end of St Luke's Drive had been fitted with blocks to stop cars using it as a rat run, and as she unlocked her own car, Cat noticed another trying to negotiate an awkward three-point turn a few yards away. It was a fast, smart Mercedes coupé. She recognised it, and waved.

'I thought satnav was supposed to know these things,' Rachel called out of the car window. 'Now look at the mess I'm in.'

'Don't worry, I'll guide you down — but stop when you're the right way round again, I haven't seen you for ages.'

The turn was managed easily between the two of them.

'What are you doing out here anyway?'

'Delivering a parcel of books. Someone impatient for new things we didn't have in stock, and they came in today so I thought I'd add the personal service element. And I was on my way home. You?'

'Seeing a patient. Listen, I've got to collect Felix and then I'm heading home. Come to tea? Glass of wine?'

Rachel smiled with real pleasure. 'Love to. I was only going to watch a film I downloaded weeks ago.'

'Sad.'

'Tragic.'

'Right, here's the front-door key to the farmhouse, go in and put the kettle on, I'll follow with the boy. Unless Hannah is already back but I doubt she will be. Sam's at cricket nets.'

Rachel caught the key, gave Cat a thumbs up, and sped sleekly off.

FORTY-ONE

For a split second after the sirens had wailed up to full volume, Ray Norman had gone through the emergency procedures in his head, beginning with total lockdown. Then, the full implication of what he had been told hit him. The escaped men were Will Fernley and Johnno Miles. He unlocked his own mobile, the only place on which he had the contact number stored. It was picked up after a single ring.

'Ray Norman. We have a breakout, two men, one of them Johnno Miles.'

'Wait a moment please.' There was a thirty-second pause before he came back. 'OK, here's the procedure. Continue with the routine as normal, lockdown, short tannoy announcement, all officers to posts on the unit, all men in the public area, rooms to be vacated and locked temporarily. No one outside the building. Local police are being informed from here as we speak, and will be with you fast. Continue with them as normal, their Chief knows the score, he will inform any others strictly on a need to know. Police units across the county and adjacent will be put on alert. Within the prison, there is no need to know, you are the only contact, talk to no one else. If the media descend, press conference only, statement as per, ensure you use Miles's legend as his only story. Repeat. Nothing to be said to break his cover. Answer questions briefly, mainly to maintain public confidence. You know what's going to happen the minute they hear "escaped paedophiles". We don't want panic, schools closing, all that. No risk, no danger, police fully deployed blah. You've got all of it?'

'When you catch up with them — and you're pretty much bound to, I'd have thought, there's no hiding place round here — then what?'

'Arrested and taken into custody. We deal with everything. But they won't be coming back to you.'

The receiver went to tone, the governor slipped the mobile into his inner pocket. Seconds later, he heard the police sirens coming closer and fast from the main road. Ray was listening to them, cursing the day he had agreed to have an undercover cop on the premises, when the first person came banging urgently on his door.

FORTY-TWO

'Flat on your back, pull the branches over you.'

Simon did as he was told with an urgency he did not feel. The police helicopter was starting to circle the surrounding area, flying low. In a few minutes, they would be right over the dyke in which he and Will were concealed — and pretty well concealed, he thought — but if the crew caught sight of anything resembling men on the run, as per their instructions, they would not drop down further to investigate. Only one or two police would know the score but the helicopter crew would be included in that and made aware that one of the escapees was working undercover, though they would have been given no further information. They would make a great show of searching, and then buzz off.

It was unpleasant in the ditch, the vegetation scratching their arms and faces, the mud and slime at the bottom rank-smelling as they disturbed it. It was close, and humid, and another twenty minutes before the helicopter went out of their hearing. They waited a quarter of an hour before Will said he felt it was safe to move on. Another hour of trudging and crawling slowly along and he stopped and turned his head.

'OK, in about a hundred yards, we climb out of here and make a short dash skirting the side of the field, to a crown of trees. Not many of those around here and I've had it marked out. We won't be seen in there, the foliage is pretty dense and the grass is high round the edge. We hole out there until dark. Then we'll make our way about five miles to a farm. The house is empty but the stables are in use. That's the next hiding place.'

'You seem to know all this like the back of your hand.'

'I do . . . and what I don't know I've mapped out for weeks — months. Only worry is if they use night-flying helicopters with thermal-imaging cameras but those will pick up horses and with luck we'll blend in with them. Otherwise, if we're in a ditch or out in the open lanes and fields, we'd be picked out as the only heat source for miles and they'd have us.'

'Listen, where exactly are we heading and how long's it going to take? I'm bloody starving and we'll need water again.'

'The bottles have to last us until we get to the farm. There'll be a stable tap.'

'All right but then where?'

'Andrew's,' Will said curtly. 'Let's get a move on, shall we?'

Half an hour after reaching the shelter of the trees, they were both flat on their backs asleep. There was a slight breeze and there was shade. That was all they needed. They lay a few yards apart, under the shelter of different trees. Simon smelled the earthy smell and the dry-leaf smell and the smell of his own sweat. It was cool now. He was exhausted, but too alert to sleep very deeply and he was the first to wake. There was a deep silence, broken far away by the sound of a tractor. He looked over at Will. He was on his side, head on his left arm, snoring slightly.

Whatever happened in the long run, he knew they were not going to be hunted down and arrested within the next few days. The London team would get what they needed from Ray Norman. His own job was the same — to stick close to Fernley and try to get names, details, everything and anything that would lead them to the paedophile ring. Until he had something, he would not be expected to run off, nor did he want to. In fact, he felt more optimistic than he had done inside Stitchford. Out here, he had far more chance of bonding with Will and ingratiating himself well enough to be let into secrets. Inside, there had always been a risk, and always others about, and a general atmosphere of watchfulness. Plus the therapists, on the alert for any close relationships and bent on breaking them up. One-to-one friendships were always frowned upon.

He rolled over and lay with his hands crossed behind his head, looking through the leaf canopy to the sky. Blue. Still. He looked over at Fernley again. Could he take a chance and try to make even the briefest contact via the device secreted on the Snoopy watch? No. Will might wake suddenly before he had any chance to cover up what he was doing. Not worth the risk.

A collared dove settled in the tree and began to coo softly. Nothing else moved. Will slept on.

Rachel came into his mind, her face clear and close in front of his eyes. Rachel. She deserved better. Any woman deserved better, he knew that. His family were used to this sort of thing, and even if they worried, took it in their stride. Not Rachel. He wished he believed in telepathy and could make it work. Wished, more mundanely, that he could contact her, or get a message to her. Knew that he could not.

He loved her. But did he ever love anyone enough to let them make a permanent home at the centre of his life? He had minded more strongly than he knew was reasonable when she had moved in and started to make her mark on his flat, leaving traces of her presence everywhere. It was a statement and he had not been able to accept it. And if that was the case, how could he conceivably think of marriage?

He couldn't.

Will Fernley woke and sat up in one single, alarmed movement.

'It's OK, nothing's happened,' Serrailler said.

'Jeez.' Will lay back. 'Nightmares. You?'

'Nope. Out like the proverbial. I'm bloody hungry though.'

'Time?'

'Half eight.'

'Christ, we've been asleep for hours.'

'We were knackered.'

Simon stood and did some arm-swinging

and stretching, trying to get his cramped muscles to ease. Lying on hard ground was not the best way to keep his back problems at bay. Will was doing press-ups but flopped onto his stomach after nine. 'Not as fit as I should be.'

They sat side by side, hearing the leaves rustle, the distant tractor, an even more distant train.

'So — this Andrew whose place you said we're going to. He the barrister guy?'

Fernley nodded. 'Top man.'

'You said he won't be there?'

'Probably not, but he comes down on Friday afternoons, and if we're still there, which I dare say we will be, we'll meet up then.'

'Is he prosecuting or defending?'

'Mainly defending. Just once in a while he takes on a prosecution but it has to be worth his while. No legal-aid stuff.'

'Charges high?'

'You could say.'

'Has he looked after you?'

'God, no. Wouldn't come within a million miles.'

'Because you're friends?'

'No, though that isn't the best thing. No, other reasons. You could call it . . . clash of interests.' Will laughed.

Simon had the feeling in the pit of his stomach which came when he sensed he was getting somewhere. It happened during questioning. They gave you nothing, blocked you, dodged, stonewalled, played dumb, and then something gave — maybe a give so slight only an experienced interviewer would recognise it for what it was, but once the hairline crack had opened up, it was almost always just a matter of time before the entire structure crumbled.

'Not sure I follow you,' he said.

'Yes, you do. He's a top barrister, he earns a mint, he gets the high-profile work. He can't afford to be careless. He can't be seen to associate with — me. My sort. Your sort. Oh, come on, Johnno!'

'Ah . . . got you. Yes. I see. Sorry — being obtuse there.'

'Too right. And while we're on the subject — don't for God's sake say anything . . . you don't know, you haven't been told a thing. He's a mate of mine, he's willing to give me — us — a place to stay for as long as it takes, but that's it. He won't talk. You don't talk.'

Simon held up his hands. Then he said, 'I've been here before. One or two — well, friends. Public profiles — businessmen. A big-name journo. Headmaster. I even know an MP.'

'Only one?'

It was easier once it grew dark. They left the open flat lands behind and skirted along the edges of hedged fields. They came to a B-road and a shack of a shop with petrol pumps attached. One jeep was pulled up getting fuel but the shop seemed empty.

'I'll go in, you stay round the back,' Serrailler said. He knew there would have been a blackout on their names and photographs being put out over the media, and if the unit had its way, a total block on any news of their escape at all, but however small the chance, in the event of any problem he was better able to deal with it than Fernley. Simon had no money. Will tossed him a fiver. He bought bottles of water, sandwiches, chocolate and biscuits. The television was on behind the counter and he glanced at it. The weather forecast. Dry, mild night, sunny day tomorrow, dry again. They could have worse. Behind the rack of crisps, he pressed a button on his watch, merely to send the pre-recorded message that he was OK.

Beside the petrol station, what had once been a garden was now a dumping ground, with a dilapidated caravan and some ancient but serviceable plastic furniture. A hedge hid them from sight of both the shop and the road. They sat there and drank and ate ravenously and in silence. Three cars and a van went past.

'How far?' Simon said, wiping his mouth.

'Couple of miles, across country again, to the stables. There's a disused airfield not far from here, though. I wondered if we could hide out in the buildings instead. I don't know about you but I'm still pretty knackered.'

'Isn't that the sort of place they'd expect us to make for?'

'There are several old airfields in this part of the world. They wouldn't have the man-power to search them all, though I guess they'll get round to it. Worth a chance?'

Simon waited before replying, staring at the ground, chewing the last of his sand-wich. Then he said, 'OK. You're probably right. They don't have the resources to look everywhere and if you add up the empty houses and decommissioned churches and airfields and God knows what else, we could be anywhere. Let's go for it.'

The night was so balmy that they lay outside on some rough grass verges around one of the hangars, rusting and boarded-up, even the danger notices falling into disrepair. Keep Out notices were attached to the perimeter fences but there were plenty of gaps and they had no difficulty getting onto the site. The inside of the few flat-roofed buildings that remained were damp, rat-infested and unpleasant. The floors were broken-up concrete. It was better on the grass. They lay on their backs, looking up at a night sky thickly scattered with stars. There was a half-moon and no cloud, so they could easily see all the way around them.

Simon was dozing, going over events, trying to plan ahead, when Will Fernley said, 'Doesn't it all seem a bit odd to you?'

'What?'

'Well, taking into account the area to cover and all of that — still, wouldn't you have expected more patrol cars and helicopters around? That petrol station sold local papers but the boards didn't mention a breakout, I looked — they were about a man being drowned and the football team. They must be throwing everything at it — they ought to be. There isn't a peep.'

'There was.'

'One chopper and one siren, first thing. If I lived around here I'd be baying for blood.

Two convicted paeds out of Stitchford? The earth ought to have stopped revolving.'

Serrailler did not reply.

'Doesn't seem odd to you, Johnno?'

'Now you mention . . . I'm not going to worry about it though. We could have gone in several directions — they're searching the others. We got lucky.'

Fernley leaned on his arm and looked at Simon, searching his face as if to find something out there. 'Why did you trust me?'

'No option.'

'Of course you had an option. You needn't have come.'

'Are you mad? Chance to get out of that hellhole? It was pretty clear you'd got it planned. I just decided to risk it. Who wouldn't?'

'Oh, a lot wouldn't. Most of them in there. You'd been there a few weeks. You didn't give it much of a go.'

'I knew it the minute I walked in. That it was a big mistake. By the time I was in the first group meeting, I was absolutely bloody certain. Therapy? All right, it works for some — a few. Though I guess it's damage limitation more than anything, but if they're prepared to go through with it, good luck to them. They're desperate. They want to change, to crawl out of their old skins and into new ones. And Stitchford is their one and only chance.'

Will rolled onto his back. 'Cassiopeia. The Plough. The Bear. The Pleiades . . .'

'Always wish I'd been able to make sense of that. Beautiful — beautiful names. I've tried endless times — got charts and so on, and it still all looks the same to me.'

'I'll teach you.'

'You couldn't.'

'You're like me, Johnno. Tell the truth.'

'I told you, the night sky all looks —'

'Fuck it, not the sky. How we are. You and me. That's why we wanted to get out. I knew it as soon as we started talking.'

'Knew what?'

'As I said — those guys want to change. Want to be different. Cured. Whatever. They hate who they are. But we don't. I don't. You don't. We don't want to change because we like what we do. We enjoy it. We're hooked. You can only change a druggy or an alcoholic if they want to be changed. Tell me I'm wrong.'

Serrailler was silent for a long time. He looked at the Bear. Orion . . . Then he said, 'You're not wrong.'

He lay awake for some time after Will had

347

rolled over and gone to sleep, head on his arm. He wondered how many of the others felt like Will, that having got a hard-won place, they had to play along with the treatment and keep their real feelings concealed. Not so many, he guessed. Will had always struck him as too relaxed and easy-going about the whole thing. Now he knew why. Will had stuck it out only because it was less frightening than being a nonce in prison, where the aggression and hostility and sometimes outright violence wore you down. But Will had also known that it might be slightly easier to escape from a therapeutic community prison than a regular one, and although security was presumed to be tight at Stitchford, he had been right. The chink in the armour had not been hard to find.

It was going to be harder from now on. Serrailler closed his eyes. The air was pleasant, it wouldn't drop down cold at dawn. He would not let himself go to sleep yet. He needed to think himself more thoroughly into his undercover persona now, to behave as the paedophile Johnno Miles behaved. If he was successful, he would not feel good about it.

FORTY-THREE

'I don't suppose you've heard from Simon . . .' Rachel said, trying and failing to sound casual.

Cat was setting out the remains of the previous day's cheese flan, and making a salad, having persuaded Rachel to stay for supper. It had not been difficult.

'I wish I had.'

'Does he have no way of leaving messages even just to let you know he's OK?'

'He may have but if so he doesn't use it. He's disappeared like this before and then simply reappeared like a genie.'

'Don't you find it unnerving? The radio silence?'

Cat set the salad bowl on the table, looking at Rachel quickly as she did so. Rachel looked back, her expression hard to read. But her eyes were troubled.

'I'm used to it and it doesn't happen often. Don't fret that he hasn't been in touch, Rachel . . . it isn't you.'

'But I think it is. I understand what you're saying about him not being able to contact anyone, only perhaps if he had wanted to as much as I want him to, he'd have found a way.'

'Perhaps.'

Cat cut the flan and passed Rachel a plate. They had opted not to drink anything other than water. Cat was having every other night wine-free and Rachel was happy without. Fine, Cat thought, but a glass would have relaxed her just enough. If she wanted to talk about Simon, she might have found it less awkward after a drink.

Instead, Rachel asked, 'Do you know a man called Rupert Barr?'

'Sir Hugh's brother? We've met a couple of times but I don't really know him. Why?'

Rachel told her about the possibility of investing in the bookshop.

'Hmm. That's a big decision. You seem very fired up about it. Are you sure?'

'Look, I have money and I need something to do, something to absorb my spare energy and . . . take my mind off Simon. If I don't I'll go mad . . . I could just waste the time away brooding about him and being depressed, or I could do something, and this is the perfect opportunity. I know what's

350

wrong with the shop, I know why Emma isn't making it work, and why she wants out, I know I can turn it around. With someone else backing me — not just financially but with their own enthusiasm and initiative — I could have a really good business and it will make all the difference to me. Whatever your brother chooses to do.'

'It sounds good — and you're right, brooding is the worst thing you can let yourself waste your life on. But listen, I'm not prying, and I have no idea what's in Si's head, because I haven't talked to him about it and that is God's truth. But suppose he comes back next week and asks you to marry him — what would you do then about taking over the bookshop?'

'Oh, that's easy. I do both.'

'I hoped you'd say that. Simon would definitely want you to say that, I do know that much.'

Rachel was looking across the table at her intently. Too intently.

I should not have said any of that, Cat thought. I should have kept my mouth shut.

'Cat . . .'

Cat held up her hand. 'I don't know anything. If anyone epitomises the "plays his cards close to his chest" metaphor, it's my brother. I haven't a clue what he thinks or feels about you or what his plans might be, if he has any. Though knowing him, he almost certainly hasn't.'

That was a lie. Simon always thought things through in detail, looked at a situation from every angle, and had a plan. She was afraid that his plan regarding Rachel was no plan. No marriage. But no split, no drama, no quarrels either. In his own odd way, he probably loved Rachel more seriously than he had ever loved anyone. It was just that, in Simon's case, that was never enough.

She wanted to tell Rachel to get out while she could, go and open a bookshop at the other end of the country. Give up on Simon. But she wouldn't waste her breath.

She merely said, 'Don't rely on him, Rachel. I've learned not to and I'm only his sister. He's wedded to the job, he'll take off without a word, he keeps his life in compartments and not ones which have interconnecting doors.'

'Are you saying he has several women at the same time?'

'No, I'm not. But you should count yourself lucky to have got as far as you did — moving in? Good God, Si has never let a mouse move in with him before.'

'Why are you telling me this, Cat? If he's

said something or if he's asked you to —'

'He wouldn't dare. I'm not doing his dirty work. I'm telling you all this to try and save you a lot of heartache.'

'I've had that already.'

'I know.'

'How many others have you made that little speech to?'

'Enough.'

'And has it worked? Have any of them taken any notice?'

Cat laughed. 'I want to know more about the bookshop. Emma really does intend to chuck it in?'

'Yes. Her heart hasn't been in it for a while. It's got so much harder and she isn't one for a fight. She just likes running a quiet, modestly profitable bookshop — but we need to do a lot more than that to survive, let alone do well.'

'Has Rupert Barr any experience of bookselling?'

'No, but he's got plenty of enthusiasm, he's been a management consultant, so he's used to homing in on what's wrong and turning things round. He's got plenty of money — not that I need a financial backer, I don't, but it will be a handy backstop. And it'll be nice to do it alongside someone, not all on my own.'

'You think you'll get on with him well enough?'

'Yes, I do, and in any case, he'll leave the day-to-day running to me. But we'll have plenty of meetings, and I'll consult him about all the changes I've got in mind and get his take on them. I'm excited.'

'I can see. Will you be in the shop yourself?'

'Yes, but not full-time. I'll need some very reliable staff, especially when we open the coffee bar.'

'I knew it! Great plan too . . . it works. People come for coffee and stay to browse the books.'

'Coffee, tea, hot chocolate and home-made cake, no food otherwise. There's only room for six small tables, but that's enough. Intimate. Books all around, and beanbags and a toy box. Shop copies of books for the children to look at without it mattering about making fingermarks. Author events — "An Evening with . . ." you know the sort of thing. Informal. Glass of wine. Someone doing a friendly interview, questions, mingling. Signing copies. Nothing fierce — I'd like people who don't usually dare come into a bookshop to find they can enjoy it . . . I know a bookshop is small beer in comparison to some ambitions, but I want to make a mark. I never have. I've been married to a wealthy man who was ill for years. I made his life comfortable and as happy as it could be, but I think whoever I was disappeared somehow. And now . . .'

'And now . . . Rachel, listen. You do this. And don't let Simon make any difference. Whatever happens.'

'What do you think will happen?' She was pleading, wanting Cat to tell her that she knew Simon loved her, would surely marry her, and Cat could not. She had learned over a long time not to trust her brother with women's feelings. He could be charming, attentive, loving. He could also be ruthless and selfish and cowardly. Cat doubted if he would ever change enough to share himself with any woman at all, though she did not doubt that he needed to. But he would stick pins in his eyes before he admitted as much, even to himself.

FORTY-FOUR

As she drove up to the front entrance and before turning past it to a door at the side, Rachel had a flashback to the first and only time she had been to the castle. Then, the drive and the entrance had been floodlit, the side area was a car park full of waiting Bentleys and their chauffeurs, and she had been walking out down the flight of stone steps with Simon, after the Lord Lieutenant's dinner.

Now, there were three or four much more modest cars parked in the gravelled area where she pulled up. There was a truck with ladders and two men lopping some branches of a great horse-chestnut tree. A food-delivery van moving off.

'Good morning!' Rupert Barr came out to her. He's handsome, Rachel thought. She hadn't taken it in before. Handsome and charming, well mannered, well spoken, well dressed. It all went together. She smiled to herself. Simon would fit in perfectly here, although he did not have the money. He had the air of easy, almost casual command, though. Was that another way of saying 'air of superiority'? Not quite but self-belief and confidence, certainly.

'Rachel.' Rupert kissed her lightly on both cheeks. 'Listen, it's such a beautiful morning, would you like to walk down through the top garden to the gazebo? We can sit in there and have our coffee and talk work.'

'I'd love that. I'm a gardens freak.'

'Well then, when we've finished work I'll show you round. It's been my brother's lifelong task to restore the grounds — they were a bit down at heel when he inherited, so he's spent a lot of time and effort on them. Nothing's been altered too much, just spruced and repaired and he did a lot of replanting — and some drastic tree felling. It looks wonderful now but I've scrutinised the original plans and there are plenty of Edwardian photographs. It's still recognisable. Gertrude Jekyll had a hand in some of the west garden.'

They began to wander down some wide stone steps onto a great lawn. At the end a magnificent copper-beech tree stood on top of a grassy bank.

'The Theatre Lawn. We host the Lafferton

Players every other year. Traditionally they do *A Midsummer Night's Dream* of course.'

'Anything else?'

'Come and see — it's next year.'

'Are the gardens open?'

'No, only for that and for one outdoor concert, but not the gardens alone. I think my brother likes people to enjoy them but he prefers to do it by invitation not as a regular thing. When he was Lord Lieutenant there were masses of garden parties for charity and I wish he'd do it again. But he feels he spent such a lot of time being on duty as a public figure, he wants to be quiet and peaceful here now.'

They walked across the lawn and along paths between magnificent borders, through a laburnum tunnel and up towards a ha-ha, on the other side of which a field of sheep were dotted about as if they had been scattered like confetti. Here they turned left and Rachel saw the gazebo, white, Edwardian in style, and overlooking the valley through a wide opening in a high hedge. As they went towards it they were overtaken by a golf buggy which stopped at the gazebo. A young man took out a container and went inside. As Rachel and Rupert followed, he was setting out coffee in a Thermos, china mugs, milk, and a tin which they found full of shortbread.

She looked out to the valley beyond. Lafferton Cathedral tower rose out of a haze in the distance. The rest of the town was hidden.

'Goodness.'

'I know.'

He let her pour her coffee. The gazebo had basket chairs but they sat at the table, looking out. A mower hummed in the distance.

'You are not going to believe this, Rachel, but I have a pretty big business and I don't always have every bit of it in my head, just the overall picture. I'm good at the overall picture. But one of the business managers was here yesterday going over various things and he brought up Lafferton. Of course I knew I owned some property in Lafferton — the old cinema, for instance . . . we're still trying to decide what to do with that. We have some apartments converted from the old ribbon factory. A couple of small blocks — mixed residential and shops. And half of one side of the street in the Lanes which includes the bookshop. Believe it or not.'

Rachel's spurt of alarm must have shown on her face.

'But I swear that has nothing to do with

wanting to take it on with you. Genuinely, I didn't realise. Does it mean you would rather not continue?'

'I'm not sure. Surely the quarterly rent —'

'Will be paid to one of the holding companies. There are several. It's quite normal in property business. I think the rent for the Lafferton buildings goes through Pendulum Estates but I can check. You can check, come to that. The lawyers and agents deal with the day-to-day stuff.'

'It sounds as if you have a lot of properties.'

'I do — or rather, my companies do. I started with three shops and a house that I inherited when I was eighteen. I expanded from there.'

He sat forward and put down his cup.

'If you want me to pull out at this point, Rachel, I will.'

'Of course not. I don't see how it can make any difference who owns the bricks and mortar. That isn't why you became involved.'

'Indeed it isn't. But thank you. Now — one thing I've discovered that goes along with all this. The antique jeweller next door to the bookshop . . .'

'I don't understand how he makes a living. He has some nice things but they're very overpriced and I never see people going into the shop.'

'Which is probably why he's closing down. He wants to retire anyway.'

'I hope something good takes it over.'

'I think it may. You'll need to look at it carefully and see if you agree but it would make a wonderful extension to the bookshop. We'll need to talk to builders but if we opened up the wall between the two we could have a children's section all to itself . . . and that part would adapt very well to events and the coffee bar . . . there would be much more room to breathe.'

Rachel leaned back and looked at Rupert with approval. 'You are the perfect business partner.'

'Or just the perfect partner,' someone said in a heavily accented voice.

The man who came into the gazebo was slim, tall, with a large nose, classically Venetian colouring and features, a face seen in paintings and frescoes in churches all over the city.

'This is Guido.' For some reason, Rupert looked slightly impatient at the interruption.

The Italian took Rachel's hand and kissed it lightly. It was difficult to tell his age. His skin was smooth, his hair thick and glossy, worn slightly longer than was now fashionable but it suited him, and it was beautifully cut.

'We're having a business meeting and the coffee pot is empty,' Rupert said.

Guido laughed. 'Fine, I only came to say I am going to London after lunch now, not tonight, and back not till Thursday.'

'OK, I'll see you before you go.'

'So nice to meet you. But only the first time. We shall meet much more often.'

'I hope so.'

'I know so.' He lifted his hand to them both as he left.

For the next hour and a half they mapped out plans, swapped ideas, made notes. Rupert did not want to be identified as landlord of the bookshop or the adjacent jeweller's but would ask someone at the property company to arrange for Rachel to look round. There was no harm in her telling the jeweller she was interested in taking it over. And although she and Rupert did not plan to make the new venture public until everything was formalised and all the work done, it would not actually be a secret.

'If word spreads like a nice piece of gossip, all the better.'

Rachel laughed. 'If all goes according to plan and we get the financial side sorted out, when do you think we might be ready to reopen?'

'Grand launch? September — but that's a good time. Holidays over, schools settled back.'

'Christmas in sight.'

'Absolutely.'

'It's a tight schedule, Rupert.'

'I like a challenge. So do you, I can tell.'

'I've never had one like this. But I'm excited.'

She was. And it would give her something to fill her mind and time, whether Simon was still absent or had returned. She had to stop making him the centre of her world.

FORTY-FIVE

Andrew Morson, QC, lived in a seventeenth-century rectory. If Serrailler had been in any other mood he would have walked round to the front and spent some minutes admiring the rose-coloured brick, the barley-sugar chimneys, the grassy path that led through a yew hedge to the side gate of the small church, whose tower had four golden angels flying from each corner, now catching the late-evening sunlight to flare and flash like beacons across the meadows beyond. It was everything he could have guessed it would be, the home of a privileged, high-earning, hard-working barrister whose cases involved shipping, commerce and company rights rather than petty crime.

Will Fernley led him round to the back door. They were filthy, hot, exhausted, footsore, and suffering from a surfeit of one another's company. Whatever the architecture of the Grade II listed house, Serrailler could not have cared less about it.

'One look at us and the housekeeper will press the alarm.'

'She knows me. I've been here.'

'Not in your present state you haven't.'

'Mr Morson said you might arrive any time.' The housekeeper was younger than Simon had expected and welcomed them as pleasantly as if they were dressed in black tie. She asked no questions, chatted about the beautiful weather and led them up to spacious rooms on the second floor.

'There are some clothes if you need them . . . though —' she looked Simon up and down — 'they might be a bit on the small size for a man of your height. I'll see if I can do better but it will be tomorrow now. Mr Fernley, you know your way around the house. It's getting on for half past eight, so if you'd like supper in an hour I'll see to that. My husband's about too.'

'Frankie,' Will said when she had gone. 'What Lynn doesn't do, Frankie does. There's the odd other person helping in the garden or the house but these two are the linchpins.'

'Whose is the Audi at the back?'

'Theirs. Andrew looks after them very,

very well. That way they stay loyal and there's no gossip around the countryside.'

'What sort of gossip?'

Will looked at him. 'You know,' he said.

The bathwater was scalding and after soaking in it for twenty minutes, and then showering to wash his hair and cool off, Simon tried on the underclothes, shirt, cotton drill trousers and light pullover left out on his bed. Lynn had been right — the trousers were a few inches short of his ankles and the pullover only came to his waist, so he left it behind. The rest were not a bad fit and he went downstairs, following Will, in loose jeans, a polo shirt and yellow trainers. Simon wore navy-blue deck shoes which would give him blisters if he walked more than fifty yards.

The drinks cupboard was well stocked and the supper straightforward — T-bone steaks, apple pie, cheese. They cleared everything, plus a bottle and a half of burgundy. By the time they were sprawled on sofas waiting for the late-night news they were mellow and drowsy and both had kicked off their footwear.

There was no mention of the breakout from Stitchford, on any channel, or on the local station.

'Odd or what?' Will looked across the room at Simon, who had his eyes half closed.

'Odd. I think maybe they don't want to put the wind up everyone. Doesn't help.'

Will said nothing.

'Do you want this left on, watch a film or something?'

'Do you?'

Simon shook his head and pressed the remote. The room was lit by a couple of lamps, and the windows were open, letting in the grassy night air. Will poured himself another measure of Laphroaig and offered the bottle to Simon, who poured a larger one.

'It's beginning to fade,' Will said, plumping the sofa cushions noisily before lying back on them. 'The ditch. The thistles.'

'The thirst.'

'The sweat.'

'The smell.'

'Before long, it will be as if —'

'— it was all a dream.'

'Nightmare.'

'What's your plan, Will?'

'Another malt. Sleep.'

'Long run.'

'Not sure. Hole up here for a bit. Can't go home — they'll be watching the place.'

'Where is home?'

Will looked at him between half-closed eyes. 'I told you.'

'Right.'

'You?'

'Countryside about ten miles from Lafferton. Know it?'

'Yup.'

'Friends there?'

'Nearby.'

Don't push it, Simon thought.

'You like it there?'

'I do actually. So long as I get right away from time to time.'

'Where's that?'

'Oh, you know . . .' He gave Will a look. 'Somewhere hot and exotic.'

'Thailand.'

'Thailand. Bali. Singapore.'

'Nice. But you don't always have to go so far to find what you want.'

'Safer though.'

Will shook his head. 'What's your username?' he asked quickly.

Simon's heart gave a thump. 'As if . . .'

'No, you're right. All right, name of the group.'

'You heard me. Anyway, why do you need to know? Thought you had your own arrangements.'

'Yup.' He took another mouthful of whisky. 'Andrew's got cigars here somewhere.'

'No thanks, make me wheeze.'

'What, asthma?'

Simon nodded and pretended to sip his malt but took only a little. He was drowsy, the drink had gone to his head faster than usual. That was a state in which he would either let his own guard down or miss something when Fernley did.

'Very, very pleasant,' Will said sleepily.

'It is.'

'Nice to have a very rich hospitable friend.'

'Aren't you?'

'Hospitable?'

'Rich.'

'Family is.'

'There you go then.'

'You?'

'So-so.'

'Thing is, Johnno . . .'

'What?'

'Forgotten.'

'Sleep.'

It was just after midnight by the time Simon was in bed. He had the curtains and windows open onto the garden, because of the sweetness of the air but also because he could see the reflection of Will's lamp. He waited for twenty minutes after it had gone out, and then took the precaution of locking his door, although that would take some explaining away if Will did come round.

Simon had found an old but freshly laundered T-shirt and boxers on his bed. He put them on, then went back to the door and listened. He turned the key and opened the door a chink. Listened again. Nothing so much as creaked. The old house and all its wooden staircases and floors must have finished its settling for the night.

Another ten minutes and he sent an 'AM OK' message via the watch then he went to lean on the windowsill and looked out onto the moonlit garden, the old trees beyond, a bank climbing up into the darkness. The smell of the cool night earth was soothing. He had the feeling that another day or two with Fernley would get him some serious information, names, venues, even something about the security technology behind their very sophisticated Internet ring, and in any case, his senses were alert to the vibes of this house. He would pick up what he could here, too, and from Morson when he eventually arrived. Morson . . . He picked up the watch again. Sent another message. 'Check Andrew Morson QC.'

The church clock chimed. His watch was slow. It was clearly not designed primarily as a timepiece. He adjusted it to a minute past the hour, got into bed, and did not wake until eleven the next morning.

Forty-Six

Cat found Elaine Dacre on a reclining chair in the garden. The chair had a canvas canopy so that her head was out of the sun and she had a small table beside her with a jug of iced lemon tea, medicines, her Kindle, a radio and phone, a notepad and pen, tissues . . .

'Jack thinks of everything and Lou is at home revising for her exams so if I need anything I've got her on speed dial.' She smiled at Cat. 'It's lovely to see you again, Doctor. You are good.'

'I finished surgery early — amazing how people find they're not feeling so unwell after all when the sun's shining. And please call me Cat.'

'Would you like some of this lemon tea? I'm afraid you'd have to get a glass from the kitchen . . .'

Cat went. The sun shone onto gleaming work surfaces and floor, and there was a faint smell of pine. The glasses in the cupboard sparkled.

'Your kitchen is out of a showroom,' she said, unfolding a deckchair and sitting down next to Elaine.

'That's Jack. It used to worry me when he was a boy. His room was always immaculate. His drawers were laid out like the ones in the outfitters, his books and toys had to be just so. It seemed a bit obsessive to me but now I think he just likes neatness and order.'

'Nothing wrong with that.' Cat sat back and sipped her tea. It was a quiet garden, but she could hear a small child chattering next door and the whine of a hedge trimmer further down.

Elaine's face had become thinner, even in the few days since Cat had seen her last, and there was a parchment dryness to her skin. The bones of her hands showed through.

'How have you been?'

Elaine shook her head. 'Tired. Just so tired. But it's odd . . . I feel as if I know something. I can't explain exactly.' She frowned in concentration. 'A lot of your life, you wonder how it will end, don't you? And you pray it won't be in terrible pain or when you're a long way from home. It's — well — it's one of the unknowns. But now, I know. I know how. Not when and not every detail but all the other avenues are closed off. I'm not going to die in a plane crash or driving my car or in childbirth . . . does this sound crazy?'

'Not at all.'

'And because I know now . . . I feel something very important is settled and I don't have to worry about it any more.'

'Not knowing is often the worst . . . I've been thinking a lot about what you said to me last time I came . . . I don't mean physical things, pain or whatever, I mean spiritual experiences — it doesn't necessarily have to do with religion but I think "spiritual" is the right word. Like your experience when your grandmother died. These things are quite common. I had a patient a couple of years ago who came out of a coma, sat up in bed and held her arms out to someone she could see in the doorway . . . and her face just shone with surprise and joy. The nurse saw it, I saw it, her son saw it . . . but when that nurse asked some of her colleagues about it and if they'd had the same sort of experience, they shut her up, or discovered an urgent job they had to do, they were embarrassed. One even said, "If you're going all spooky, you'd be better off on a different ward." '

Elaine leaned forward, trying to reach the jug, but took a deep breath and sat back. Cat jumped up.

'So silly. I can't even do a little thing like that sometimes. Is this how it's going to be from now on?'

'Not necessarily.' Cat handed her a glass. 'You'll have better days and worse days . . . but you will get more tired, yes.'

'If it's only tiredness . . .'

'We have good pain and symptom control now and you'll get it, I'll make sure, but there's not a lot to be done about tiredness. It's natural. It's part of the process.'

'Well, it's annoying but I can just sleep can't I? I thought there was so much I wanted to do, but you know, I'm not sure there is now. I don't mean things like wanting to watch Lou grow up and so on, I'm sad that I won't be here for that, won't know what career she goes for and who she marries and if there'll be any great-grandchildren. But I find I'm not really interested in climbing Mount Kilimanjaro or going to Disney World.'

'I think it helps being able to accept.'

'Is there any alternative?'

'Some people never can. They fight, they struggle, they go down every medical byway and every alternative one, they don't hear

what you tell them, they won't believe
they're mortal at all . . . and I can understand that, I really can. But it makes it
harder and it means even if there were
someone who would talk with them, they
can't do it because they're in full denial.
I've been asked for referral to specialists in
Australia and how many more courses of
chemo before it starts to work and they'll
be cured, when they've had the maximum
already and it's ravaged them — but if they
were told they could have a terrible treatment that would make them live another
day, they'd go for it.'

'Do you believe in anything, Doctor —
sorry, Cat?'

'Yes. It's often very hard but I do think
my Christian faith has sustained me through
an awful lot and it still does.'

'What if it isn't true?'

'I've got to this position, Elaine — I got to
it a year or so after my husband died — that
if you try to follow the essential teaching
then that's got to be a good way to live, and
besides, I love the Church of England. I love
the services and the language and the music
and the prayers. I love the traditions, I love
our cathedral . . . that sustains me as much
as anything. And I decided to go on loving
them and believing because of the way I'm

sustained by it all — and if I'm wrong, well, I shan't know anyway. None of us will. But meanwhile, it's given a point and a purpose to life and made it better. It's religion twisted by men to back up their own desires which has caused so much harm, don't you think? I haven't much to say in support of the Crusades.'

'There's something else I wanted to tell you . . . it was years ago but it was so strange and I still think about it. It's come back to me vividly these last few weeks. When I was a young wife and Jack was a toddler, our next-door neighbours had a daughter of fifteen, and a younger son. He was a monkey but Sally took the biscuit for being naughty — not bad, just full of it. I never knew a child so full of life and high spirits and — she was up for anything, scared of nothing and so full of bubbliness. Jack adored her, absolutely adored her, and one year, he was three I think, Sally came round and started to talk to him about how it was going to be Mothering Sunday and he had to pick some flowers for me and make a card. It was sweet — they sat at my kitchen table and made this card, and I wasn't supposed to see it . . . and then on the Sunday, Sally came round and took Jack into the hall and shut the door. When they came back in he'd got the card in his hand and a little bunch of freesias . . . when I say "bunch" — there were three. I think she'd taken them out of the ones her mother had been given but I didn't say anything, obviously. I put them in a vase, and they smelled so strong — even just three of them. Such a sweet smell . . . it was a real joy. I propped Jack's card next to them on the windowsill.'

Elaine had closed her eyes.

Time and memory, Cat thought. Death throws them up in the air and they fall in a different order. Ageing does it more gradually. It occurred to her that she and Chris had avoided conversations about his dying. He had shut himself off and dealt with it alone, she had thought stoically. But perhaps not. She had been afraid, wanting precious time with him not to be stained by death talk, and for Chris, that had always seemed pointless except in the purely medical sense. How would he have felt if Elaine had wanted to have this sort of debate with him? Did it matter whether they had talked enough about those things not just towards the end but all through their married life? She knew now that it did. It mattered to her.

FORTY-SEVEN

On Sunday mornings, the main streets in Montcuq were packed with market stalls and people. Judith loved it, loved buying cheese and olives, bread and honey and lavender soap, wandering among the rolls of fabric and piles of baskets. But if you arrived late, the cafes were packed and it was impossible to get a seat. She and Richard were not early risers in France — they preferred staying up late into the soft warm nights in the garden of the gîte. But this was not market day, they had parked under the chestnut trees in the shade and walked up to sit under the umbrellas of the Café du Centre. Next to them, four elderly Frenchmen drank small glasses of rosé. It was hot. Nothing moved. Dogs lay in the deepest shadows they could find, heads down on the stone pavement.

'I can't imagine a group of men drinking rosé at eleven in the morning at home.'

'Odd habit,' Richard said, his head in the previous day's *Times* which he had just bought.

'Do they start young and just carry on? I suppose their metabolism is used to it.'

'Highest rate of liver cirrhosis in the world.'

'But they're not alcoholics.'

'Not as such.' He turned a page.

He looked well. Relaxed, tanned, fit, happy. He had been a different man out here, his old self.

'Perhaps we should live here,' Judith said, watching a woman lift a tiny chihuahua out of her shopping bag and set it down beside a saucer of water. Its collar and lead flashed with diamanté and it snarled viciously when someone nearby moved her foot.

'Actually,' Richard said, putting down his paper, 'I was going to say just the opposite. Time we went home.'

'Oh, darling, do you really want to? It's so lovely just being here with you, no pressures, nothing to do but potter and sleep and read and eat.'

'I'm sick of duck.'

'I never cook duck.'

'No, but if we go out to eat that's all we get. It's a myth about wonderful French cooking.'

'So you often say.'

'Look at the marvellous places we can eat within — what, a five-mile radius of home?'

'You often say that as well.'

'Am I a bore?'

Judith put her hand over his. 'Darling, you have never bored me for a single moment since I married you.'

'Do you want another coffee?'

'I'll try and catch his eye. Do you want the same again?'

He did not reply but bent his head to continue scanning the newspaper. He was only just finishing it when the ever-unsmiling waiter brought their coffees.

'Interesting?'

He folded the paper. 'Just medical stuff. But yes.'

'You miss editing the journal, don't you?'

'Not really. Bit of a chore in the end.'

'You should write a book.'

'What on earth about?'

'All eminent doctors have a fund of stories.'

'So they may. I was not an eminent doctor.'

'Of course you were — but whatever, you still have plenty of things to say, stories to tell.'

He shook his head, draining his black coffee. 'Come on, let's saunter.'

The long street was dusty beneath the trees. Today there were no boules players on the sandy patch.

'Did you mean it, about wanting to live here?'

Judith turned to look at him in surprise. 'I don't know. No, I don't think I meant permanently. It's too far from the family and it isn't any warmer here in winter than at home. And you'd hate the life of an ex-pat . . . all that sitting about chatting to other expats just because they speak English.'

Richard groaned. 'But a little place to spend a month or two at a time — the families could come.'

'Not too little then.'

'If we turn round, we can go past the estate agent's window again.'

'Are you serious about this?'

'I don't see why not.'

'Half an hour ago you were ready to go home.'

'Was I? I'm not sure there's anything to rush home for.'

Judith slept for a couple of hours in the afternoon, but Richard only dozed in a chair for twenty minutes. The living room of the house gave onto a small terrace which had a vine growing over to give it deep, cool shade and he took his book out there. He had read the English papers earlier and found nothing to concern him, but the memory of his conversation with Tim continued to trouble him. He had been sanguine after he had put the phone down. Tim was his friend, Tim was a sensible man, Tim had been annoyed, understandably, but Richard was sure he accepted what he had said and wouldn't make any fuss.

But his concern would not go away. If Shelley refused to listen to her husband, if Shelley talked to a friend who then persuaded her not to let the matter drop, if the newspapers got hold of it . . .

He nodded off, still going over the scenarios. Judith's phone woke him.

'Dad? How are you both? I was a bit worried . . .'

'Why? We're fine, enjoying the sun. Nothing to worry about at all.'

'I'm relieved. Judith usually sends the odd message but she's been quiet on that too.'

'As I said. France is extremely relaxing. We're thinking of coming out here to live.'

'What?'

He gave a grunt of amusement. 'Not permanently, but we might buy something.

Spring and summer and so forth.'

'Gracious. But why not? It makes sense, I suppose.'

'I presume this isn't an emergency call? Felix hasn't stubbed a toe or something?'

'We're all fine, thanks, Dad. Miss you both.'

'You miss the extra childminders, that's all.'

'Not so . . . I said we miss you.'

'Judith's having a nap. I don't know how she can sleep in the middle of the day.'

'Heat.'

'Doesn't trouble me. I assume your brother's still underground or whatever they call it?'

'I presume so. No word.'

'They do enjoy their games.'

'I should think it's something more than a game to keep him under the radar for so long, Dad.'

'Hmm.'

'Have you no idea at all when you might be home?'

'None whatsoever. Why, has anyone been asking about me?'

'Only in a general way.'

'Who?'

'I can't recall . . . no one in particular.'

'Good. Well, don't let me keep you,

Catherine.'

In Lafferton, DCI Austin Rolph twisted and untwisted a paper clip, as an aid to thought. He had been reminded by a call from St Catherine's that Shelley Pendleton was still intent on pressing charges against Richard Serrailler and they wanted an update on the police response.

He threw the paper clip in the bin as he went out towards the CID room.

'Where is everyone?'

'Out and about, sir.' The only body present looked up from her computer. 'Anything I can do? I'm just signing off a missper as "Found", that's all.'

'Yes.' He swung the seat beside her desk round and sat. 'Rape case.'

'Oh good. I mean, not good. But . . . I mean . . .'

'All right, all right, just listen up.'

Ten minutes later, DC Clarke had Cat's home and mobile numbers. Then decided the face-to-face approach might be better.

When her car drew up at the door of the farmhouse, Sam was looking out of the window.

'Mum — there's a woman — silver VW Golf 1.4.'

Cat was changing into jeans, having just got back from a committee meeting at the hospice, and shouted down, 'I'm not expecting anyone. Probably wants to sell me something. Say no, politely, Sam.'

'I don't think so.'

'Why, do you recognise her?'

'No, but I can tell.'

Cat came down the stairs, pulling on her sweatshirt.

'She's a cop,' Sam said.

Cat froze, looking at him.

'It's OK,' he said, 'if it was . . .' But she had pushed past him and opened the door.

DC Clarke was already holding up her warrant card.

'Oh God,' Cat said. Sam had come to stand close to her. 'It's all right,' he said quietly.

'Dr Deerbon, I'm —'

'Just come in. Are you alone?'

Ellen Clarke looked surprised. 'Is that a problem?'

'Yes. No.' Cat's heart was banging in her chest. 'I thought — if it's bad news, aren't there usually two of you?'

'If you mean accidents and so on, then yes, but it isn't like that.'

'But it's my brother?'

'Sorry? Oh, the Super . . . No.'

'Where he is?'

'I don't know. As I said —'

'I'm so sorry, come into the kitchen. Sam, homework.'

'I want to make sure you're OK.'

'It's fine. But thank you. Go.'

He shrugged and wandered out slowly. Cat looked across at the officer and made a gesture to her to wait before saying anything else. She knew Sam's ability to lurk silently at the foot of the stairs, not wanting to miss anything.

'Sam . . .'

His footsteps went loudly and meaningfully up.

'Can I give you some tea? I'm making it, I haven't been in long.'

'Thank you. Yes, white, no sugar — thank you.'

Cat gestured to a kitchen chair, pushing a pile of papers and her laptop out of the way.

'You're sure this isn't about Simon?'

'Absolutely. I don't know anything at all about the Super, where he is or what he's doing. We just haven't been told.'

Making the tea, Cat went through things fast — speeding, jumping a red light, out-of-date car tax, lost purse, lost child . . . None of those.

She set down the tea.

'Dr Richard Serrailler,' the DC said.

'My father? Is . . . ?' No, of course there wasn't — if there had been an accident one CID constable wouldn't be here alone and calmly drinking tea. Would she?

'No, no bad news, everything's fine. Well, so far as we know.'

'My father and stepmother are in France on holiday, have been for a few weeks.'

'We need to make contact with him fairly urgently. We've had no response from the landline or his mobile, and as the Super is away as well . . .'

'Can you tell me what it's about? I might be able to help, save them having their holiday interrupted. Presumably it isn't anything serious?'

'Sorry, I'm afraid I can't tell you any more.'

'Meaning you don't know or you won't say?'

'Meaning we need to talk to Dr Serrailler.'

She hadn't quite left the textbooks behind, Cat thought. How old was she, twenty-seven? She checked herself, remembering the stiff little phrases she had used as a very junior doctor.

'Well, beyond giving you Judith's number, I can't give you any more information.'

The DC left without finishing her tea.

Sam watched over the banister.

'You all right, Mum?'

'Fine, thanks, Sam.'

'Uncle Si?'

'No.'

He came a few steps further down.

'Do CID ever carry weapons?'

'Lord, Sammy, I don't know! In the absence of your uncle, google it. Why do you want to know?'

'No particular reason.'

Cat heard him go back and close the door of his room, then she put the tea things away before ringing her father. The phone went straight to his irascible and curt voice-mail.

'Serrailler. Leave a message if it's important, don't if it isn't.'

Judith woke when the late-afternoon sun lanced through the half-open shutters onto her face. But the ringing of a phone echoed faintly in her ears too.

Silence.

She closed her eyes again and let herself relax back into a semi-doze, in which she seemed to be floating just above the surface of the bed. She had not felt like this, so rested, so peaceful, so unhurried and unconcerned, for a very long time, but France, this golden corner of the South-West, the slopes terraced by heavy vines, the wide fields of ripening maize and melons and sunflowers, the quietness and the slow pace of everything, had returned her to a tranquillity and a contentment she had almost forgotten were possible.

Somewhere in the fields across the valley, a tractor hummed. The birds were silent. Only the pigeons murmured of high summer.

An hour later she came out of the shower to find that Richard had set glasses and a bottle of chilled Sauvignon on the terrace and was refilling the anti-insect lamps with citronella. He smiled.

'You were right,' he said.

'Was I? Thank you for this, darling . . .' Judith poured out their wine. 'You look pleased about something.'

'I am. I rang the owner about staying on here for another six weeks. That should give us time to find somewhere to buy and sort everything out . . . French bureaucracy and all that.' He sat down and raised his glass. 'Here's to a life in France.'

'Well . . . Some life in France anyway.'

'I can't think of anything drawing us back, can you?'

'Of course.'

'Oh yes, yes, but they can come out here — plenty of the summer left . . . Look, aren't we happy at the moment? Aren't you? You look so well and rested.'

'You know I am.'

Richard frowned. 'You're willing to stay on for a few weeks now?'

'I think so. Unless anything happens.'

'What do you mean, "happens"? Accidents? Illnesses? Don't be neurotic.'

Judith did not reply. The edge to his tone made her uneasy. She did not want to irritate him, or to make him think badly of her.

'No, you're right,' she said eventually. 'Of course we should stay. Maybe we should go over to Preyssac tomorrow, try the estate agents there?'

He smiled. 'I can see through that one, my dear.' He refilled her glass. 'Tomorrow is Preyssac market day.'

'The thought had never occurred to me.'

She drank her wine, happy to be teased, glad of anything to make Richard happy. She would not like to spend half of the year in France, for all she loved it, but she would not say so. Not now. Not yet. And perhaps there would not be a house they liked enough to want to buy after all.

Her phone buzzed from the living room.
'You stay there, I'll go.'

'It's bound to be Vivien or Cat — or maybe David. Unless there's news of Simon . . .'

But he had gone out of earshot. The buzzing stopped.

'Hi, Judith, I'm leaving this on your phone as well as Dad's. You're probably sitting at a cafe table somewhere, and good for you. We're all absolutely fine, and no news from Simon, but if you get this first will you tell Dad to ring Lafferton Police Station? Not sure how urgent it is but one of them came here because they couldn't get hold of him, so he ought to call. Try you both later, or ring me, I'm at home. Lots of love . . .'

Richard listened to the message again, deleted it, and set the phone back on the table. When Judith asked, it had been a French number and a bad line.

FORTY-EIGHT

Luxury, Simon decided, was a power shower that could be switched in a nanosecond from scalding hot to ice cold. He spent a long time, alternating between the two, letting the freezing needles dance over his skin until he couldn't bear any more, then changing to hot. He had already had a very hot bath. Somehow, he needed to keep sluicing the stain of this house and Will off his body.

It was when he was putting on the clean shirt that had been laid out on the bed for him by the ever-efficient housekeeper that he realised his watch was missing. Snoopy. He went back to the bathroom but he knew he had not showered with it on. He had taken it off for the hot bath. So, it must be beside the bed.

It was not.

For the next five minutes, in a blind panic, he scoured the room before noticing that as well as bringing him a clean shirt, Lynn had taken a few clothes to be washed. She had also removed the two newspapers which he had read and which had been on the bedside table. The watch had probably been underneath them and been scooped up with the pages. He thought that he had never done anything so stupidly careless in his life.

'Johnno?' Will held up a bottle of beer, smoking with cold from the fridge that was tucked under the bookcases. 'Gin and tonic? Vodka?'

Serrailler nodded to the beer.

The double doors were open onto the garden, and the smell of night-scented stocks was a powerful memory of those his mother Meriel had always grown, up the path to the kitchen door at Hallam House. His teenage years, his youth, his return visits home during university and then as a rookie copper in the Met, evenings with a beer lying in the hammock after a cricket match . . . All, all of it came rushing back down the long corridor of time, to where he sat now, next to Andrew Morson, QC. Will Fernley was a yard away, head tipped back to let the icy Beck's slip down his throat.

'I didn't think you were usually home on a Thursday,' he said after a long drink.

'Adjournment. Nothing doing till Tuesday now.' He rattled the ice round his glass of vodka.

Whatever picture Will had given him of the barrister had been wrong. He was rough at the edges, where Simon had assumed smooth, short where he surely would be tall, his voice held a strong trace of Estuary/cockney, where he had expected plummy vowels. He was entirely bald, his skull polished and shining, as if it had never grown hair at all. It looked likely that he had alopecia. His features were small, snub, almost porcine, but his eyes were unusually large and wide open, and exceptionally blue. A medical condition? Cat would know at once. The fingers holding his glass were short, the hands very small, the backs as hairless as the head.

But he had welcomed him easily, was a relaxed host, asked no questions.

Those, Simon thought, would come any moment now.

It felt surreal, drinking chilled beer, smelling the stocks, enjoying the comforts of this house, forcing himself to remember who he was, why he was here, and to plan, to speculate, to work out how he could make contact. He glanced at Will. To him, surely, it must be even stranger. He had been in the prison system for five years, and yet he was relaxed, apparently comfortable, looking young, looking handsome, looking as if he had no anxiety. Presumably that meant he had none. Morson would look after him. Morson.

The man was looking at him. Simon's skin prickled.

'Another?'

'I'm fine thanks.'

Morson got up and refilled his own glass, handed Will a second bottle of beer without asking.

'So you were a schoolmaster, Johnno,' he said.

Serrailler's brain clicked into place.

'Hard to believe.'

Andrew smiled. 'I bet. Small boys?'

'God, no. Thirteen plus.'

'Couldn't trust yourself with prep-school boys?'

'Nothing like that. As Will knows.'

Fernley smiled.

'Just didn't want to be a nanny. I like good brains — clever young men.'

'Sciences?'

'Nope. English. And cricket.'

Andrew gave a short laugh. 'Cricket, what! Nice for you both.' He nodded at Fernley.

'Probably why they put us next to each

other at Stitchford.'

'My God, the OB network spreads its tentacles bloody wide.'

'You have a problem with that?'

'With public schools as schools? Not really. With the lifelong privileges it gets you — I think so, Johnno. I think so.'

Morson sat silently for a few seconds, swirling the drink round his glass, before he shook his head slightly, looking at them both.

'So, when do you reckon it will be safe for you to leave here? No rush as far as I'm concerned, place is yours for as long as you like. But I should think you want to move on? Abroad or something?'

'Couple of weeks,' Will said. 'Maybe ten days. Johnno?'

'Thing is, we're safe here — and thanks, Andrew, by the way . . . thanks for this. I don't underestimate the risk you're taking.'

Morson laughed. 'Not really. Not the French Resistance.'

'All the same . . .'

'Eminent QC hides nonces in luxury mansion.'

'The QC would go, for starters.'

'There'll be a surveillance on our homes, twenty-four/seven.'

'Still . . . You've got friends.'

'I've got friends.'

Simon remained relaxed, legs stretched out, tone casual. His sixth sense was alert. Morson's eyes did not leave his face, when he said, 'Like to watch a film?'

A split second. 'Great.'

'Thought you might.'

Across the hall. Through a door. Along a passage. Short flight of narrow stairs, with the ceiling so low, Simon had to bend his head and shoulders.

'Did you see this? Help yourselves if you're interested.' He had opened a door and switched on a light, showing a long room with a full-size billiard table, and a dartboard on one wall.

'Drinks in there.' Morson pointed to a dark wood cupboard. 'Fridge inside. You play, Johnno?'

'Badly.'

'Yeah, not really a public-school game, billiards. Come on through.'

He led the way to a door in the panelling at the far end. Another room. Small. When the door was closed Simon was at once aware of the soft deadness of a room with full sound-proofing. A sofa. Deep matching armchairs. Low table. Another drinks cupboard. A wall-mounted screen.

Morson switched on a lamp, and opened

a cupboard below the screen. 'Take a look. Anything you fancy?'

Rows of DVDs. Major feature films — westerns, horror, crime, adventure, drama, even musicals.

He'd been wrong then.

He bent down. *The Magnificent Seven . . . True Grit . . .'*

'Fred Astaire?' There was a mocking unpleasantness in the barrister's voice now.

A row of complete operas. Wagner. Mozart. Donizetti.

Above, films of old steam-engine journeys, vintage cars, Second World War light aircraft.

It was the collection of a man who bought by the dozen, everything he fancied, everything his guests might fancy. He could come down here, have his supper brought, watch for hour after hour, glass always topped up.

Nice.

'Nothing?'

He noticed that Will Fernley was standing back, thumbs in the belt of his jeans, waiting.

Serrailler said nothing.

'OK.' Morson slid one of the racks of DVDs aside. It moved easily. Behind was a large wall safe. He bent in and positioned himself so that they could not see as he turned the combination several times.

When the door swung open, Simon saw that the safe was set back deeply into the old wall. The click of a switch. A low light. He did not try to peer in, just waited, next to Fernley.

Rows of DVDs in plain boxes. After a moment or two, Morson stepped back with half a dozen in his hand, swung the safe door to and re-locked it. Slid the concealing shelf back into place.

'Do for a start,' he said. 'Make yourself comfortable, Johnno. What can I get you to drink?'

The vodka bottle came up from the fridge.

The remote control was on the arm of Morson's armchair. It controlled the lights in the room as well as the screen and the sound.

Serrailler's stomach tightened. One lamp was left on, in the corner a yard away from him. If he closed his eyes, it would be noted. He took a deep breath and let it out slowly. Will was sitting slightly forward on the sofa, glass in hand, eyes fixed intently on the screen.

The first forty minutes were among the worst Serrailler had ever endured. He tried to distract himself from the horrifying pictures and desperate sounds by counting, by remembering Latin conjugations and the Greek alphabet, by working out chemical formulae, by trying to put his own images — of places, of his family, of the Venice lagoon, of cricket — between his eyes and the screen. None of it worked, none of it blotted out what he was forced to watch, and several times, he was aware that Morson was glancing at him, wanting to share his own excitement, so that he could barely blink let alone close his eyes. He remembered that the CEOP teams watched this sort of thing day in, day out, and wondered again how they could bear it.

The screen went blank for a second. Morson fast-forwarded, then went to Pause.

'Here we go then,' he said. He turned to Simon. 'Hope you enjoyed the warm-up.'

What he had seen was inside his head and could never be unseen, never be erased, it would haunt his waking and sleeping and bring him nightmares that caused him to break out in a sweat. But a few minutes into the next film, he stood up quickly.

'You all right?'

'No. I'm sorry, but I don't do this. This is where I draw the line. Not me. Not my thing.'

Morson went to Pause again.

'I'm surprised,' he said. 'I had you down for a man who would relish a snuff movie. Like Will here.'

'Nope. You had me wrong.'

Serrailler found the door, and the dark steps, the passageway. Found himself, about to vomit, in the wide entrance hall of the house. He went out.

The garden smelled of night, after the heat of the day, smelled sweet and cool and earthy and green. He walked straight ahead, across the grass, under an archway, alongside a stone wall. There was a half-moon, enough to see by. He reached a huge old beech tree and leaned on the trunk, breathing deeply, feeling the nausea churn in his belly. The bark was cold and smooth under his fingertips and oddly comforting.

What he felt most of all, over the sickness, the disgust, the shock of what he had seen, was anger, like a hot nail driving down through him, anger, and a passionate resolve. He would have Morson, he would bring him down and, with him, however many others there were in his ring of evil and degradation. He would break them open and pick them off, as many as there were. He punched his fist hard into the tree trunk. The thought of going to his room, to bed, to try and sleep after what he had seen, was terrifying. Perhaps this was how men felt when they had been in war, witnesses to unspeakable sufferings. But they were so often helpless in the face of such things. He was not. He could not be. He had drifted through his recent days, as he had simply put his head down and got on with his time in Stitchford, slightly detached, listening and trying to find out what he could, yet with an odd sense that he was playing some sort of game. Not any more.

He thumped the tree again and again, until his knuckles bled.

FORTY-NINE

'Judith, at last! I've been trying and trying to reach you, I've left messages — I was beginning to worry.'

Judith sat on the edge of the bed, looking out through the open windows at soft summer rain veiling the garden. She had woken to it, and to the refreshing smell of wet grass.

'I haven't had any messages, darling, but I think there might have been something wrong with my phone.'

'And I've left them for Dad . . . I know you're in France but it isn't usually as bad as this.'

'Is everything all right? You sound a bit frantic.'

'I am a bit frantic. Listen, I've no idea what it's all about, almost certainly nothing, but I've had the police here asking for Dad, and before your blood pressure soars, it's nothing to do with Simon — no news at all there. It's Dad they want to talk to — is he there?'

'No, he's gone into Cahors to try and get his reading glasses repaired. But what's it about?'

'No idea, but will you get him to pick up his messages? — I've left the CID woman's number for him?'

'Of course I will. And what about all of you?'

'Fine, and there's something else you might tell Dad — just pick your moment, he might not be remotely interested, but I've been asked to give the second Caxton Philips lecture at Bevham General.'

'Cat! And of course your father will be interested, he'll be thrilled to bits.'

'Hmm. Anyway, I'm pleased — the first one was given by Dame Irene Higgins. Follow that.'

When the invitation had come, she had been astonished, and then immediately decided to refuse. The American philanthropist George Caxton Philips had been the largest benefactor to Imogen House, and for a time had lived near Lafferton with his young wife, but he had returned to the States and died shortly afterwards. The lecture in his memory was well endowed and prestigious. What had she to say for an hour to a lecture hall packed with medics, the great and the good? She did not understand why she had been asked at all. But Judge Gerald Hanbury, who was on the lecture committee, had persuaded her that she ought to accept.

'Caxton Philips virtually built the hospice. He loved Lafferton — that's why he endowed a lecture here, and not at some big London hospital. He would have been very unhappy about what's happened recently because of our financial problems — if he'd been alive we would have gone to him for help. He knew you, you've been one of the driving forces behind the hospice for a long time, and you have sound experience of palliative care, you're informed, you have opinions . . . Come on, Cat. Next time we can find some prof from out there, probably the States, but I've no doubt that this time it should be you.'

Certainly, she had plenty of opinions she wanted to air, even more since she had been to see Elaine Dacre. She felt a spurt of excitement at being given such a platform. She wanted to throw out challenges, encourage people, speak out about what she believed had been brushed aside for too long by too many people.

After talking to Judith, she went upstairs

to change. Would her father be pleased? Proud? If he was he would never in a million years tell her so.

She put it out of her mind. She was going out into the garden to pull up a large dead rose bush that had been killed by last winter's frost, and whose bare greyness, in the middle of the otherwise lushly flowering border, had been annoying her for weeks.

As she went across the landing, her foot caught against a cricket ball, lurking against the skirting board, and she almost crashed over. She picked it up and went into Sam's room, put it in the middle of his desk and looked for a pen — *'I might have killed myself tripping over this. PLEASE DO NOT —'* She stopped in mid-sentence, seeing the printed-out sheets, half a dozen of them, with photographs, descriptions, and some brief notes at the sides in Sam's handwriting. At the bottom of the last sheet were a couple of mobile phone numbers, and what might be a name — Zak M.

Digging up a well-rotted old bush was hard work and it kept her from pacing about the house waiting for Sam to come in, but it could not keep her mind from running round like a hamster on a wheel, question after question popping up and not one of

407

them easily answered or dismissed. Leaning on the garden fork for a moment's rest, Cat suddenly felt the chill of aloneness. Everyone was away or out of contact or dead.

'Help me please,' she said, half a prayer, half a message to herself.

But although still a believer, still dependent on her faith and practice, she knew that whatever her Christianity was about, it was not about magic.

She pulled up the fork and attacked the dead roots again in a fury, but dealing with the bush did not help her own feelings.

She sat on the old bench beside the gate and got out her phone.

'CID.'

'I'd like to speak to whoever is standing in for DCS Serrailler please.'

'This is DC Pitman. Can I help you?'

'Not unless you can put me through, or give me a name.'

'Who is it calling?'

'Dr Cat Deerbon — I am Superintendent Serrailler's sister.'

'Hold on.'

She held on, was put through to two other people who were not standing in for Simon, could not get a name out of anyone, and left a message without much hope of it reaching the right place. She could think of no good reason why they needed to keep the identity of someone's deputy a dark secret, but the frustration of it made her feel even more isolated.

The phone rang after supper.

'Dr Deerbon? This is Kieron Bright — Chief Constable.'

She sat down. 'Oh no . . .'

'No, it's all right, I'm not ringing with bad news — or with any news at all about Simon — but I found out that you'd called the Lafferton station. There wasn't any reason why you shouldn't have been put through to the acting Super — his name is DCI Austin Rolph, by the way — but in future, will you come straight to me? I may not be available there and then but I will always ring you back.'

'Thank you — thanks so much. You're sure you're telling me the truth — nothing's happened to him?'

'Listen — there is a very limited amount I can say and you'll have to understand that I'm not able to give reasons but I don't want to do this over the phone. I'd prefer to talk face-to-face. Can I come out and see you?'

FIFTY

A soft knock on his door.

'Brought you a beer.'

Simon was standing by the open window, listening to an owl in the copse and trying to let its gentle hooting soothe him. He had washed his knuckles under the cold tap but the gash he had inflicted on himself still smarted.

Will had closed the door behind him and now he stood just inside the room, holding the beer bottle. He was the last person Serrailler wanted to talk to, except perhaps Morson.

'You OK?'

He did not reply.

'Listen . . . there wasn't much I could do. That last lot of stuff . . .'

'I can't take it . . . not snuff movies. Never could. Just way too far.'

'Not sure about them myself, but Andrew's always been into them. He's got tapes where —'

'Shut up.'

'Well — have the beer.'

'Can you just put it down there?'

He clenched his fist in spite of the injury. He wanted to smash it into Fernley's face. Into Morson's face. He knew he was on the verge of being unable to control himself.

Instead of leaving, Will came to stand by him at the window. The owl hooted again.

'Love that sound. When I was a small boy, I rescued a newly fledged tawny — it had fallen out of the nest onto a ledge. I climbed up and got it, put it higher up. The mother came and fed it there . . . kind of good deed, I thought.'

Simon turned to look at him. His face had softened with the memory. He was a good-looking man. He spoke quietly. How? How, how, how? Thinking of what Will had just sat calmly watching in the basement room, watching with such greed and excitement, his head swam. He had heard Fernley in the group therapy sessions, explaining what he had done, how he felt about it. He had listened and he might have been listening to an actor in a play, spouting out a false confession, working up their emotions, sweating to try and convince those men how he belonged, was one of them and worse than some. Just as he himself had done.

But tonight, the reality of it all had come home to him, the reason he had been there and was now in this house he was desperate to get away from, a vile, tainted, depraved place which would leave its stain on him for the rest of his life.

'Andrew's happy to get us to the next stage — cars, drivers — perfectly safe.'

'He can't know that. It's not safe.'

'He's done it before. OK, not exactly the same — but people needing to move somewhere discreetly.'

'Right. I might head north.'

'Do you have somewhere?'

'Probably.'

'Listen, Johnno . . . I don't know what's got to you. Is it just what we did catching up with you or is it something else? Can't just be that stuff tonight, you've seen plenty of that, for God's sake, or why are you here?'

'Sorry.' Simon put a hand on Fernley's shoulder. 'Delayed shock . . . I get nightmares — because if we're taken, it's not going to be back to Stitchford, is it?'

'You had a bad time, didn't you? They beat you up?'

'You could say. Rather not talk about it at this time of night.'

'I'll go. Want me to slip down and get you

a Scotch to chase the beer? Or Andrew will have some pills, make you sleep like the dead.'

'I'm OK. Thanks for the drink.'

A door slammed somewhere. Footsteps hard up the stairs.

'Shit.'

They turned as Morson crashed into the room. 'They've hacked into Blind Runner . . .' He leaned against the door jamb to catch his breath.

'It isn't possible.'

'No, it isn't, but they've done it all the same. They've got into the back room, which means they've got the lists, contact emails.'

Fernley's face was white. 'For fuck's sake . . . are you sure?'

'Of course I'm bloody sure!'

'How? *How?*'

'A leak. Has to be.'

'No way.'

They were talking across Serrailler. He might not have been there. There was panic on their faces, in their voices — controlled, but still panic.

'I need to talk to someone,' Will said.

'PAYG mobile in my desk drawer, right-hand side, with the pens. Bring it up here.'

When Will had bolted out of the room,

Morson seemed to calm down and relax. He wandered over to the open window and stood listening. The owl was still there, its soft hoot filling the garden.

'You're OK, are you, Johnno?'

'What about?'

'Your network, you idiot.'

'Don't know — haven't had a chance to check. Anyway, it's a long time since I was on there, isn't it?'

'I wouldn't know. You might have had all sorts of things set up from Stitchford.'

'You're kidding.'

'Deprived, then, I take it.'

'You get used to it.'

'Did he?' Andrew swung round. 'Will? Must have been frustrating and he's an impatient sort of bloke. I'm surprised you threw in your lot with him.'

Andrew's eyes did not leave Serrailler's face.

'Right. You can get online from here.'

'Better not.'

'Be quite safe.'

'Not given what's gone on with yours, I don't think so. Can't risk it anyway.'

'What's your username?'

'As if I'd tell you.'

'Safe with me.'

Simon shook his head. 'Can I use the

phone after he's done?'

'Be my guest.'

Will came back with a basic-pay-as-you-go phone in his hand. 'You sure this is OK?'

He looked strained.

'Perfectly. Unused. It's the safest way. I'll leave you to it. When you're done Johnno here wants a turn.'

Left alone, Serrailler stood, thinking, thinking. If they had managed to black out a member of the paedophile ring Morson was central to, they would have enough information to trace a lot of people. It was a breakthrough, certainly, but it had put him in more danger. He needed to alert his contact and plan a getaway. He *needed* Snoopy . . .

When Will brought the phone back, he checked it out. Nothing. Whoever had been contacted, the number and message had been deleted. Using it, though, to send a covert police message was chancy. Cat. One text? No. If there was the remotest chance that Morson could call up the number, it could put her in danger. He had learned over many years that there is no such thing as absolute safety, or any move that was entirely without risk.

He made up a number, sent a text that

said *Am OK* and deleted it all. Not to have done so would have looked suspicious.

He lay on his bed, fully dressed, waiting for the house to fall silent, time to pass.

He had to find his watch. If it had gone with the old newspapers Lynn might have put them in the recycling bin, in which case he would find it. If it was with his dirty clothes, he hoped to God she had not put it through the washing machine. If she hadn't, and it had dropped out of the bundle, he could either go and ask her the next day, or hope she would return it to him. But to-night, he could at least do one search.

He waited until a quarter to three, then put on the old cotton jacket Morson had found for him and which fitted loosely, took two bananas and an apple from the fruit bowl, and the now-tepid bottle of beer. Nothing else because he had nothing else. He was only taking extreme precautions. Chances were he would be back in his bed safely, watch intact, within the hour. But he had an odd sense that he might be at risk, and he had learned long ago not to ignore his gut instincts.

He moved with infinite patience and care, one small step, barely the length of his foot, then stop, listen, wait, one small step. The wood settled into itself, the boards shifted, but he had become used to the sounds the house made of its own accord and tried to work with them and not make more of his own. It took five full minutes to cross the landing to the first staircase, after which he stood for another minute, scarcely breathing, not touching the banister, hands against his sides. One step down, millimetre by millimetre. Ten minutes to go down the stairs. Five on the second landing, and here, he was even more careful, if that were possible, because Morson's room was a couple of yards to his right. He heard a faint snore. There was not a sliver of light.

His hand bumped very slightly against the head of the banister and he froze. Nothing. Two more minutes. Three. Four. He moved again.

It was easier once he had reached the wide hall, and started to inch his way to the side door. He was unsure if anyone had a room on this side of the house but took no chances, still moved at snail pace and with the greatest stealth, still paused, listened, holding his breath. There was no hurry other than to do it all before the sun rose, and before the others surfaced out of the deepest sleep into a lighter one during which they might become aware of sounds.

He slid bolts. Found the key on the shelf.

Turned the lock. It made a slight click but the noise was deadened by the thick walls on either side. Wait again.

He pulled the door to gently behind him but did not close it.

He had to work out where the bins might be. Two false tries, and then he found them, under a wooden overhang next to the wood store, and accessible by the dust cart beside the back entrance. There were three bins, one for garden refuse and two others. So far as he knew, there had not been a collection in the last three days. Waste disposal of any kind is never a quiet operation but still might well not have been heard from upstairs and right round on the other side. He lifted the lid of the first black bin. It was full to the top, the lid barely closing. The second was not much emptier which meant collection was imminent.

The watch and newspapers would have gone into a recycling sack and there were several.

The top bag was obviously full of plastic bottles and boxes. The next was extremely heavy. He felt about and his hand touched what felt like something made of metal. Even the owl had fallen silent now.

He hauled out the bag and saw not a bag but a large cardboard box underneath it, full to the top with papers. It would not be difficult to sort through them, though it would take time to pick each newspaper up, shake it, put it to one side, take up the next. He was about to bend down and make a start when he was half blinded by a bright blue-white light shining directly into his eyes.

'Have you lost something, Johnno?'

FIFTY-ONE

'I can't believe you mean this, Shelley —
after everything that's happened, everything
you've gone through up to now.'

'I do mean it.'

'You haven't thought it through.'

'I *have* thought it through, I've done nothing else but think it through, and inside and
out and upside and down. I haven't slept
for thinking it through.'

'Something's happened, hasn't it?'

'No.'

'Something's happened, someone's said
something. Was it Tim? You haven't told
anyone else, have you?'

'Tim's been the same from the start. He
didn't want me to go this far and he's never
wavered.'

'Then what, Shelley? Don't you think you
owe it to me to tell me? Last time you were
here you were rock solid — you were pressing charges, nothing more certain. Today

you come in and you've changed your mind. Something must have happened.'

Shelley stared out of the window at the summer rain. The traffic below moved along silently, sound muffled by the double glazing in the consulting room. She did not look at Tina because she felt ashamed of meeting her counsellor's eye.

'Listen . . . a lot of women who come in here are not only like you, frightened, in shock, hurt — physically hurt, emotionally hurt — they're also all over the place and the one thing they want to do is blot it out, run away, have it over with, and they're often women who are terrified of what will happen to them if they do press charges against the man — assuming they know his identity. If they don't, they're terrified the police will find him and that will put them in danger . . . they're not women who are very familiar with the police and the court process — or if they are, it's not in a good way, I can tell you. They might have been up before the court themselves, in prison even — and once that's happened, they're convinced no one will believe them, and with good reason. It shouldn't affect things but I'm afraid all too often it does. If they get even as far as us they're doing incredibly well. But you've no reason to fear the police, you don't have a criminal record, you're — well, let's just say you're the kind of woman a court is likely to believe. Why would you go this far? Why would you lie? What possible reason could you have? Shelley, listen to me — I'm here for you, this place is behind you, all of us, the whole system, everything we can muster — you can afford a top lawyer —'

'So can he.'

'All right, but —'

'I know what sort of man he is, Tina, because, basically, he's the sort I married, other than the fact that Tim would never in a million years do what Serrailler did. But he's a pillar of the community, doctor, highly respected, Freemason, all that . . . they're not going to take my word against his, of course they're not. That's what I suddenly realised. I'd be mad to go into court against him. And when I lost, which I would, how would that play out in the future? With my life, with my marriage, for both of us living here? Think of what it would be like every day, when I went shopping, if we ate out, just everyday life . . . think how people would look and point, you try putting yourself into that place.'

'I have,' Tina said quietly. 'I do it every day.'

Shelley started to cry. Small, silent, pathetic tears rolled down her cheeks.

Tina pushed the box of tissues across the low table. She waited. Shelley got up and turned her back, staring out of the window at the rain. Tina poured some water, drank it all. Looked at Shelley's back. Looked at rain dashing against the windows. Waited.

Eventually, and without turning round, Shelley said, 'One more week.'

'That's brilliant!' Tina got up and went to hug her, but Shelley stiffened. She used to hug and kiss easily, had always been affectionate with everyone, from her two small nephews upwards. Now, she couldn't bear anyone to come close to her. She had to brace herself when Joshua and Luke clung round her legs, wanting to be picked up. She could not let Tim near her at all.

'Sorry,' she said.

FIFTY-TWO

Cat had only met Paula Devenish, the old Chief Constable, a couple of times and she had found her formidable, though she knew Simon had liked her, worked closely with her, and been sorry when she retired. He had said nothing about her replacement before he had disappeared.

CC Kieron Bright was surprisingly young, though she smiled as she caught herself thinking so.

She made coffee and they went into the sitting room. The rain was over and the sky had cleared to a hazy blue. Drops of water caught in the hollows of leaves and petals glittered in the last rays of the sun.

He was a relaxed man, leaning back in his chair with an easy manner, out of uniform and wearing pale blue chinos and a sweat-shirt, but his expression was alert, on a long-nosed, wide-mouthed face. There was a sharpness in his look. He would not miss

424

much. He had drunk his coffee straight off and accepted another, saying little though doing so amiably, but when he set his mug down, he leaned forward.

'Right. Simon,' he said. 'The first thing is for me to reassure you — I have no bad news. All I can tell you is that he's under-cover, on a very sensitive operation, and I am the only person in the station who knows where and why. I'm not his direct contact but I'm next in line. If I hear anything at all that I can tell you I will. Listen, you're aware of his work with SIFT, you've had him vanish for days or even weeks before now, you know how it is.'

'Yes, I do, and I know better than to probe, don't worry. He'll surface.'

He leaned back again and smiled. 'He will, trust me.'

'Dangerous thing to say. I very much appreciate your taking the trouble to come out here though.'

'Thanks.' He paused. The sharp look again. Then, 'That wasn't your only reason for ringing the station, was it? You had a visit from a DC, asking about Dr Richard Serrailler but not saying why.'

Cat was taken aback. Chief constables did not usually concern themselves with the small stuff of everyday police enquiries, they had the broader picture to worry about. So perhaps it was not a trivial matter and all she could think about was that it was to do with Judith. But Judith would never in a million years go to the police about anything personal, no matter what he had done. She had never even admitted that Richard had been violent towards her.

She suddenly felt sick.

'I've no idea why my father is supposed to be contacting the police but please don't keep anything from me.'

Kieron said nothing for a long moment, and looked out of the window, thinking, working something out. She liked the fact that he had not come with a stock set of bland phrases which told her nothing, that he was not impulsive or glib.

'Right,' he said. 'You're a doctor, you know all about confidentiality. So do I. Legally, I may be doing the wrong thing here but I'm going to live with that because I think you should know, if only to be prepared. But can we assume for a moment that you are in the surgery and what I say is under that seal?'

He waited for her answer.

'I think so. Yes.'

When he told her, his voice was calm. Cat thought that few people, especially few men in his position, could have said what he had to say to her with such tact and gentleness.

It did not take long because he could not give her much detail. When he had finished, her first reaction was a clear-headed and unemotional one. She was not surprised. The fact that her father was to be charged with rape should have been shocking, upsetting and horrifying. It was not. It was as though many things which had been floating about apparently at random in the depths of her mind now clicked together and she saw a clear picture. She did not doubt that it was true.

'Thank you,' she said to Kieron Bright. 'I'm grateful for your honesty and the fact that you've told me won't go any further.'

She was very tired, deflated, but quite composed. Perhaps the facts had not gone deep enough for her to feel anything else. Perhaps she would start to cry, or shake or be angry before long.

No. No, she decided. She was as she was. Her first concern was that Judith had to be prepared and looked after, her second that everything should be put in train as soon as possible.

'He has to come back,' she said. 'I'll talk to him. He obviously must know what the calls were about and he's deliberately avoiding any sort of contact, but he has to. I'll phone him later tonight. Judith will make him talk to me.'

She heard the sound of a car in the drive — the Lawsons, bringing Sam home after cricket. Seconds later, the front door slammed and he was in, calling for her, slinging his bag across the hall.

'A hundred and seventy-four!' He came dancing in, punching the air, and stopped dead.

'Oh.'

'Sam, this is Kieron Bright — Chief Constable Bright. My son Sam.'

'Having scored massively by the sound of it.' Kieron stood up and shook Sam's hand, clapped him on the back. 'Good man.' Exactly as Simon would have done, Cat thought.

Sam scrutinised him for a second. 'Why does your force still use the Remington 870?'

'Not for much longer.' The Chief didn't miss a beat. 'I'm phasing it out.'

'For the Glock 17?'

'Yup. Much better gun.'

'Most forces use the Glock. The Met does.'

'You interested?'

Sam shrugged. 'Yeah, well . . . Nice to

428

meet you.' He turned at the door, his face anxious. 'There's nothing wrong with Uncle Si, is there?'

'No,' Cat said, 'he's fine. Did you eat enough at teatime?'

'No, rotten tea, shop cakes as well, but I had fish and chips with the Lawsons. Cheers, then.' He banged out and up the stairs.

'I think what Sam just asked you lifts a bit of a cloud.'

'Unusual question — interesting. Why?'

'Oh, I found a load of stuff in his room about guns . . . pictures of guns, write-ups about guns, clips out of gun mags, downloads from the Internet. He hadn't hidden them or anything but, well, you know . . .'

He laughed. 'Take your point, but just think — better than a stash of spliffs or a pile of porn mags.'

'I wasn't so sure at the time. Kieron, I'm in need of a drink. Can I get you a glass of wine or a beer?'

He hesitated. She knew he had driven himself, so he probably wouldn't want alcohol.

'Or just more coffee?'

In the second during which she sensed that he was going to accept, his mobile rang. He glanced at her in apology but answered at once.

'Kieron Bright.'

He said nothing else, just listened. Something about his expression made Cat stop. Wait.

'OK,' he said. His face did not give away much. Just enough. 'I've got to go.'

The words 'Sorry. Thanks . . .' came back to her as he raced to his car.

She stood there, watching the dust rise as he hit the road, knowing the call could have been about any one of a thousand police matters, dreading that it had been about Simon. But if it had been, he would have stopped just long enough to tell her as much.

It was not her brother she was most concerned about now.

FIFTY-THREE

'Can you get that light out of my eyes please?'

Andrew Morson stepped forward, to stand beside Simon near the bins. He wore a waxed coat over his pyjamas, and wellington boots. He was smirking.

'Just worried about you going through my bins. But you seem to have found what you wanted, Johnno.'

He was too quick. He had grabbed the watch before Simon had time to realise what he was doing. He shone the torch on it, turned it over, examined the small buttons on the side.

'Odd, don't you think? Where did you get this?'

'At a service station, a fiver with a fill-up of diesel. Can't remember exactly.'

Morson held the watch up. 'Really worth all that cloak-and-dagger stuff just to get this back?'

'Just didn't want to lose the only timepiece I've got.'

'You're behaving like a kid that lost his teddy . . . Interesting array of knobs here. You get this sort of thing on a Patek Philippe or a Rolex.'

'Hardly. They're just dummies, aren't they?'

'Are they? Let's give them a go.'

Simon shrugged. He knew that the buttons only worked if pressed in the correct sequence, and the chances of that were fairly low — but on the other hand, there were only four buttons.

Morson fiddled about for a moment. Nothing. Or, at least, there were no beeps or flashes.

'So why bother to come down and sort through the bins at half three in the morning? Maybe I'm missing something obvious. Am I? But in my job, it never pays to do that, so generally I don't.'

His voice was silken, his head was cocked slightly on one side, and he was almost smiling. But not quite. His eyes, as they met Serrailler's, did not blink. Simon's left hand twitched.

'Well, never mind. You're here now, whatever time it is. Odd though. Can I keep this? It's only worth a fiver. I'll give you a fiver.'

Serrailler took a pace back. 'You'd be welcome to it except that I don't have another, and to be honest, I've got a bit attached to it. I've had it inside for a long time.'

'Like your old teddy bear. Your constant companion. Sort of talisman, is it? I understand totally. I feel like that about my ancient shooting jacket. Still, I've taken a bit of a shine to it, Johnno.'

He pressed the buttons: one, two, three, four.

Simon lunged forward suddenly, and the torch went out as Morson hit the ground and he ran fast into the darkness.

The side path led to the drive, and he knew that the gates could only be opened by the activation of an electronic barrier. They were impossible to scale. He kept close to the high wall and ran to where the garden gave onto a rising meadow which had a ring of trees at its crown. There was no hiding place here but the rise dropped down quickly on the far side, and then towards a thick hedge. Beyond that was open country — too open. He expected an alarm to have started up but there was silence and the security lights had not been switched on. It was possible that he had knocked Morson out cold and now had a head start. He did not let himself think further.

It was still pitch dark but he found a weak gap in the hedge, and pushed his way through, tearing his shirt and his arm on brambles. There was a ditch on the other side. He dropped down and lay until his breathing slowed. He had no means of making contact with base and no idea at all of what Morson might do.

However, he had come to suspect that Johnno Miles was not Johnno Miles; now he would be certain of it, though he had no way of finding out his real identity. That was irrelevant. He had been clever enough to start probing. The explanation about the plastic watch being a beloved object because it had been with him in prison had not held water for a moment. But when he came round, he might play about with it until he discovered what happened when everything was pressed in the right order. Nobody would reply, there would be no voice, no beeping, but Simon was certain that Morson was suspicious enough to investigate further, and perhaps even discover that 'Johnno Miles' was an undercover cop.

Something scurried close to his feet at the bottom of the ditch and he got up quickly. A rat bite was the last thing he needed.

He had to hide out, moving across country, until he came to any sort of house, service station, farm. Even better, if he came to a village he would be able to get access to a phone — probably by simply asking for it. The news blackout on their escape meant that he would not be recognised, and although he looked scruffy, he thought he could provide a plausible explanation for that.

He stayed long enough to eat the banana he had taken from the house, which gave him a shot of energy, and then moved on. He had about two and a half hours before dawn. The countryside was silent, he had not heard a single vehicle or seen any headlights. It would be safe, at least for a time, and much faster, to get onto a road.

Morson was winded and disorientated. He was also angry. He had come round after ten minutes, realised that he was not badly hurt and unlikely to suffer any damage beyond a sore head. He got up cautiously. Took a few deep breaths. Went back into the house, to make two phone calls.

A few minutes later, he heard the Range Rover start up in the yard.

Painkillers and brandy took some time to work on his blinding headache and he lay thinking, not about 'Johnno' — that would be taken care of now — but about how the ring could have been cracked and then disabled, who had let anything slip, what information might have leaked out. Email addresses, servers, ISPs, they all led somewhere in the end.

Everyone had been alerted on a separate server and gone offline. There were other ways of keeping contact going though it would be unwise to use them.

No one knew better than he did how big the risk was now, how high the stakes, but most of them had everything to lose if it came to public exposure.

FIFTY-FOUR

Three men, one woman. The small room was one of the few in the building with a light on. They were staring at an enlarged Google Earth map showing an area of open country. It was 3.30 a.m.

Someone came in without knocking. 'Guv — we've got a red.'

The officer whistled. 'Where is he?'

The man who had come in bent over to the screen of the laptop. 'Not that far away from where he last showed up.' He scrolled, clicked, enlarged. Homed in.

'This is still very rural. Now — he's within this area . . . two square miles or so of this point.'

'Shouldn't be too difficult.'

'You're taking the piss.'

They scrolled down. Fields. Hedges. More fields. Ditches. A farm. A cluster of buildings and a church marking a village. Big house and garden next to the church. Three more houses. Two footpaths, one B-road, one lane. One pond.

'Signal's dead.'

'Shit.'

They stood about in silence, staring at the computer screen and the map as if they might come alive and tell them what was happening, what they should do.

'I'm getting Craig out of bed,' the DI said.

'He won't thank you.'

But the Super was awake, making tea in his Ealing kitchen because his mind was crowded with problems, none of which had straightforward solutions, and he had indigestion after a late curry. He listened, drinking his tea too hot. Thought for half a minute while the DI was silent, knowing he would get a clear and coherent set of orders.

'Right. Serrailler's safety is now first priority. I'm on my way, and meanwhile, here's what we do.'

FIFTY-FIVE

It would be light by half past five. He would keep moving until then, hope to reach a place where he could get to a phone. He had no money but he would find something, even persuade a newsagent to let him make a call to the nearest police station. If he hit a town where there was a station, even better. Morson would now know that he was not Johnno Miles but what could he do about that?

Ten minutes later, alert but judging that it was safe to leave the shelter of the hedge, he came out into a lane and started to jog. Running would have been faster but he wanted to conserve his energy.

He didn't hear the car. The headlights were behind but then suddenly all over him, covering him in what seemed to be a single piercing, brilliant light. He had nowhere to go. The man was out of the 4 × 4, onto him and had brought him down before he could get out of the way. He felt a blow to the back of his head which did not knock him out completely, and then a punch in his solar plexus which sent him reeling, fighting to breathe.

He was choking as he felt himself kicked off his feet then lifted over the back of the vehicle so that he tumbled forward. His chest burned and his throat ached with the effort to get two consecutive breaths and, when he did so, he was kicked in the stomach, winded again, and hit with something that made the inside of his head flare briefly like a bonfire being set alight, then go black.

The last thing Frankie wanted was to drive too fast and hit a random cop car on night patrol looking for stolen vehicles. He kept to the speed limits. The van heading up to meet him would do the same. But it was quiet, even on the dual carriageway. No sound from behind him. He'd knocked the man out, that was all. It was up to the others to do the rest.

He turned on the radio low — traffic news, weather, phone-ins from the miserable and the desperate and the idiotic, uber-cheery presenter, seeing you through the small hours. Another twenty minutes and he was heading into a town. Another twenty, he'd start to look out. He knew the meeting point.

He wasn't bothered about any of it. All in the night's work. He'd done plenty of unusual jobs and Lynn never asked questions. Why else did they get paid so much, plus the coach house, the cars, the food and drink, the holidays, the account cards? They'd never cheated. He was proud of that. Everything they spent was accounted for and the statements transparent. Meanwhile, pincers straight from the furnace wouldn't get a word from him of what he knew — and he knew everything.

They were already there, lights doused, as he turned into the slip road that led to an industrial estate.

It was done in less than five minutes. The man was out cold and stayed out when they hauled him from the boot and threw him hard into the back of the van. None of them spoke a word other than to identify themselves with the names Morson had given. They wore dark clothing and balaclavas over their faces.

Frankie waited until the van moved off, then sped over the bridge and back on the road home. He didn't give the guy he had knocked out a second's thought.

FIFTY-SIX

The first call had worried him but not unduly. The second, in the middle of that night, had him up and dressing as he answered.

'No, you listen to me — this is one of my senior officers, he comes under my command, he's my responsibility before he's yours and I'm in on everything. I don't care what your bloody protocols are — so far as I'm concerned they don't exist. This started on my patch, we've a vested interest. I owe it to Serrailler.' He listened again briefly, then said, 'Forty minutes, I'd guess, but the pilot will radio in.'

The police helicopter was scrambled and down into the small park across the road from the Chief's house ten minutes later, another three and they were airborne, heading east.

Local special forces were alerted; the London team would be meeting them on the edge of the mapped-out area. There had been no further signals from Serrailler's electronic bleeper, which was now assumed to be dead.

'Let's hope,' the DI said as they loaded up, 'it's the only thing that is.'

It was still barely dawn when the police vans, choppers, unmarked cars and a large body of officers stood in a field belonging to Daffern Farm, getting orders. The air was heavy with early dew, the cows on the other side of the high hedge were undisturbed.

'Bloody good job it isn't sheep,' someone said. 'Half the county would have heard, racket they make.'

'OK, Daffern Farm. Jim Weston is the farmer, there's a wife, son and daughter-in-law, all live in. We're going up in single file, we knock them up, I've got the warrant, but no barging straight in, wait for the word. Might be no problem, chances are it's nothing to do with them and they know nothing, but we have to start somewhere. Outbuildings — cowsheds, couple of barns — around the house, usual load of old vehicles and derelict caravans, and we're searching everywhere — and that means everywhere. Heads up.'

They went forward in silence, boots brushing long grass. There was a single light on in an upstairs front room.

The hammering on the door set a dog barking inside. The police dog handlers held theirs back on short chains.

'Jim Weston?'

'Good God, what's this all about?' The man peered out, his unshaven face bewildered. But he listened without protest. 'Nothing here and nobody, but I suppose you wouldn't come without some sort of reason, not this lot of you. I've got nothing to hide. Go where you like, only let me get the women warned and dressed before you go barging through the house if you don't mind.'

'That's all right, sir, you do that, get them downstairs quick as you can, and whoever else lives here.'

'Nigel, only he's away, not back till Thursday.'

Minutes later the house was swarming with police. Others, plus the dogs, were into every corner of the outbuildings, as the first streaks of dawn showed pale in the eastern sky.

Frankie drove past as they were regrouping, having drawn a blank. He slowed a little and glanced in their direction, because it would be odd not to, took everything in, and then put his foot down.

Serrailler came round because someone had trained a power hose of freezing water onto his head. He was lying on concrete. He saw a thin paring of what might be the moon and a thin line of light on the horizon, both of which confused him, so that he closed his eyes. The hose hit him again at full power.

'Open your eyes, Johnno. Open your fuckin' eyes . . .'

He opened his eyes. But Johnno? Who were they talking to? Someone else. Not him. The concrete was ridged and cold against his back and pain was everywhere, he could barely breathe for it, squeezing and knifing his lungs and ribs when he tried. He saw boots. Denim legs. Tried to look up but the pain in his head would not let him. He wanted to see their faces.

'Get up.'

He lay.

'Get the fuck up, Johnno . . .'

A kick in his thigh, then another in his ribs which made him yell. He tried to move his legs. One moved. Not the other.

'Pull him up then.'

They pulled him up and then had to prop him against a wall and hold him. The light swirled. Some sort of building ballooned out then shrank, and the light grew wavy until he threw up suddenly, could not stop himself, or the pain as he did so.

'Hose him down again, he's not going fuckin' unconscious.'

The ice-cold jet on his face and head and neck and chest, stinging, powering into him.

But then, he was fully awake. His sight settled to normal.

There were three of them. Dark clothing. Faces covered.

Morson. It had to be, though he couldn't work out how.

'Where is this?'

'Ha . . . he's with us.'

'I said —'

They came at him as one man and he felt himself sliding down the wall and hitting the ground and hoped he was dying. The water jet brought him back to life.

'Get up, nonce.'

'I'm —'

'Shut up. Get up.'

He managed it, but he was only on his feet for seconds, before the punches came again, and then something like a huge stone crashing into the side of his head, the other side, the back, his chest, his belly. Then fists again. It went on and on until the end of time and he couldn't pass out, couldn't die, couldn't do anything but pray. 'God, let me die. God, let me die.'

He heard a voice from a long way off, with an odd echo behind it. 'Watch the time, Al . . . they start up . . .'

Then he heard someone screaming, bellowing like a bull, howling in pain, and the sound was pushing through his ears and into his brain and after a moment he knew that it came from him.

He realised with a flare of relief that his prayers were answered, that he was going to die, but it did not seem to be happening quickly, the pain went on, different forms of pain, and of fear. Time had sped up, time had slowed down, but now there was no time, everything that happened was endless and in one permanent present.

'I said fuckin' move it . . .'

'I'm enjoying this.'

'Finish it, Al.'

That was the last voice he heard on earth, a whining, nasal voice, worming itself into his head and repeating, repeating . . . 'Finish it finish it finish it . . .'

The pain in his legs and back could not surely get any worse but then increased off the scale of pain. He vomited again. Then, at last, the merciful last blow to his skull, which cracked open as everything went not black but a blazing, fiery white, splitting into fragments behind his eyes.

'We taking him?'

'We're fuckin' leaving him.'

'We can't —'

'Shut the fuck up or you'll be in there with him.'

The kid laughed. 'I get you,' he said with a terrible pleasure.

He helped drag him, helped lift him. Helped throw him, up and over and down.

'Now fuckin' move.'

Morson, always decisive, woke Will Fernley. Lynn was already packing a couple of hold-alls. The morning was grey, the sun not yet up.

'Shit,' Fernley said.

'There's a hotel won't ask any questions. Get a bloody move on.'

'Johnno coming with us?'

'No.'

Morson walked out of the room. Frankie had both bags downstairs and into the boot by the time Will came running.

'Shit,' he said again. He was hung-over and not properly awake.

'Shut up, Will. You're being taken care of, what more do you want? All right, Frank.'

Frank nodded and started the engine.

They plunged fast down the drive to the gate and reached it as the police arrived on the other side.

'Shit,' Fernley said, before he jumped out of the car and started to run.

FIFTY-SEVEN

'Chief, you're welcome to sit in, but I'm not sure it's correct that you do these interviews.'

'Because this is your patch not mine?' Kieron Bright was angry.

'Not exactly, but our guys . . .'

'Serrailler is my officer and I'm responsible for him. Technically, you're right, and someone else can interview the housekeeper — my guess is that she's peripheral. But I have to take the men apart to find out where my officer is and you would do the same.'

Privately, Kieron doubted it. The Superintendent was a robotic box-ticker, not a man who thought much for himself or would ever stray from the rules.

'All right,' he said now, 'but I'm putting it on record that I'm not happy.'

After that, they walked down the corridor to the interview rooms in silence.

Frankie Webster came in with his head up. He sat back in the chair opposite Bright, folded his arms and met his eye.

'What did you do with him?'

'With who?'

'You know who.'

'I'm not a mind-reader.'

'Don't mess me about, I don't have the time or the patience. Where did you take him?'

Silence.

'Listen, Webster, you're deep in already, you'll get more for keeping your mouth shut. Where did you take him?'

Silence.

'How long have you worked for Morson?'

'Twelve years.'

'And your wife?'

'She's not my wife but, yeah, the same.'

'Gets a lot of visitors, doesn't he?'

The man shrugged.

'Unexpected ones. Like Will Fernley and Johnno Miles.'

'Nothing wrong with that.'

'Did you talk to Johnno Miles?'

'Only in the way of my work.'

'Do you go into Morson's basement?'

'No.'

'Have you ever been into it?'

'No.'

'What, not even "in the way of your work"?'

'No.'

'Where is Johnno Miles?'

Silence.

'Did he go into the basement?'

'Yes.'

'How do you know?'

Silence.

'Does Morson lend you the stuff?'

'What stuff?'

'DVDs , . . films . . .'

'No.'

'What's your username?'

'What?'

'To get into the website. Username.'

'I don't know what you're talking about. What are you charging me with? You can't hold me —'

'Oh shut up, Webster. Listen. You are going to tell me where he is. In the house? In the grounds? No. He's somewhere you know about though. Why won't you tell me? We'll find him, we've got clothing from the room he slept in, the dogs will find him.'

'Don't need me to help you then.'

'Where is he?'

Silence.

'You'll go down for as long as your boss, you know that?'

Frankie snorted.

It went on for another ten minutes. Frankie had not given an inch.

Morson's face was grey and he looked sick. Bright looked at him in silence for a long time, until the QC shuffled, met his eye, dropped his gaze again, leaned back, leaned forward.

'You are scum, Morson, but before we go there and I ask you how many deaths you are responsible for, you tell me where Johnno Miles is.'

'I don't —'

'Yes, you do.' Kieron put his arms on the table and stared. 'You dare to sit there, you dare to walk the face of this earth, with the letters QC after your disgusting little name?'

'What did you mean just then? You can't just say things like that. I am not responsible for anyone's death — you'll retract that accusation.'

'You'll tell me where he is.'

'I don't know.'

'Who has him?'

Morson rubbed a pale, fat finger to and fro across the tabletop, his mouth twisting.

'You are going to prison for life, Morson. You can't save yourself and you know it. Your career is in ruins, your name will be

muck, you will be reviled and abused —
well, you should know all about that — and
you'll be begging for solitary and an armed
guard to keep them away from you. You've
seen the last of your grand house and your
rich life and your basement room full of
vile, nasty secrets. And a hell of a lot of
people are going to have their collars felt
during the next couple of days, and when
they open their newspapers, they'll know
who to blame. So just find it in your stink-
ing, filthy, miserable little soul to tell me
where he is, and who's got him and what
you told them to do. All I need is a mobile
number, Morson. Just one number and you
can go back into the cells to rot. Come
on . . .'

'One mobile number isn't going to tell you
anything.'

'One mobile number.'

Morson's face was contorted into a sneer.
Bright clenched his fists under the table.

'Give it to me. Come on, come on.'

'Why should I?'

'Right — there *is* a number.'

'If there was I wouldn't remember it.'

Kieron sighed. 'As well as the deaths of
children on your conscience, children murdered so that you could watch abuse and
snuff movies, you want the death of a cop

spreading the stain as well? How many times a life sentence is that?'

Quite suddenly, the man crumpled. Something Bright had said had gone home. Something had penetrated to the place where he acknowledged it all, admitted it to himself — something he had probably never done. The Chief could see it on his face, in his eyes, hear it in his voice when he muttered the digits of the mobile number.

He wrote it on the back of his hand as he ran out of the room.

It took even less time than he had hoped.

'They've got it, Chief. The mobile has been traced to Grays, Essex. Owner is Jason Anthony Smith, 147 Rondella Road, and the signal is within a couple of streets of that address.'

'Anything on our Mr Smith?'

'Oh yes. History of GBH, robbery with, armed robbery . . . dangerous man, but he was found not guilty last time, and if he's done anything since, he's been clever.'

'Can you find out the name of the counsel who got him off?'

They came back within a few seconds.

'Andrew Morson, QC.'

FIFTY-EIGHT

Lex Tindall prided himself on being at work before anyone else, so his motorbike was roaring up the slip road and onto the industrial estate by five to seven. Ten minutes later, he was rolling the first dumpers out ready for the day's collection, which happened around eight thirty.

It was a warm morning already, with a cloudless sky. Another evening out on the scramble bikes then, until maybe ten o'clock. The day wouldn't go fast enough but he liked his job and didn't fret about it.

He moved over to the row of huge metal bins and loaded the first one. It was hauled up into the air and tipped over, tipped back and brought down again. He rolled it off, and wheeled the second bin up. The mechanism seemed to jam and it failed to engage and lift. Then he got it moving but it stuck a few feet up. This went on for long enough to be annoying. He got the bin back down, disengaged it, and inspected the lifting gear. It seemed to be all right, smooth and without any jams. But when he tried again, the same thing happened. There could be a jam higher up.

Lex got a safety ladder, and a hard hat, and climbed up steadily. The big container bins were twelve feet in height and held a large volume of compressed rubbish. He reached the top, fully aware that this was against every safety rule and that if anyone came up now and found him . . . but no one else would be here for another quarter of an hour.

He could see nothing wrong with the haulage mechanism that tipped the contents, but he leaned over a little way to peer in.

Twenty seconds later, he was on the ground and making fast for the office and the phone, yelling, yelling as he ran.

The police cars, ambulance and fire engine arrived at the industrial estate around the same time as half a dozen officers pounded on the door of 147 Rondella Road and, when they got no reply, broke it down, found Jason Smith and arrested him. Jason's mobile phone had stored numbers including that of Andrew Morson, and the record of his call the previous night.

It was difficult and dangerous work and took what felt like hours for the firemen to scale up the outside and then down the inside of the refuse container. The man was easily seen, but had to be moved with extreme caution.

'You got him?'

One of the firemen raised his arm, but it was a slow job to get the gear, and a stretcher, into place, then load the man onto it. The fireman looked carefully, without touching, glanced up at the others and grimaced.

By then, Kieron Bright and two others were on their way, blue lights and siren and 110 mph, to the scene. They arrived just as Simon Serrailler, aka Johnno Miles, was being lowered with maximum care to the ground and the waiting paramedics. Seconds later, the whirr of the air ambulance was overhead, coming in to land on an open stretch of tarmac.

Bright pushed his way through and looked down at the body on the stretcher.

'God Almighty,' he said, and felt a surge of the purest coldest anger.

The chopper blades were still turning as the doctors ran across, rucksacks of medical kit bumping against their backs.

'He's gone,' someone said. 'Has to be.'

The first doctor was kneeling, the second unpacking his bag.

'Do we know what happened? Do we know how long he's been in there?'

They worked fast as they asked the questions to which no one had answers.

Kieron Bright turned away. He paced around the area, turned, paced back. He had given up smoking twenty years earlier but he felt the need of a cigarette. One of the officers who had driven down with him came over. 'Shall I find out if they've a kitchen or a machine in there?'

'Thanks.'

'How's he looking?'

Bright shook his head. Serrailler looked dead. He was so beaten up as to be almost unrecognisable and there had been no sign that he was alive.

'My best officer by miles.'

'Shit.'

'Yes. Go and see about drinks, will you?'

As the man went, there was a shout. 'Chief . . .'

He knew what they wanted. He had to stand there while they formally pronounced Serrailler dead at the scene and got his permission to take the body away.

The doctor was kneeling, leaning back on

his heels. 'Christ knows how, but he's got a pulse,' he said, and then looked warningly at Kieron. 'Barely detectable but it's a sign that he's not dead.' He did not have to add 'yet'.

'What are you going to do?'

'It's a tough call. He's lost a huge amount of blood and he's deteriorating. My guess is that aside from what we can see, which is a lot, he has internal injuries and bleeding. Frankly, there's so much that I wouldn't know where to start if we keep him here.'

'Has he been conscious at all?'

'No, thank God. I think what we're going to do is move him as carefully as we possibly can and get him airlifted to a major trauma centre. If he survives being moved, if he survives the journey, then that's the only place where he stands the slightest chance.' He stood and began to give orders to the others.

Kieron watched hopelessly.

The helicopter was airborne as there was a shout of 'Drinks!' from the building behind them. The remaining men walked across in silence.

FIFTY-NINE

Elaine Dacre had had a bad night. The hospice nurses were coming in regularly now and one was there as Cat arrived. Now that there were no beds in Imogen House, they tried to give the same care to patients in their own homes, though it wasn't always possible and the physical comforts of special beds and equipment were lacking. The GPs did not come out after hours either — some would not make home visits at all, even to the dying. That left a gap which no one else could fill, Cat thought.

The room was suffused with early-morning sunlight and the window was open onto the garden. A neighbour was cutting grass nearby and the smell came drifting up, making Elaine smile. 'Summers of childhood,' she said. 'Smell of grass . . . sound of the sea.'

Cat sat beside her and took her hand. All the flesh seemed to have melted away now, leaving skin stretched over bones, and bright, bright eyes.

'It's so good of you to come. You know I like to see you. Tell me what's happening in the world.'

Cat laughed. 'Not sure you want to know.'

They chatted for a while. Elaine's voice was weak now but she was still ready to laugh. Once or twice she closed her eyes and dozed. Angie brought in coffee for Cat, but after looking quickly at her mother-in-law, was struck by the need to rush off on some urgent mission.

Cat wondered, as ever, why people were afraid of death and the dying, and decided that the usual explanation certainly held true, that it was because death was now pushed away to the far edge of everyday life instead of being put in the centre of it. She remembered one rare patient, a young woman in her early thirties, who had insisted on having her three children in and out of her room, on her bed, even going to sleep with her, through her last weeks, and talked to them about what was happening, never failing to answer their questions, never allowing them to be sent away if they wanted to stay. How rare that was.

She drank her coffee as Elaine drifted off. She would die within the next few days and how would the family cope, if they were alone with her when it happened? Leave her by herself? No, but until the last second they would be in denial, and if Elaine wanted to talk, they would stop her, kindly, firmly. Cat felt helpless but knew that what she could do, she was doing now. There was nothing else.

It was warm and quiet and the sun was on her face. Her sleep was deeper, but for now she was comfortable. When Cat's mobile rang she did not stir.

'This is Kieron Bright.'

An hour and a half later, she was there. 'My father and stepmother are coming back from France now.'

She looked at the Chief, trying to read his face.

'I want to see him,' she said.

'The trauma team are working on him — they won't let anyone else in for now. You know the form. Come to the canteen, I'll tell you everything.'

'I want him to know I'm here, Kieron.'

He hesitated.

'Listen, I'm a doctor. It's important they know that, and that someone tells him I'm here, in case he comes round. Even if I'm not allowed in I want him to be told.'

He found them a table, bought coffees, and went to get someone to relay her message. Whether they would, and how much point there was, he did not know.

'Thanks,' Cat said. Her hand was shaking as she lifted her coffee but she steadied it with the other.

'Different,' she said, 'when it's your own. Being a doctor isn't relevant.'

'No.'

'It's the same with the police, isn't it?'

'Yes.'

'All right.' She drained her cup and set it down. 'I'm focused now. What happened?'

She listened without speaking, head bent, thinking, imagining everything, going over the probable injuries. Judith rang in the middle of it, and she answered, said she would call back when she knew more.

'It's not good,' she said. They had to be prepared, as she was now.

'You can't stay here with me, you've got a force to run. Go back, Kieron.'

'Simon's my officer and my responsibility, I'm staying until there's some definite news.'

The CEOP team from London would take over and he would be kept up to speed. They would collect what they needed not only against Morson but against the whole paedophile ring, though it would take time and Morson almost certainly would have been able to warn some of the others. The local area would deal with Jason Smith and however many other thugs it had taken to put Serrailler between life and death.

They went to walk in the corridors, and outside where ambulances came in and out, and the lobbies which were crowded with outpatients. They drank more coffee. Several times, he tried to get news of Simon and failed. He took endless calls, one about Richard Serrailler, which he did not mention to Cat. Kieron ordered everyone to hold off. Another day or two before they took Richard in for questioning would not matter once he was back in the country.

They were standing in the sun by the entrance doors. Conversation had petered out. He had to stay to support her until there was news, however long it took, but there was nothing he could say and Cat clearly did not want pointless small talk. He took his cue from her.

'Excuse me . . .'

The doctor was young, calm, and his focus was still in the trauma unit.

Cat jumped up. 'You've got some news?'

'You are?'

She told him.

'Right . . . you're his next of kin?'

'No, my — our father is but he's on his way back from France.'

'Right . . .'

'I'm a doctor.'

'Ah. Right.' He went over to sit on a low wall. Cat followed. 'Right.' He seemed to gather himself together and work out where to start. 'OK, he's still alive. God knows how he survived — we don't know how long it was after the attack that he was found but . . . well, it's amazing that he's alive. He has multiple fractures, including his skull and his pelvis . . . the thing we're concerned about most is the internal bleeding, but we've had him in surgery and they've found the tear that was causing most of it and been able to repair that. He's had seven pints of blood . . .'

Cat closed her eyes.

'He'll probably lose one kidney, and his spleen . . . He's had a CAT scan and although he does have a skull fracture, as I said, there doesn't appear to be any brain damage. One of his eyes may have been blinded but we have to wait till the tissue swelling goes down and ophthalmology can assess. He had his left arm badly crushed — we don't know if we can save that yet. But he's more or less stable for now. As you'll know, the next hours are critical . . .

466

if he gets through twelve hours, he's a small chance. If he gets through twenty-four —'

'Do you think he will?'

He held out his hands.

'Come on . . . chances? Percentage? In your opinion?'

'I'm not the consultant.'

'Your opinion?'

He shook his head.

'Please. Fifty–fifty? Less. More?'

In the end he said, 'Less.' But would not be pushed further.

'Can I go in to him?'

'I'd say no, only you're a medic, you've seen all this.'

She had. Except that this was not a 'case', this wasn't some stranger being brought in by ambulance from a road accident, while she waited, as a junior doctor doing her A & E stint, to help assess the injuries and be given her job. This was Simon.

'Yes. Let's go.'

The young doctor got up. Kieron said, 'I'll wait for you. I've got some calls.' But she did not hear him.

Simon was barely visible. There were more machines than she had ever known together beside one bed, more tubes, lines, clips. More flashing lights. More beeping. He was

467

lying flat on the bed, intubated, bandaged, his chest and arms bare and covered with monitor pads. His hair was shaved at the front. He looked bloodless. No longer human.

She managed to find a bare patch on the back of his hand and stroked it.

'Simon . . . oh, sweetheart, what have they done to you?' She choked on her own tears. 'I'm here. I'm not going away. Si . . .'

The nurse touched her shoulder. The monitors were beeping and flashing, the trauma team swarmed round again. She had to go and she could not explain anything to him. He would not know she had been there. Somehow, that was the worst of all.

It took another hour and a half of waiting, outside, in the canteen, in the visitors' room, the corridors, before anyone came back, a different doctor this time, then the consultant. Still too young, Cat thought. How could they possibly know?

How ridiculous.

'We want to put him into an induced coma. You're familiar with that?'

Cat nodded.

'It's the best chance of helping him while the brain swelling goes down a bit. His body is fighting on all fronts and he's a fit man, but he's sustained some major traumas.'

'Yes.'

'Anything you want to know? I can't give you much of a prognosis yet, you'll understand that.'

'Yes, but . . . just give me a percentage . . . just . . . come on. Chances?'

He thought for a moment. 'It's guesswork, pretty much. You know what's happened to him — you could probably guess as well as I can.'

'No. You.'

'All right,' he said. 'The worry is spinal injury, his arm and possible brain damage, though I'm less concerned about that. The scans didn't look bad but while there is such a lot of swelling we can't get the full picture. He'll almost certainly lose his spleen and one of his kidneys but we don't want to risk any more surgery for now . . . we can stabilise all that. I don't know if the orthopods will hold out any hope for his arm. They're all attending to RTA victims at the moment but as soon as one can be spared from those they'll give his arm a proper assessment.' He put his hand on hers for a second. 'Listen . . . he's not going to be awake for some days . . . maybe longer. There isn't any point in your staying — we wouldn't try and wake him without letting you know in good time so that you or someone else in the family can be here. Go home. Get some rest. And go easy on yourself.'

She watched him go. Back to Simon. Back to the twilight world where he was poised between life and death. Back.

Kieron came towards her.

'Will you take me home, please?' she said.

■ ■ ■ ■

PART FOUR

■ ■ ■ ■

SIXTY

The shelving looked good. Very good. They
had had many a design discussion over coffees, teas, wine, suppers, and every time Rachel had suggested economising and pro-
duced brochures of plastic-coated metal,
Rupert Barr had expressed disgust and
pushed them aside.

'Wood. You can't improve upon wood. It
looks good, it's strong, you can paint it
whatever colour you like, and then repaint
it in a few years' time, it sets off the
books . . . there's just no alternative. Wood.'

He had waved mention of the cost away,
as he had done about the paint, the carpet,
the seating, the desk, the computer and
software, the signage.

'And when you stock — and I'm not going to interfere much there, I've said so —
but when you do, don't stint, don't pack
the shelves with cheap paperbacks. We want
some handsome hardbacks, some art books,

a table with some limited editions. Make sure the children's end has lots of shop copies and buy some of those beanbag things, but top quality, no point in getting cheap ones and have them burst open in a few weeks. This shop is going to be the best independent bookshop in the south, Rachel.'

'Which is something to aim for but it'll take more than expensive fittings, you know.'

'It will take you and whoever you choose to employ, someone knowledgeable and enthusiastic. And that's another thing — we pay him or her properly. Wages in retail are deplorable. We don't just want to get the perfect person, we want to keep them.'

Now, she gazed round the empty shop with pride. The carpet was dark blue, the walls pale blue, the wood painted white. The shelving had been made by a local firm of fine craftsmen and it looked very good. The sign was going up later. And tomorrow, stock would start arriving.

She picked up her mobile from the desk and rang Rupert again. She wanted him to come down now, if possible, and see it before the books arrived, then come and help with putting them out. She and the new assistant manager, Chloë, whom she was delighted to have wheedled away from a large bookstore, one of a major chain, would be working from dawn till dusk to meet the opening date. But that was fine, she was up for work and so was Chloë. Together, they made a formidable team.

'Rupert, it's Rachel again. Sorry to keep ringing like this . . . Maybe your phone's out of battery. Or signal. Anyway, ring me when you get this. Everything's looking really good here, I want you to come down and see.'

The door opened on Chloë, smiling happily.

'This is sooooo exciting.'

She gave Rachel a hug. 'Let's go!'

They worked all morning, and broke for a salad lunch at the brasserie before going back to it.

Rachel was standing on the step-stool putting some books on a high shelf, when her mobile rang. She gestured to Chloë to hand it up to her.

'Rupert? Is everything all right?'

'It's not Rupert, it's Cat. Where are you, Rachel? I can't do this over the phone.' Her voice sounded different.

'It's Simon, isn't it? What's happened? Oh God . . . I'm in the shop . . . I'll come. I'll come to you.'

Rachel clipped a corner as she turned onto the country road and narrowly missed a cyclist as she sped round the next bend. She took a deep breath and slowed down. A couple of miles on, a river of sheep was being moved from one field to another, and she was caught behind them, inching along, watching the two dogs chivvy the bleating creatures on either side. She banged her palm on the wheel and the dogs scurried to and fro but the sheep took their time.

'Cat?'

Rachel could not take in the change in her. She looked twenty years older, pale, hollow-eyed and oddly blanked out, as if she were not fully functioning. Always, anyone who arrived was offered coffee, tea, a glass of wine. Now, Cat did not even ask her to sit down.

It did not take long. Cat's voice was almost robotic, as if she were reading from a prepared script. She listed Simon's injuries, the stats, the prognosis, without pausing, without emotion.

'I want to see him,' Rachel said, when she had fallen silent. 'I have to go.'

'They won't let you in. Dad and Judith are on their way. Not that it makes any difference. He won't register anyone.'

'I can't just be here waiting.'

'Yes, you can. I am.'

'Where are the children?'

'School. Cricket. People are taking over. People always do. I forget how many real friends I have until there's a crisis.'

'Do they know?'

'Sam does. Hannah's got her show in two days, I can't tell her. Felix . . . I don't know. He doesn't have to know now, does he?'

'No.'

'I'm so sorry. I'll get us some coffee . . . what time is it? I don't even know what day it is.'

But she didn't move and so they sat at the kitchen table, not looking at one another, not speaking. Neither of them really there.

SIXTY-ONE

The room was crowded, with some of the officers standing at the back. Everybody was jubilant, and everybody was grim-faced.

'This has been one of the biggest ops in our history,' the DCS said, 'and this ring is one of the worst we have ever cracked. We're not dealing with dirty old men downloading a bit of smut, we're dealing with men who have abducted children, kept them, abused them and filmed that abuse, and who have murdered them and filmed those murders. I have been sickened to my stomach watching the stuff on those hard drives and DVDs we took. So have you. I understand totally how each one of you feels. Counselling is ready and available for any of you, and if you feel at all concerned about yourself, if you are finding it difficult to cope, if you cannot get these images out of your head, if you are having difficulty focusing on anything else — anything — then I urge you to take advantage of this counselling. I thought I was tough and not easily affected until I saw these images. We work in this unit, day in, day out and we are never hardened but we do find ways to cleanse ourselves mentally at the end of the day. This time it will be very, very difficult — it may not be possible. There's no shame in getting counselling and no pride in playing the iron man — or woman.

'I'd like to thank you all for the work you've done on Operation Sparrowhawk, the hours you've put in, the days off and nights with your families you've given up. I'm proud of you — I can't say how proud.

'You all know that an officer attached to these investigations, Detective Chief Superintendent Simon Serrailler, is fighting for his life at the Royal London Hospital and we're all of us praying to God he pulls through. We owe it to him, as well as to all the children who have suffered at the hands of these evil men, to bring this op successfully to a close and to see justice done.

'This is a big mop-up, but the arrests are pretty much confined to two areas — in the south and the east. This has been a paedophile ring among people who either know one another, or live in the same parts of the country. Very controlled, highly professional.

If DCS Serrailler had not gone undercover, we might not have broken this ring for years, if ever.

'This time tomorrow, we should have eighty-seven men in custody. There may be more — we need to do further work on some hard drives, and we also need to break down a few people during questioning. I am convinced that is not the full total of members of this ring, nowhere near. I'll be issuing a press release, and as you would imagine, there will be considerable media interest — this is a huge story. It clears up several unsolved cases involving the disappearance of children and the locating of some of those children in terrible circumstances. You can feel proud of yourselves, every last one of you.'

The names on the list of those arrested and charged with sexual assault and making, possessing and distributing indecent images of children included those of one public-school headmaster and three senior masters, one consultant forensic psychiatrist, two Anglican clergymen, one Nonconformist clergyman, one Deputy Lord Lieutenant, one senior HMRC chief tax inspector, one GP, four solicitors, eight company directors. A number of those arrested bore titles, including those of Viscount, Baronet, and Knight Commander. It also included seven barristers, two of them QCs. Among those arrested and charged were:

Andrew Morson, QC
James Linkhurst-Brown, QC
The Hon. Christopher Lomax
His Honour Judge Gerald Hanbury
Viscount Sarsden
Sir Alan Drummond-Peach, MB, FRCS
The Rt Revd Jasper Murray, Archdeacon
  of Bevham
Gordon Barkmore, Deputy Headmaster,
  Cathedral School, Lafferton
The Hon. Rupert Barr
The Hon. William Fernley

Fernley had been picked up by local police three hours after his escape. He was back at Wandsworth.

Cat was reading out the roll call from the front page of the *Bevham Gazette.* Rachel was sitting on the kitchen sofa, Wookie on her lap, Mephisto beside her with one paw on her knee to stake his claim.

'Dear God,' she said. There was silence. She looked across at Cat. 'It's a ring within a ring. It's like a vein of poison spread all around us. It's unbelievable.'

Cat stared at the newspaper.

'Cat?'

Rachel saw her expression.

' "The Honourable Rupert Barr",' Cat read.

After a few moments, Rachel began to say, almost in a whisper, 'I don't believe it. I don't believe it,' over and over again. Her life had fractured and gaped open like a fault line.

Cat dropped the paper and got up. Simon. Her father. Now this.

She went to the cupboard. Poured them both a gin and tonic. Put in the ice. Set Rachel's beside her. She wondered how long it would be before the next news broke and her father's name took over the front page of the paper. Did Judith know? Had the police even arrested him yet, given Simon's state?

She now knew what Simon had been doing, though not in detail. Kieron Bright had rung and told her briefly.

It was a warm early evening, and they both wandered out into the garden to the deckchairs under the beech tree, and sat, still in silence, for what was there to say?

SIXTY-TWO

'Shelley?'

Shelley woke from dreaming about the buildings of her old school, long closed and demolished.

'I'm sorry . . . I overslept . . .'

'Don't worry about it. But I need you to come in as soon as possible.'

'What's happened?'

'Richard Serrailler was arrested late last night, and charged with rape.'

It was terrifying to hear the words spoken. Shelley was shaking.

'What happens now?'

'He'll appear before magistrates, he'll ask for bail which will almost certainly be granted. Then it goes to the Crown Prosecution Service and they decide whether there's a case to answer.'

'And . . . and how long does that take?'

'Usually between a week and ten days — the CPS in this area are actually pretty quick. Once they decide there is a case to answer — that's when the waiting starts, I'm afraid. It could be quite a long time.'

'How long?'

'Six months or more before a hearing is set.'

'But . . . what happens to him in the meantime?'

'Nothing.'

'But I might meet him . . . he might come here.'

'No, he won't be allowed to — one of his bail conditions will be that he doesn't come near you. If you meet by chance, you just turn round and walk away.'

'But — if the CPS decide if . . . that . . .' She gripped the phone.

'Listen, Shelley, it would be best if you came in to see me and we can talk about this face-to-face. Can you do that?'

'Yes. Yes, of course . . . I'll . . . I just feel . . .'

'If you think you're not safe to drive, get a taxi. All right? I'll see you in half an hour?'

As she put the phone down, she heard the front door.

'Only me. I need to get my head round all this paperwork in peace and quiet so I'm doing it at home. Are you all right?'

'Yes. No . . . Yes, of course I am.'

Tim came closer. 'You're white and you're trembling. What's happened?'

'Nothing. Can you take me into town?'

'Not if I want to get this finished. Something wrong with your car?'

'No . . . I just felt a bit . . . sick. I think I've eaten something.'

'Well then, don't go into town, silly girl.'

She stood, not knowing what to say, do, decide.

'Where were you going, anyway? Can I do it for you?'

'Oh no. No, it's fine. I'll be all right.'

She picked up her bag and the car keys. But she knew she wouldn't be safe to drive.

'I'd like a taxi please, to —'

'Shelley?' He took the phone from her and disconnected. 'Of course I'll take you in if you really have to go but not before you tell me what on earth is going on.'

She told him.

'You're really going ahead with this charge? For God's sake, Shelley, what's this about?'

'It's about him raping me.'

'He didn't rape you. Listen — sit down. Now listen to me . . . please, drop all this!'

'Well, it's too late. He's been charged. The case is with the CPS. I can't.'

'Yes you can. Just go into the police station.'

'At St Catherine's —'

'Bugger the rape crisis centre, leave them out if it — they've got a vested interest.'

'Don't be so stupid.'

'As I say, go to the police — I'll take you and I'll come in with you — and simply say you're withdrawing the charges. All charges. That you won't proceed, there's no case to answer, you won't appear in court — make it crystal clear. They'll tear it up. They've no alternative. And then it'll be dealt with and you and I will go away and you'll start to get over it.'

Shelley looked at her husband's angry face. He loved her, she had no doubt of that, but he had not for one moment believed what she had told him and he cared too much about the things that did not matter. About reputation. Public show. Appearances.

Quite suddenly, everything fell into place and she was calm again. She redialled the taxi firm and walked out of the front door, to wait for the five minutes they had said it would take.

SIXTY-THREE

No news. There had been no news for two weeks. She had telephoned every hour, then every few hours, then twice a day. They were very patient, very kind. She should ring whenever she felt the need. But there was still no news.

Hannah and Felix were in bed, Sam at his friend Jake's. The house was quiet. She sat at the kitchen table with her laptop, because it was more comforting than the study which in any case was on the cold side of the house. It was still quite warm and she had the window open to smell the second flowering of the Cecile Brunner rose. And the night. The smell of the night.

He could not see the sky or the outside world, and in his room there would never be dark, only bright white lights, and never silence, only the bleep of the machines, keeping him alive.

Cat went back to her draft notes for the

lecture. It was not happening for months but so many ideas seethed inside her head that she needed to get them down roughly every day. There was so much to say, but because of Simon, it somehow seemed both unreal and very temporary, as if what happened to him might change how she thought at any moment. But it wouldn't.

Mephisto bipped in through the cat flap, stalked about for a moment, then bipped back into the garden again. Wookie leapt up, chased his retreating tail, gave up on the game and returned to his basket.

She had discovered an American research paper about how dying patients are affected positively or negatively by the voice tone of medical staff around them. It was not new but it was significant. She would print it off and read it later. The novels on her bedside table were gradually being pushed aside by medical papers, but she would always find time somehow to read fiction, she knew that. She had two collections of Alice Munro short stories waiting, plus the re-reading of *Middlemarch,* and Marilynne Robinson's *Gilead.* It was not the fault of the research papers that she had neglected novels. Everything that had happened, not least the sudden absence of the bookshop, had somehow put her off fiction as viruses put one off food. At the moment, only clear, concise medical facts and deductions seemed acceptable and satisfying.

She poured a small glass of wine. Work had always been her salvation and it would be now. Kieron Bright had called twice but what else could he do? Until there was news, nothing at all, and even then?

The phone ringing suddenly in the quietness made her start and drop the glass. Wine mingled with shards spread over the floor.

'Cat? Oh . . . sorry . . .'

'No, it's fine, just a spill, but I should clear it or the animals might cut themselves. Can I ring you back, Judith?'

'I . . . yes . . . but — no, don't. Can I just come over?'

Tone of voice.

'Of course. You don't need to ask. Just come.'

So, Judith knew. Had her father told her, or had she found out some other way?

She dropped the fragments into the bin.

Or perhaps it wasn't that. Perhaps the hospital had rung — as they would, rung her father, Simon's next of kin. That was why Judith was coming. To break it to her.

Suddenly, what she wanted more than anything was for Sam to be there.

■ ■ ■ ■

When she heard the car she went to the front door. Face it. You have to face it now.

Judith got out of the car but instead of coming straight to her, quickly, she went round to the boot. Opened it. Two, three suitcases. A holdall. A tote bag.

'Here, let me . . .'

It was difficult to read Judith's expression but she was not distressed, not hurt. She was — angry. Yes. Angry and quite calm.

'I'm sorry, darling. It's only for now, until I sort something out. But I'm not going back, you see. My other stuff can wait and follow eventually.' She put her hand on Cat's shoulder. 'I'm not going back.'

Cat felt tears in the back of her throat but pushed them down.

'Good,' she said.

'You knew?'

She nodded. 'But I was told in absolute confidence. I couldn't say anything. I'm so sorry . . .'

'That's all right, of course it is. What could you have done anyway?'

Wookie, having managed to push the door open a bit wider, came racing towards them.

'I need a drink,' Judith said, bending to

490

pick him up.

'Does Dad know you've come here?'

'I presume he'll guess.'

Cat handed her the glass of wine and Judith drank half of it before she sat down.

'He's denying all charges, did you know that as well?'

'No.'

'He'll pay a fortune for a good QC of course and that will be that.'

'No, a good defence is his right but money doesn't automatically buy a not-guilty.'

'Would you bet on that?'

Cat sat down opposite her stepmother. 'I am so angry with him,' she said. 'Not just this — I'm angry because he's thrown away a good loving marriage, and for what?'

'He threw it away some time ago, Cat.'

'Yes. But I thought . . .'

'Did you? Yes, well, perhaps I did. In France we seemed to be back where we had been — but we weren't and "seemed" so really is the word. There was some secrecy, some deception, always there.'

'You can stay here as long as you like, that goes without saying.'

'I know and you're always generous but it won't be for too long. I want to be independent and I can be.'

'Just not yet. God, this has been a bloody

awful summer.'

She looked across at Judith. She had aged. Well, nothing stayed the same but did it have to change like this, overnight, everything gone?

It had done so before and they were still here, somehow.

But Simon?

SIXTY-FOUR

'Shelley?'

She closed her eyes briefly. But then she clenched her fist. She had talked herself through this so many times, imagined standing in the witness box in front of judge, lawyers, jury. In front of him. She was ready to go.

'Do you have any news, Lois?' she said calmly.

'Can you come in?'

'No. No, I can't right now.'

'OK . . .'

'Just tell me. It's fine.'

A pause.

'Shelley, the Crown Prosecution Service don't feel there's a reasonable chance of conviction. I'm really sorry but the case can't go forward.'

SIXTY-FIVE

He could not sleep. He usually slept for six hours without stirring, woke and got up. Now it was one thirty and he had been in bed, sleepless, since eleven o'clock. The bedroom felt chilly. He went downstairs and poured himself a whisky. Into the kitchen. Topped it up with a splash of tap water. Looked around.

Tidy. Clean. Silent. Empty.

He sat at the table.

What should he feel now? Relief. It had washed over him briefly, when he had learned that the CPS had decided he would not be prosecuted, but it had slipped away like the tide and left him. He felt depressed. Irritable. And lonely.

No. Richard Serrailler would never admit to loneliness, even to himself. He was self-sufficient, practically, emotionally. He had never needed others and yet he had been surrounded with them all his life.

He was angry. He drank another mouthful. He was angry that Shelley had been so stupid and so deceitful, so manipulative, and so treacherous. She had always flirted, and the flirting had become more obvious. He could not have mistaken the signals she had sent out to him so often. Of course he couldn't. He wasn't a man who went looking for other women. But when a woman behaved as she had behaved . . .

A corner of him felt disappointed that he had not gone into court, with his excellent defence counsel, and been able to watch Shelley backtrack, contradict herself and, finally, crumble under questioning. But on the whole, no. He would not wish that on her. Let it be. She must have learned a lesson, even from the process of bringing a charge.

The tide of relief began to creep up towards him again. He had been spared not only a difficult hour or two in court, but also, far worse, having his name and reputation spread over the papers. It was unlikely to have reached the national press, but if it had, that hardly mattered. It was the local papers that would have hung him, and life in Lafferton would have become intolerable. He and Judith would have been forced to retreat, probably to France.

Judith.

He finished his whisky and poured another.

Judith.

He had loved her. Did love her. That was the truth. But marriage had been constraining, as it was with Meriel, except that they both had time-consuming, demanding work, the children had been growing up, there had been Martha . . . there had been no energy to spare on a marriage which had functioned well enough. Being retired, even if he had a few leftover jobs on the medical journal, and a couple of committees, had meant he and Judith had spent a lot of time together. Too much time.

The house was too big for one man. But he shrank even from the suggestion that he might move.

He wanted to be alone, but not alone.

Shelley and Tim were happily together, so far as he knew, but the way she had led him on had cost him his own marriage.

He put the glass in the sink and turned the tap on hard so that the cold water splashed up and soaked his pyjama jacket.

He needed Judith back.

SIXTY-SIX

Sam went quite slowly into the small room, his eyes flicking about anxiously before finally resting on the bed. Cat watched him. He looked much taller and as his face changed with adolescence he had also begun to look more like Simon. The same bone structure was coming out, the same nose, the same forehead. His hair was quite different and his eyes were darker but the resemblance was still strong.

Hair.

Simon's head had been shaved and the white-blond hair was only just coming through again.

'Hi,' Sam said, but the words barely came out. He cleared his throat. 'Uncle Simon? It's me. It's Sam.' He looked round at the machinery, lights, tubes, wires, monitors.

Beep-beep. Beeep. Beeep. Beep-beep.

'You can sit down on the stool there,' the duty nurse said.

Cat was looking at the stats. No change. No change. No change.

Sam leaned forward. 'Hi.'

Bipbipbipbip.

After twenty minutes they went to get drinks.

'He's going to be OK,' Sam said, nodding.

'Well — every day that goes by means he's survived a bit longer but he's still in danger, Sammy. His brain recordings — but no, I'm not a neurologist, I shouldn't try to draw conclusions.'

'I just think he'll be OK. Thing is — will he go back to his job or what?'

'Long way ahead.'

'Who else has been to see him?'

'Just your grandfather and Judith.'

'You know what? It just makes it really, really clear.'

'What?'

'About what I'm going to do.'

'Which is?'

'I told you.'

'No, you didn't, you left me to guess . . . which I can, obviously.'

'I thought of going to uni and then doing a fast-track, but then, I could go straight in when I'm eighteen. I talked to the Chief about it.'

'You didn't tell me that either.'

'Oh. Well, I did. I emailed him and he said to go and see him so I did. Obviously, if Uncle Si hadn't been in here I'd have talked to him.'

Cat looked at the boy who was poised between child and adulthood, now a seven-year-old, now a grown man, according to how he turned his head, the way he looked at her.

'So . . . what's the plan?'

'Kieron says uni.'

'Did he ask him to call you that?'

'Yes. So what do you think?'

'Fine. It's your future, Sam. Do you agree about university?'

'I reckon.'

'What would you read?'

'English. Or English and history. Or just history.'

'Where?'

Sam shrugged. 'Wherever they'll have me. Can I have another Coke?'

They went back to the room, before setting off home. No change. No change. Bipbip-bipbip. Bleep. Bleep. Bleep. The nurse looked round.

'The neuro consultant is around if you want a word.'

They waited in the corridor, but when he appeared he led them into the relatives' room.

'No change,' Cat said.

'No, but that cuts both ways — no change for the worse either.'

'I presume everything else will heal?'

'Not my area but it seems likely everything will be fine bar his arm. The leg will recover though it will take a long time but the arm is still a major cause for concern. You'll need to ask the orthopods about that. It's a long road, either way.'

'What's your best bet?'

'I never bet.'

'No. I understand. Thanks.'

'But you should keep coming to see him, keep talking to him, touching him . . . it's surprising what's registered. I'm an old-fashioned believer in the power of the familiar voice to work miracles in this sort of case.'

'Come on,' Sam said, 'we're going back.' He led the way.

No change. No change. Bipbipbipbip. Bleep. Bleep. Bleep.

'Hi,' Sam said, and put his hand firmly on Simon's forearm. 'It's me, Sam. We'll keep coming back to see you . . . as often as we can. I've got loads to tell you. Good about work and stuff. Cricket, erm, not so good this season. You won't want to know. Only two people can come here at once, but maybe next time Mum will bring Hannah instead. She can yatter away to you. You'll get so cheesed off you'll wake up just to tell her to shut it. So . . . hang on in there, Uncle Si. Love you.'

At the door, he said again, 'Love you.'

Cat put her hand on his shoulder as they went away down the corridor, but he only let it lie there until they were in the main concourse full of people, when he dodged away expertly and then over to the shop to buy yet another can of Coke.

The phone rang as she was setting off for the surgery. She and Hannah had been to the hospital the previous day, two weeks since she had taken Sam.

No change. Hannah had been more upset than Cat had expected and wanted to leave after only a few minutes. But there was no change. No change.

The room seemed like a hallucination.

She answered as she got into the car.

'Mike Newburn. Thought you'd want to know that we're going to try and wake him up. We've got to know what's really going on.'

'You're withdrawing the meds?'

'Yup. We do it slowly. He might surface, he might not. If he does it might be almost instantaneous or take a little while. We really won't know till we do it.'

'Oh God.'

'If he does come round we'll try and extubate him, see if he can breathe on his own.'

'Yes. What do you think will happen?'

'I don't know. It's suck it and see.'

'The worst being that he doesn't come round.'

'Brain tracings are no different.'

'No worse.'

'It's marginal but the swelling has gone down. This is the right moment to try, Cat.'

'Yes.'

'Do you want to come in now? I can hold off until you get here.'

Yes, she did, but how long would the drive into London take at this time of the morning? Judith had gone to her daughter, Richard was, she supposed, at home but he was the last person she wanted to speak to. She dithered, needing to ring the neurologist back and tell him either to wait for her or not, needed to calm down if she was to be safe to drive, needed to ring the surgery and arrange cover, schools and . . .

Seconds before she knew she might go

into meltdown, she picked the phone up.

She had been in fast cars but never like this and yet she felt completely safe. Kieron Bright's police driver was solid in every sense, burly, and rock-like. They might have been doing 25 mph in a built-up but deserted area.

Kieron had cancelled what he described as a dull public-duty day and they had been at the farmhouse fifteen minutes after she had called him.

'There's bottles of chilled water in the well under the armrest, sir — Doctor,' Keith, the driver, said. 'And chocolate.'

She had been silent for some time, but it made tension worse.

'Can we talk about my father?'

'Of course.'

'Is that it now? Nothing will happen?'

'He was given a caution, which he accepted.'

'I haven't spoken to him. I can't imagine when I might want to.'

'Has he tried to contact you?'

'No.'

'Difficult.'

'Kieron, did you honestly think he'd get off scot-free?'

'I did think the CPS might say there was

insufficient evidence, yes. In the end, it was one word against the other and that simply isn't enough.'

'But she had . . . there was forensic evidence, her frock was ripped, she . . . All right, I know. Evidence but not of rape.'

'No. Rape cases are the hardest to get right . . . they rarely come to court and when they do, they often result in a not-guilty. I think it's probably better that it happened this way.'

'I don't. I'd like to have seen him sweat it out in front of a good prosecutor.'

'And then get off and be able to boast about it?'

Cat smiled. He was right. She was still angry but concerns of any kind about her father dwindled into insignificance now. She felt a sudden flutter of — of what? Hope? Dread? Excitement? Yes, all of them.

The car sped down the fast lane. The last green fields. The outskirts of London. Sunshine. They overtook everything easily on a dual carriageway and, somehow, traffic melted, lights turned green. They slowed and made way once only, for an ambulance racing out of the hospital as they turned in.

The neurologist had warned her. No promises. Nothing certain. Nothing might change.

Kieron took hold of her arm as they neared the room. 'I'll be outside.'

'No, you . . .'

He shook his head. 'There isn't room, they'll be at full strength in there.'

She hesitated. Looked at him. 'Rock,' she said. 'You are.'

The door opened. But there were only two neurologists and the nurse. The room was quiet, apart from the usual machine sounds. She looked at the bed.

'We started about fifteen minutes ago,' Mike said. 'It's a slower process than bringing someone round from anaesthetic in the usual way.'

'How long could it take? Hours?'

'Anything's possible. If he hasn't surfaced into some sort of conciousness in twenty-four hours it will be worrying. And he might surface and then regress. Neurology isn't an exact science.'

'What is?'

She moved closer to the bed. Simon was still intubated. His hair was thicker now. He looked like someone who resembled himself, just a little. The bruising on his forehead and left cheek had faded, the cuts closed up and less livid. She sat, holding his hand. Saying his name. But she could not chat away easily, as Sam did. Just his name.

Hers. 'Hello. It's me.'

'That's everything,' Mike said. 'The drug clears out of the system quite quickly though obviously longer-term doses take longer for all the effects to subside.' He looked at the monitors. Adusted a syringe. 'I have to pop up to ITU to see a patient, but I'll come straight back and Ian here will stay.'

But as he turned to go, there was an odd, choking noise. Simon had moved his head to and fro and tried to lift it, and in doing so, had expelled the breathing tube from his throat.

There was a second, gurgling noise. A rasping low cough.

And then his eyes opened, and he looked at Cat. For a second or two, confusion, bewilderment, panic. Then he focused on her face. Recognition.

Cat pressed her brother's hand. And after a moment, she felt a weak but absolutely unmistakable and real pressure back.